J. C. Stagg, Frank Pettingell, Edwin J. Brett

The king of the school, or, Who will win?

J. C. Stagg, Frank Pettingell, Edwin J. Brett

The king of the school, or, Who will win?

ISBN/EAN: 9783741106040

Manufactured in Europe, USA, Canada, Australia, Japa

Cover: Foto ©Andreas Hilbeck / pixelio.de

Manufactured and distributed by brebook publishing software
(www.brebook.com)

J. C. Stagg, Frank Pettingell, Edwin J. Brett

The king of the school, or, Who will win?

[COMPLETE.] [PRICE SIXPENCE

THE KING OF THE SCHOOL
OR
WHO WILL WIN?

EDWIN J. BRETT, Limited
Harp Alley, Shoe Lane, West Harding Street, London, E.C.
And all Booksellers.

THE KING OF THE SCHOOL;

OR,

WHO WILL WIN?

"HE LAID HOLD OF BAYNES, AND ADMINISTERED A SOUND CASTIGATION."

No. 1.

THE KING OF THE SCHOOL;

OR,

WHO WILL WIN?

CHAPTER I.

BACK TO SCHOOL.

BACK to school!

There could not be the least doubt that such was the business, and the ultimate destination of a dozen or more well-dressed lads, varying in age from ten up to sixteen years, who had met at one of our great London railway stations.

Hearty greetings passed between them.

All the little differences that had arisen during the previous school term had been forgotten during the holidays—old friendships remaining unchanged.

"Not many fellows here yet," observed a tall youth, dressed rather *loudly*. "I shall do a weed while these porters are putting the train together."

To prove that he was in earnest, he produced a cigar-case, and took from it a very thick regalia, which he lighted, and proceeded to smoke with a pretence of enjoyment.

"Any of you fellows feel inclined to blow a cloud?" he added, handing his case round the group.

Two or three accepted the offer.

By way of introducing this young gentleman to our readers, it will be necessary to observe that his name was Albert Marsham; he was the son of a very rich city merchant, and, though not entirely bad by nature, had some faults.

He drank quantities of beer after school hours, backed racehorses, and *went the pace* gaily; yet, during the hours allotted to study, he was tolerably steady, though he gained no prizes.

His friends, Burton Templeton, Gerrard Stanhope, and George Lascelles, imitated him to a certain extent.

"Here comes Charlie Fitzgerald;" suddenly exclaimed the last young gentleman; "and who is that with him?"

No one was able to answer the question.

Charlie Fitzgerald came forward and shook hands all round.

"Who is your friend?" asked Lascelles.

"One of the jolliest fellows living His name is Frank Egerton. Frank let me introduce you to my friends and schoolfellows, Stanhope, Lascelles, Marsham, and Templeton."

Egerton at once made himself friendly with his future companions.

"Here comes Baynes!" observed one of the party; and a youth entered the refreshment-bar of the railway, where all the party where assembled.

"I don't think I shall like him," whispered Frank Egerton to his friend Fitzgerald.

"Why not?"

"He looks like a sneak."

Fitzgerald smiled as he replied—

"He is one, and a bully as well."

"He had better not bully me," said Egerton, half clenching his hands.

The youth had remarked that Baynes was received on all sides with far less cordiality than he had received—a circumstance which he attributed correctly to the fact that they all knew his disposition and habits.

Baynes ordered a glass of sherry at the bar, muttering something about "low beer-drinking fellows."

"Do you mean that observation to apply to me?" asked Fitzgerald, who, with Egerton and the others, had been indulging in some bottled stout.

"I mentioned no names," replied the bully.

"So much the better for you," observed Egerton.

"Why?"

"Because if you had spoken of me in such terms, I should have——"

"Hush!" interposed Fitzgerald, in a loud whisper; "don't quarrel here, whatever you may do when you arrive at Lexicon College."

For a few moments there was silence, then the door of the refreshment-bar was pushed open, and a ragged urchin, some ten or eleven years of age, crept in.

"What do you want?" inquired Baynes, roughly.

The dark blue eyes of the tattered boy almost filled with tears, and his cheek flushed, at being thus abruptly addressed. For a few moments he seemed unable to speak.

Egerton, however, spoke to him more kindly, and then he replied—

"I am very hungry, and I can't get anything to eat unless I steal."

"Which you know how to do well enough, I'll be bound," said Baynes. "Out of this, you young ruffian, or you'll be robbing some of us."

"Shame!" exclaimed Egerton.

Baynes, however, took no notice of the exclamation, but gave the poor boy a hearty slap on the face, with intent to hasten his departure.

"You deserve to be well thrashed," shouted Fitzgerald.

"I should like to know who is able to do it," replied the bully, aiming another blow at his victim, who, however, avoided it, and ran behind Egerton.

"I can," said the last-named individual.

And, suiting his action to the words, he laid hold of Baynes by the collar of his coat, and with his walking-cane administered a sound castigation, to the great delight of Marsham and the others.

The operation was continued for some seconds, till the guard of the train came in and separated them.

"Come, gentlemen, can't allow no fighting 'ere," observed he. "It's 'gainst the bye-laws; you can settle it when you gets down to the college."

"And I will settle it with a vengeance," growled Baynes, as he moodily walked away, and ordered another glass of sherry to heal his bruises.

"I shall be very happy to give you an opportunity of doing so whenever you please," answered Egerton, amid cries of "Bravo!   Served him right!"

"But let me see," continued Frank, addressing the cause of this dispute. "You said you were hungry. Take this pork-pie and pitch into it."

"What a lark it would be take this youngster down to Ballsbury!" said Marsham.

"What could we do with him there —or, rather, what could he do?" asked Fitzgerald.

"He could make himself useful."

"In what way?"

"Why, I am going to have a couple of terriers down, and as old Whackley won't let them be kept within the boundaries, I shall want some one to look after them. I'll give him five shillings a-week."

"He can look after my rabbits, too," observed young Webber, a boy who, for some time past, had devoted himself to the consumption of buns. "That will be five bob more."

"What say you, youngster? Will you go? or don't you care to leave your parents?" asked Fitzgerald.

"I don't know anything about my parents, sir, and I should be very glad indeed to work for any of you—except——"

He glanced timidly at Baynes, who

was consoling himself by a flirtation with one of the barmaids.

"Never mind him. I'll see he doesn't hurt you," interposed Egerton.

"Have you made up your mind?" asked Marsham. "You are promised ten shillings a-week for certain, and no doubt you will pick up five, or, perhaps, ten more."

"A sovereign—all in one week!" ejaculated the boy.

"Yes; isn't it enough?"

"Oh, yes, sir—a great deal more than I ever had."

"Here, then, get yourself a third-class ticket."

As Marsham spoke, he handed the delighted boy a half-sovereign, with which he ran off to the booking-office.

"Here's the change, sir—three shillings and a ha'penny; the ticket cost six and 'leven pence ha'penny," said the boy, as he returned.

"Keep it," was the response.

The delighted boy thrust the coins into the pocket of his ragged trousers.

"Times up, gentlemen," said the guard, thrusting his head in at the doorway.

"We are going in your van, Snooks," observed Lascelles.

"It's against the rules, gentlemen."

"Bother the rules. You must find room for us."

"Any more for the train?" shouted a porter.

"Come along, Frank," exclaimed Fitzgerald, and the boys raced along the platform till they reached the guard's break van, into which they leaped.

Marsham was last to enter, driving before him in a good-natured way the ragged boy who had been befriended by Egerton.

The guard felt rather inclined to be angry at the presumption of the boy in forcing his way among his betters; but the state of the case was soon explained to him, and, when he had received one of Marsham's thick regalias, and a drop of brandy from a pocket-flask, he so far relented as to smile upon the lad as he sat up in one corner, devouring the pork pie.

"What's your name, you young beggar?" asked Lascelles, when the boy began to show signs that his hunger was satisfied.

"Harry, sir."

"Harry what?"

"Well, sir, they call me Harry Smith, because I used to lodge at old Mother Smith's in Parker Street, but——"

The boy paused.

"Then Smith I suppose is not your real name?"

"I think not, sir."

"You think not. What do you mean?"

"I can just recollect when I was a very little chap, I used to live in a very large, fine house, but I don't remember whereabouts it was?"

"How did you come to leave it?" asked Egerton.

"That I can remember very well, sir."

"Tell us," exclaimed all the other boys crowding round him.

"Well, gentlemen, I can just remember that one day the nurse took me out into one of the parks, that was when I could walk and speak a little, and I remember as well as if it only happened yesterday, a big soldier came up and spoke to the nurse, and she put me down on the grass while she was talking to him. I wandered off, and when I looked round after a little time, I could not see her.

"Then I began to cry, and a strange woman came up and asked what was the matter. I told her I wanted to go home, and she said she would take me; but instead of doing so she took me to a low place, where I was stripped of my good clothes and dressed me in rags.

"I remained with her a long time, then she used to send me out to sell matches; if I did not sell a good quantity she would beat me. One day after she had been beating me I ran away, and began to sell matches on my own account; and with that, and holding gentlemen's horses, and one thing and the other, I have managed to get along."

"Where have you lived lately?" asked Lascelles.

"Nowhere in particular, sir; I sleep sometimes in the park, and sometimes under an archway."

"Poor little beggar," muttered Marsham. "Well, you won't have to do that again for some time to come."

After a ride of about three hours, the train approached Ballsbury.

"There's old Lexicon College," said Fitzgerald, pointing to a large, antique, red-brick building which stood among some trees close by the tall cathedral.

Frank Egerton looked rather anxiously at his future home, and finally came to the conclusion that if the interior arrangements were as good as the external appearance, it would not be such a very bad place to spend a few months in.

A few minutes after the train drew up at the platform, cabs were procured, and the whole party—with the exception of the ragged boy, who was instructed to procure a lodging and a cheap suit of clothing—moved off to Lexicon College.

But our hero's introduction to that celebrated educational establishment must form the theme of another chapter.

CHAPTER II.

THE COLLEGE AND THE TOWN.

LEXICON COLLEGE stood within the precincts and beneath the shadow of the venerable cathedral.

It was a large place with a central building, in which the masters resided, and two wings for the use of the scholars.

The college had been founded by a rich clerical dignitary in past ages for the education of the cathedral choristers; the presentation to the chief mastership was in the hands of the dean and chapter, and was always held by one of that august body.

At the time Frank Egerton made his appearance there the post was filled by the Reverend John Whackley, D.D., a canon of the cathedral, renowned for his orthodox principles, the purity of his Latin, the soundness of his logic and his floggings, on which latter point the writer can give his testimony without the slightest doubt or hesitation.

The door was opened by a footman in livery, who was instructed to pay the cabman and see to the luggage.

Fitzgerald then led the way to the study, in which the man of learning was seated.

"I am glad to see you again," said the doctor, as the boys entered, holding out his hand to Charlie. "And your friend——"

"This is Frank Egerton, Doctor Whackley."

"Ah, you are welcome. I have heard something of you from your parents, young gentleman; they tell me you are rather wild. Is it so?"

Frank blushed, and looked down for a moment, then, fixing his eyes full upon the doctor's face, replied—

"I am very fond of any kind of fun, sir."

"Very good. Now I don't object to fun provided its object is not to annoy or injure anyone. I like to see boys enjoy their youthful flow of spirits, and be fearless of danger; at the same time I strongly discourage recklessness. Your friend, Fitzgerald, will now show you over the place, and introduce you to some of your schoolfellows who have already arrived."

Both boys then bowed, and were about to leave when the doctor again spoke.

"No doubt Fitzgerald will also take you through the town; while so doing I shall feel obliged if he will point out to you certain streets in which I do not allow my pupils to be seen. Any infringement of the rules in that respect will be very severely punished."

"Well, what do you think of him?" asked Fitzgerald, when they had left the study.

"I fancy that if he would grow a moustache, and wear spurs, he would make a first-rate officer of dragoons."

"Why?"

"Because he is so awfully straightforward and determined. He would no more allow the enemy to infringe upon his rules than ourselves. Show me round, Fitz."

Fitzgerald conducted him over the central building and the right wing.

"Let us have a look over the other side," said Frank, when he had seen his own sleeping apartment, the class rooms, and various other objects of interest.

"You had better wait a day or two till all our fellows are here."

"For what reason?"

"That is Nightingale Grove."

"What a queer name! Why is it called so?"

"That's where the singing-birds stay."

"What singing-birds? Explain yourself."

"The singing-birds are the choristers. There are always forty boys from the town boarded and educated free in that part of the building; twenty-four of them are choristers in the cathedral, and the others are training to take the vacancies that occur when some of the elder ones retire."

"But is that any reason why we should not go there?"

"Yes. They are too many for us now. Our fellows hate the nightingales, and we very often have rows with them. Here comes a nightingale."

"Where?"

"Coming from the cathedral door. That fellow with the snuff-coloured jacket, and the big white frill round his neck, making him look as if he carried his head in a dish."

Egerton saw a boy approaching whose costume was as Fitzgerald had described it, with the addition of a *mortar-board* cap.

As he came up, Egerton began to whistle a bad imitation of the notes of the nightingale.

He of the snuff-coloured jacket flushed up, clenched his fist, and said,

"Wait till I get a few of our fellows together, you'll learn to whistle another tune."

"Can't *you* teach me?" responded Fitzgerald, you must be very bad musicians in your wing if it takes a dozen to teach a pupil."

The nightingale, however, saw that his natural enemies were too strong for him, so he walked on.

"Let us take a stroll in the town," suggested Fitzgerald. "I'll show you about the place."

"With all my heart."

They had not walked twenty yards from the school, as it was generally called, when they became aware of a dashing-looking youth, on a more than half-bred horse, cantering up.

The cavalier reined in his steed as soon as he saw our two friends, exclaiming—

"Ah, Fitzgerald; glad to see you, old boy. Who's your friend?"

"One whom you will be pleased to know; a gentleman after your own heart. Spouts Greek like Porson, and mills like Tom Sayers. I have very great pleasure in being the means of introducing the Earl of Pembridge to my friend Francis Egerton, Esquire, of Mount Grange, Suffolk, and Hill Street, Berkeley Square; and now, perhaps, your lordship will condescend to extend a fin to a poor commoner."

"With all the pleasure in life, Fitz; but where are you going?" asked the young earl.

" For a stroll round the town."

" I am with you, then; I'll leave Mercury at the 'Red Lion' stables. Do you know Baynes has arrived?"

"We came down with him," said Egerton.

"And he is not the least bit improved. Do you know I saw him, with his friend Crawley and another, tormenting a poor boy as I came down the High Street?"

Fitzgerald and Egerton looked at each other.

" Our young friend," said Frank.

"No; only a poor chap. He looked as if he had no friends about this part of the country."

"We brought him with us from town. Baynes gave him a blow, for which he received a good thrashing."

" From whom?" asked the earl.

" Our friend Egerton."

" Hurrah! I am glad the fellow has found his master at last."

"It was only a caning affair; the fight has yet to come."

" That's not quite so rosy-looking. Can you fight, Egerton?"

" Pretty well," replied Frank. "When I was at a private tutor's, I used to practise with the gloves for nearly an hour every day with the grooms at some livery stables."

" Baynes is very clever with his fists, and you'll be obliged to fight; so mind what you are about."

By this time they had passed through a gate, over which stood a statue of King James I., and were in the High Street of the town.

The Earl of Pembridge conducted them up a turning on the right hand side, and left his horse at some stables.

While he was so doing, Egerton heard shouts at some distance, and looking, saw his young protégé surrounded by a dozen or more town boys, who were urged on by Baynes, and two or three other *gentlemen* from the college, to pelt the poor London outcast with stones and mud.

Egerton, Fitzgerald, and the Earl of Pembridge rushed forward, and, after a brief skirmish, succeeded in rescuing the boy.

The first-named then turned to Baynes.

" Are you not ashamed of yourself?" he said.

" I am not; but I shall be if I submit to any more of your impertinence. I shall be in the old chalk-pit at three o'clock to-morrow afternoon if you dare to meet me there. Any of your friends will show you the way."

" I will find the way, and be in time."

The two parties then separated.

Crawley exclaimed to his friend Baynes, as they walked down the street—

"That new fellow must be taken down, or he will make himself King of the School!"

" He shall not while I have either strength or cunning left. I mean to lick him into a sense of his proper position to-morrow."

" Quite right."

They walked on in silence for some time, till they reached a tobacco shop, over which hung a red lamp.

"Do you play billiards, Crawley?" asked Baynes.

" No."

" Well, come in here and I'll teach you."

He walked through the shop, pushed open a green baize-covered door, and ushered his companion into a large room, lighted at the top, in which stood two billiard tables.

Round the room stood racks for cues, and all the usual furniture found in such places.

Both tables were occupied, so Baynes and his companion were compelled to look on while others played.

While so engaged a tall, bushy-whiskered individual, buttoned up to the chin in a frock-coat, and carrying in his hand a riding-whip, entered the room.

Baynes flushed slightly when he saw the man enter.

Don Whiskerandos, after a quiet glance round the room, went up to the schoolboy and held out his hand.

" Glad to see you again, Mr. Baynes," said he; " we have been very quiet since you gents went away—haven't we, Chalky?"

"'STOP TILL MY MAN HAS HAD A LITTLE BRANDY,' SAID CRAWLEY."

The last question was addressed to the marker, who responded—

"Blooming dead and alive, I can tell yer, Mr. Baynes. —— Twenty-four—eighteen; no cannon;" he continued, as he scored the game.

"By the bye," continued the whiskered individual, still addressing his conversation to Baynes, "you remember—"

His voice became so indistinct that no one else in the room could hear what he was saying.

"I could not, Captain Robinson," replied Baynes.

"Nonsense! You could do the one thing easy enough; you ought to have done t'other. A chap, like you, as has got plenty of tin, should never say, ' I couldn't.' "

The ungrammatical, though forcible, arguments of the captain, as he was by courtesy styled, produced very little effect upon Baynes, who turned away to watch the play.

"Now, look here, I ain't goin' to be treated like this. Do you know what your character in the school would be worth if I was to write to Dr. Whackley?"

"About as much as your commission in the army would sell for," replied Baynes.

"But what if I should take it into my nut to write home to your pa!"

The youth first flushed red, then turned pale as ashes.

"Ha, ha, now I know the soft point," continued the captain. "Don't want your pa to know, eh! Afraid he'll stop the dividends! Ha, ha! Master Baynes, now will you do as I politely request?"

"You really must wait a little time— a week or two. I can't ask the governor—"

The remainder of the sentence was heard only by the captain.

"To-day is Monday; I can wait till Friday."

"But I dare not ask my father for at least a month."

"What am I to do in the meantime, Mr. Baynes?"

"I don't know."

"I know how we might both make a good pot of money," said the captain, again sinking his voice to a whisper.

"How ?"

"Come here; it won't do to let every-one hear."

The so-styled captain led Baynes into a recess, and for some time was engaged in a whispered conversation with him.

When at length they turned once more towards the players, the school-boy's face was very pale, and big drops of perspiration stood upon his brow.

"I dare not," he said, in answer to the captain's proposition.

"I never thought as you was a coward," responded Robinson.

"Nor am I."

"You are, or you wouldn't make such a fuss about a little bit of——"

"Hush! Let me have time to think it over. I will see you again to-morrow night."

"Very well. *Only if I don't see you I shall consider that it is all right for this day week.*

The conversation then turned upon the game, which, according to the marker's showing, stood at forty against forty-three.

The highest scorer was about to make another stroke, and, the balls being in a very easy position, would probably have scored, when his opponent winked at the captain, who repeated the signal to Chalky the marker.

Listen to the consequences.

Just as the player was in the act of making his stroke, Chalky managed to let fall the *rest* with which he had been moving the slides on the marking board.

The noise distracted the player's attention, and instead of adding five to his score, as he would otherwise have done, he gave one to his adversary, who immediately played out.

Captain Robinson professed to be highly indignant with Chalky, and expressed a strong desire to kick him all the way to the next town; but, when the loser had departed, after paying all the bets he had made, the sham military man handed over five shillings to the marker.

"Take it, Chalky; you put a sovereign in my pocket by dropping that rest. Ha! ha! ha!"

All joined in a boisterous outbreak of laughter, in which Baynes joined.

"You are getting very sharp here, captain," he observed.

"We are obliged to be, Mr. Baynes. Flats is more wide-awake than they used to be, and we are obliged to use all kinds of dodges. Remember, Mr. Baynes, to-morrow evening, if I don't see you, *I shall get everything ready for next Monday night.*"

"Yes," responded Baynes, in a dreary, mechanical way, as though he hardly understood the words he was uttering; and then he quitted the billiard-room.

On arriving at the college, he found that Egerton, Fitzgerald, and the Earl of Pembridge had returned before him.

Remembering, however, that a challenge had been given and accepted, he said nothing, and the evening passed over in peace.

Supper was served for those who chose to partake of it at nine o'clock, after which meal all retired to bed, Frank Egerton's apartment being shared with Charlie Fitzgerald.

It was a tolerably roomy, double-bedded apartment; at least, so Frank found it when he had an opportunity of looking round, which was not till another candle was brought by Fitzgerald.

"What is the matter, Frank?" asked the latter.

"Some one has been having a joke with me."

"Ha, ha, ha!"

Fitzgerald laughed most heartily at the dripping appearance presented by his friend, who stood, half amused, half angry, shivering, while water ran from every part of his dress.

Some ingenious wight had placed a water jug upon the door, which had first been partly opened.

The jug itself was tied by a string to a nail driven into the wall above the door, so that on attempting to enter, Frank Egerton had caused it to over-turn, his punishment being the receipt of its contents upon his head and shoulders, the vessel itself remaining dangling at the top of the doorway.

Fitzgerald's laughter brought out the occupants of the other rooms on that floor.

"Why, Egerton, you look like a modern Leander!" exclaimed the Earl of Pembridge. "Have you been swimming across old Whackley's water tank, in order to win the affections of one of the housemaids?"

"Don't chaff a fellow so awfully," replied Frank. "Some of you have played a very good joke—rather old though; but I'll take care you don't catch me again. Good night. I must make haste and change, or I shall catch cold."

"Are you really very wet, Egerton?" asked the earl, coming forward.

"Soaked."

"I am very sorry, indeed; I did not think of the consequences to you when I foolishly perched that jug up there. It was I who did it, Egerton, and I ask your forgiveness."

"Which is given as soon as asked," replied Egerton, holding out his hand to show that he bore no enmity.

CHAPTER III.

SINGLE COMBAT.

THE night passed away quietly enough, the pupils of Lexicon College not being quite in the humour for any large amount of practical joking.

In the morning the second classical master held a preliminary examination of the new pupils, for the purpose of assigning them their various positions in the school.

Frank Egerton acquitted himself very well, having been well trained by a private tutor, and was sent to the fifth form, not far below his friend, Charlie Fitzgerald.

Then came the first morning of school discipline and instruction, and the old scholars found they had a formidable rival in the new-comer.

Baynes gave him several very savage glances by way of reminding him that he had not forgotten the challenge of the previous night.

However, Egerton took no notice of him.

At length they were dismissed.

As soon as they had reached the playfield, the Earl of Pembridge came up.

"Who is going to second you in this mill, Egerton?" he asked.

"I suppose Fitzgerald will. I have not asked."

"Then let me have that honour; will you, old fellow?"

"Certainly."

Some twenty or thirty of the boys who were aware of the acceptance of Baynes's challenge then made their way to the old chalk-pit, which was situated at the bottom of a steep hill, just outside the town.

"I don't see our adversary," observed Pembridge.

"Here he comes, though," said another.

Baynes appeared a few minutes after-wards, attended by Crawley; a ring was marked out on the green turf within which the two combatants were placed, and the spectators were warned not to intrude.

Both then delivered their hats, coats, and waistcoats to their seconds, and, advancing into the centre of the ring, assumed defensive attitudes.

All the spectators were breathless with suspense, as the two combatants prepared to commence hostilities.

Baynes was a strongly-built youth, not too fleshy, and possessed of a great deal of self-confidence.

He had already fought two or three severe school fights, on each occasion proving the conqueror, though there were ugly whispers abroad that he had not fought fairly.

Egerton was about his equal in height and size, and felt full of enthusiasm, remembering the line—

"Thrice is he armed that hath his quarrel just."

Before going to the place of combat, he had practised for an hour with the gloves, and had found himself able, without much difficulty, to overcome both his friends, Fitzgerald and the Earl of Pembridge.

This inspired him with confidence.

Baynes, nothing loth, relying upon his former victories, and the reputation he had gained as a bruiser, stepped forward, and—

The combat commenced!

ROUND THE FIRST brought out the sparring qualities of both.

Either combatant was anxious to discover the other's weak points.

Baynes assumed a more busy action than his opponent, but considerable fistic science was displayed by both.

After sparring for some minutes,

Baynes had the good fortune to plant his left fist very cleverly upon Egerton's forehead, without the least chance of a return blow, thus gaining the first advantage.

Frank, however, took it very coolly, having made up his mind to win the fight, no matter what difficulties might stand in the way.

He showed quite a confident bearing, while the other, elated by his first success, smiled quite as joyously as he toed the mark.

"I'll bet two to one against your man," said Crawley, who acted as Baynes's second.

"I'll take you with a great deal of pleasure—sovereigns, of course?" replied the Earl of Pembridge.

The bet was booked, during a few seconds of very cautious work between the combatants, which precluded a rally at close quarters, in which Egerton managed to give his antagonist a sounding blow upon the chest, which he endeavoured to repeat, but, in so doing, caught another heavy blow on the forehead.

The Crawleyites applauded greatly, and Frank Egerton's seconds began to look rather down in the mouth.

"I'll repeat the bet," said Crawley.

"Certainly," replied Pembridge; "I should be a very poor second did I refuse to put my cash upon my principal."

"I am with you on the same terms, Crawley," observed Fitzgerald, who had been very intently watching his friend's boxing.

The ground being rather slippery, after a long term of wet weather, they paused for a moment, looked at each other with a smile, and then recommenced.

Egerton's length of arm now began to show to advantage, and enabled him to "draw the ruby," as a *Bell's Life* reporter would style it.

Some close and hard hitting followed, at the end of which Baynes fell, the first round being thus slightly in favour of Egerton.

"If you like to acknowledge yourself beaten you may withdraw your man," said Pembridge.

"Thank you, we decline to take a licking," replied Baynes's second.

"You will be compelled to do so sooner or later," was the response, at which Crawley shook his head incredulously; but he did not offer to renew his bets.

Round the second then commenced.

Egerton, with great self-possession, advanced to the attack, being the first to leave his second's knee. There was a slight symptom of discoloration on his forehead, and Baynes's mouth was a little puffed.

The latter, however, met his adversary with great determination, and had the good luck to give Egerton a heavy left-hand blow upon the shoulder, receiving in return one on the crown of the head.

Both then *sparred for wind;* that is, kept on the defensive while regaining breath, then resumed the conflict. Baynes first attempted to put in a hit, but Egerton was clever enough to stop it, and returned right and left, drawing blood again. Then Baynes rushed in, and began to wrestle, when both fell at the same time.

Their seconds picked them up, and employed some few minutes in preparing them for a renewal.

Egerton looked fresh, and his face was tolerably free from marks, while Baynes had several severe bruises, which were beginning to exhibit different hues. Frank quickly came up, to the scratch, and put himself on guard.

"Now, then, where's your man?" asked the Earl of Pembridge.

"Here he is," replied Crawley; "the referee has not called 'time' yet. We shall be up in time to beat you."

"Had we not better hasten on to the end of this miserable affair?" asked Frank, speaking for the first time.

"Stop till my man has had a little brandy," replied Crawley, "then we shall be delighted to finish giving you a thrashing."

As he spoke, he placed a pocket-flask to Baynes's lips

"Time!" said Marsham, who acted as judge and referee.

The combatants being both upon their mettle, commenced the third round with great spirit.

Egerton, with much dexterity, put in two tremendous hits on Baynes's left cheek.

In return Baynes, after several abortive attempts, managed to give his adversary a left-hander on the throat.

For a moment Frank was almost stunned, but rapidly recovering, he closed in and both fell—Egerton being underneath this time.

Crawley's party cheered loudly.

"Shall I have the pleasure of booking you again at the ole figure?" asked Crawley.

"Certainly," replied Pembridge.

"I don't mind taking your offer," said Marsham; "for I certainly think—"

"Pardon me—we can't allow the referee to make a bet, and his opinion should be reserved till asked for on either side."

Round the fourth was extremely short. Baynes managed to deliver another blow on the throat, knocking Egerton fairly off his legs.

Baynes's few friends cheered loudly, and began to look upon the battle as won, for it seemed as though Egerton would not be able to renew the combat.

"Are you sufficiently thrashed?" asked Crawley.

"By no means!" responded the Earl of Pembridge. "Here, one of you fellows cut to the 'Six Bells,' and bring up a bottle of brandy."

The "Six Bells," an old-fashioned hostelry, happened to be close by, and in a few moments, under the influence of the spirit, Frank Egerton began to rally. When Marsham again called time he was able to appear at the scratch with a smile upon his face.

The fifth, sixth, and seventh rounds were quickly fought, with no great results on either side. It was evident to all that two or three more would decide the conflict one way or the other, for the combatants not being professionally trained pugilists, were beginning to show scantiness of breath, and other symptoms of distress.

Both took more brandy, then rose once more from their second's knees.

As Egerton advanced towards his opponent it was evident that his throat had been severely visited by the swinging hits administered in the previous rounds.

However he went forward steadily, evincing every disposition to fight it out.

He brought his left hand to bear with stinging severity on Baynes's mouth, bringing more blood.

That young gentleman feinted, and stepped back, but was rapidly followed by Egerton, who dashed in, regardless of consequences, delivering both right and left upon the right eye and again upon the mouth.

Baynes fell heavily, and was immediately picked up by his second.

Crawley wiped the blood from his face and mouth, and once more applied the brandy flask to his lips.

Baynes, in a very listless manner, swallowed the spirit, which had not the usual effect upon him, and failed to revive him.

He sat upon his second's knee, staring vacantly around.

Egerton, though flushed and slightly fatigued, was able to walk round the ring, to keep his blood in circulation.

"Had you not better give it up, and confess yourself beaten?" Pembridge again asked.

"By no means," was the reply. "We are quite able to beat you yet."

"That remains to be seen."

"Less chatter there," interposed Marsham. "Time's up; bring your men to the scratch."

Frank Egerton as he commenced the ninth round saw that the victory was his own.

Baynes walked with a tottering step, and seemed hardly conscious. However, he made a show of putting up his fists, and was immediately knocked down by Egerton.

Some minutes elapsed, and then Crawley, finding that his principal still remained insensible, said sulkily—

"We acknowledge ourselves beaten."

"Hurrah, hurrah!" shouted Egerton's friends, who outnumbered the others three to one. "Hurrah for Frank Egerton."

"Who has proved himself THE KING OF THE SCHOOL!" added Pembridge.

Half-a-dozen of them then seized him and bore him in triumph to the "Six Bells."

The host was accustomed to see the pupils of the college slightly bruised after a visit to the old chalk-pit, so forebore to express any surprise till he heard that it was Baynes who had suffered defeat at the hands of our young hero.

"What, Mr. Baynes whopped!" he exclaimed.

"Yes," replied Pembridge, "licked after a splendid mill which lasted fifty minutes—nine rounds."

"It must have been a hot 'un, for I taught Mr. Baynes to box myself," said Grimes. "But come, sir, let me tie this bit of raw meat over your eye; it is a stunning thing to take out all the inflammation."

Frank submitted, and, after sundry bottles of Bass had been consumed, and he had recovered his breath and strength a little, he and his supporters set out to return to Lexicon College. Crawley and his friends, supporting Baynes, were some distance ahead.

CHAPTER IV.

PROFESSOR MOERITZ

"*Ach Himmel! Wer ist dieser jüngling?*"* exclaimed a stout, middle-aged man, with fair long hair, as he saw the conquered one come towards the college.

Having carefully adjusted a pair of blue spectacles upon his nose he gave another look, which seemed to satisfy him as to the youth's identity.

"Mein gott!" he then exclaimed in slower and more guttural tones, "Mein gott! it is Baynes, and he shall have been fighting.

The speaker was Dr. Franz Moeritz, professor of German mathematics, and natural philosophy in Lexicon College.

Professor Moeritz was most decidedly a popular man among his pupils, a strict disciplinarian in class-hours, a splendid scholar, and a profound thinker; in the playfield a burly, genial giant, who delighted to take part in the sports patronised by the Boys of England.

    * Oh, Heaven! who is this youth?

None laughed more heartily than he when he made some ridiculous blunder in the midst of a game of cricket, or became the victim of some practical joke.

"Ah, Meinheer Baynes, so you have been at ze box. Dat is bad."

Baynes looked down, and said nothing. He felt very weak, and heartily longed to retire to his bed-room.

Finding the professor was not inclined to put any more questions, he tottered away.

Then up came Frank Egerton.

"Zo you are ze new poy. You haf begun well, sir; you haf beat Baynes till he shall no come home with a blue eye."

"I was challenged, sir."

"Ah!"

"Of course I could not refuse to accept a challenge. Even you, sir, I think, would fight under such circumstances."

"FRANK THREW OFF HIS JACKET, THEN IN HE PLUNGED."

" Yes; but vot haf you done that he challenges you?"

" I gave him a good caning, sir."

" Ja! I should challenge any man dat beats me mit a shtick."

" It served him right, Dr. Moeritz; he behaved in a most cruel manner to a poor little homeless boy only half his size," observed Fitzgerald.

" Was ist grausamer !".* ejaculated the German, holding up his hands. " I should haf in Vaterland. haf beat him mit a shtick, and he would haf challenged me. But we should not fight mit ze box as you Englanders always do."

" How then, doctor?" asked the young earl.

" I would fight mit a degen—sword, as you call him."

" Ah, yes; I have heard of the way German students fight," laughed Frank. " They pad themselves till it is almost impossible for a sword to penetrate their thick dresses; and then, if one gets a scratch on the finger or wrist, his courage cannot be doubted."

" It is not always so," responded the professor. " Look."

He pulled off his hat—of the true republican shape—and shaking back his tawny locks showed a long deep scar extending right across the skull.

The boys gathered round him curiously, as though waiting for an explanation.

" It was done when I was at the Heidelberg University."

" Tell us how, doctor;;" I should like to hear a story of a real duel," said Pembridge.

Doctor Moeritz hesitated, but being pressed by all the boys, at last consented to tell his tale. In repeating it to our readers, we shall take the liberty of making the professor speak good English, a thing he was not accustomed to do.

" It is twenty-five years since I first entered the University of Heidelberg.

" I was then a young man, and entered with heartiness into all the

* What is more cruel?

freaks and jokes of university life, though I certainly did not neglect the lectures.

" In fact, I always devoted at least three hours every day to hard reading.

" Of course, most of you have heard that in Germany the students do little except drink beer and smoke.

" That is wrong; many of them are accomplished students, though it is also true that many more are confirmed tavern haunters.

" I tried to hit the medium; if I spent my days in study, I saw no particular harm in passing the evenings in the society of my fellow-students.

" It was at one of these convivial meetings that I first met the man who gave me that wound.

" He was an Englishman, too, and bore the same name as you."

The professor pointed to Frank Egerton as he spoke.

" That is strange," muttered our hero.

Dr. Moeritz, without heeding the interruption, went on—

" His name was Fairfax Egerton——"

" The name of my uncle who went to America years ago, and has not since been heard of," said Frank.

" It is indeed a singular coincidence," replied the professor. " However, as I am unable to tell whether it was your uncle or not, I can only finish the history of my duel.

" We met one night at the hostelry renowned for the excellence of its beer.

" Of course the guests were all students, and among them was one named Fritz Leiderwold, a poor weakly youth, who had only just joined the university.

" He was the only son of his mother, and she was a widow; a circumstance which, combined with the bad health Fritz had always suffered, had led to his having been brought up in a very effeminate way.

" He could neither ride, swim, shoot, nor fence!

" The Englishman knew this well, and neglected no opportunity of reminding Fritz of his want of manhood.

" Egerton, I should say, was not like

some other Englishmen who were at Heidelberg; they were manly fellows, while he, though possessed of great personal strength and considerable skill with the sword, was known to be very cautious with whom he quarrelled.

"On this particular evening he seemed more insulting than usual.

"As I entered the tavern I heard him say—

"'It's a great pity such babies as you are allowed to go about without their nurses. Now I very nearly mistook you for a man.'

"'You pride yourself upon your strength and skill, Mr. Egerton,' replied Fritz. 'I have never yet handled a sword; but you will not dare repeat those words this day six months.'

"'I dare pull your nose now,' said the ruffian, but before he could carry out his threat I dashed a tankard of beer full in his face.

"Of course, after that he could not avoid challenging me, nor could I, under any pretext, refuse to meet him.

"Friends on either side proffered their assistance, and a meeting was arranged for the following Wednesday.

"It was on a Saturday the quarrel took place.

"We met.

"It had been settled that no padded dresses were to be worn, and that sabres were to be used—a very different affair from transforming your adversary into a cotton bale, and tilting at him with a knitting-needle.

"I found my adversary knew the theory of sword-play quite as well as I did myself.

"It was also very evident that having entered on the affair, he wished to come out of it with flying colours.

"He fought very carefully.

"At length I managed to give him a slight wound on the arm.

"That seemed to fire him with a determination to be revenged, and a few seconds afterwards I received the wound I have shown you.

"I just had strength enough left to return the compliment when I fainted;

our seconds interposed, and declared that we had both acted like men of honour.

"It was a week after the duel before I was permitted to leave my chamber.

"I inquired about my late antagonist, and was told that another week must elapse ere he would be permitted to rise from his bed.

"A few days afterwards I was looking out of my window looking towards the Konigsthul,* when I fancied I saw people walking upon the summit. I took down my telescope, looked carefully, and saw that one of the two persons was my late antagonist, Egerton, the other being a female whom I could not recognise.

"Some mysterious influence urged me to go also to the Konigsthul. When I reached the spot where I had seen Egerton he had disappeared, nor have I set eyes upon him since; but I found a piece of paper which I still preserve, partly as a memento of the combat, and partly in the hopes that some day it may prove of value to some honest man."

Thus ended the professor's tale; but little thought he how soon he was to be called upon to fight another though less harmful combat.

*   *   *   *   *

Next morning found Baynes unable to rise.

The thrashing he had received, together with the mortification attendant upon a public defeat, preyed heavily upon his spirits as well as body.

On being informed of the cause, Doctor Whackley at once asked Frank if it was true.

"Yes, sir," was the unhesitating reply.

The doctor looked stern for a minute, and said—

"I don't approve of fighting; but, as there seems to have been some provocation in the shape of a challenge, I feel compelled to overlook it. I am glad, too, that you, like most of my pupils, know how to speak the truth."

"Rather an impertinent remark,"

* King's seat, a hill on the south side of Heidelberg.

thought Frank to himself, but then neither he nor the other pupils of Lexicon College knew that Baynes had been guilty of prevarication when questioned as to the fight.

Two days after the combat, Baynes wrote the following note to his friend Captain Robinson—of the black-guards, said Pembridge.

He did not tell any one of his friends, not even the renowned Crawley, what he was writing about; but we, using the author's power of seeing farther through a brick wall than other people, shall take the liberty of peeping through the envelope and reading it.

It was worded thus:—

" DEAR ROBINSON,—Since I saw you the other day I have had a tremendous mill with one of our fellows, and, you will be sorry to hear, got the worst of it I cannot leave my bed for a week, so that you see it will be quite impossible for me to do anything towards Monday night's adventure. But don't be alarmed, old fellow; put off the affair for a week or two, and I will find some means of paying you the £20.

" Yours faithfully,
" HILTON BAYNES."

Captain Robinson swore when he received the note, and vowed that he would not be baulked by a boy, and that Monday night would find him— Baynes knew where!

⤙⤙⊠⤚⤚

CHAPTER V.

" HARRY, THE HEIR OF A NOBLE HOUSE."

IT is time now that we should enlighten our readers as to the doings of the boy whose appearance at the station was the cause of the fight between Baynes and Egerton.

After being rescued a second time from his tormentors, " Harry, the Heir of a Noble House," as young Webber called him, hunted about, and with a little trouble managed to find, a decent and cheap lodging, which he immediately took possession of, and enjoyed such a night's sleep as he had not known for many months.

The next day—that is, the day of the great fight—he entered upon his duties; gathering green food for Webber's rabbits, looking after Marsham's dogs, and grooming the Earl of Pembridge's horse.

The work suited him admirably, and so kindly was he treated by his young masters, that he blessed the day he was tempted to go into the railway station to try to beg a penny.

Things went on very pleasantly till he had been in the good old town of Ballsbury a week.

On that day—which, of course, was the Monday of which Captain Robinson had spoken so impressively—he was, by Marsham's instructions, taking the two terriers (which were kept at the " Six Bells ") out for exercise.

He walked till he reached a wood at the top of the hill above the old chalk-pit.

Suddenly Pincher and Billy bolted into the underwood, most probably in pursuit of a rabbit.

Harry called and whistled in vain, they would not return to him, nor had he any very definite idea which way they had gone.

Not knowing much about such matters, it struck Harry that it would not be a bad idea to climb a tree; then perhaps, his range of vision being more extended, he would be able to see something of the truant tykes.

Accordingly he ascended a young oak, the trunk of which was thickly covered with ivy.

No dogs could be seen, but he suddenly became aware of footsteps and voices approaching.

Now the London boy had heard terrible tales of the horrible punishments inflicted by the bloated aristocracy of this land upon small boys, poachers, stick-gatherers, and other hardy trespassers.

The idea flashed through his mind swift as lightning that the approaching individuals were two gamekeepers in the employ of the tyrannical proprietor of the wood—that they had heard him calling the dogs, and, therefore, would immediately imprison him for poaching, or perhaps some crime of greater magnitude.

The first law of Nature—self-preservation—was obeyed immediately.

He crouched among the ivy that clustered about the fork of the trunk so as to completely conceal himself.

The voices approached nearer and nearer.

" Surely they can't be gamekeepers," thought the boy. " Why, they are not talking about me !"

That was quite true.

Any thing or body appeared to be the theme of their conversation, though it seemed they had some kind of *game* in view.

Harry listened more attentively.

" Old Whackley is rich enough for a Jew," said one.

" And ever so much stingier," replied the other. " I did the petition dodge up there once; widow and six children burnt out, and all that sort of thing. I'm blest if he did't send it back, saying that he believed I was an impostor, and he'd a good mind to send for the peelers."

" That, of course, didn't suit your book ?"

" I should say not. Well, young lively, who thinks he can play billiards, owes me twenty pounds ; and as he can't pay, and won't——"

The speaker dropped his voice to a whisper, and Harry could only catch a few disjointed words.

" In his bed-room—good plan—we collar—all the blame on him—splendid swag."

" Why, they must be thieves," thought the boy; " and they mean to rob Doctor Whackley."

He waited till the men had passed out of sight, then slid down from the tree, and hurried back to Lexicon College.

Just on the outskirts of the town he saw Doctor Franz Moeritz, the German professor.

Recognizing in him some one high in authority at the academy, Harry stopped him and hurriedly told him what he had just heard.

" Good boy," exclaimed the professor, " I vill gif you a great reward von day. I vill *lehren* (teach) you ye science of mathematics for *nichts* (nothing)."

" Thank you, sir," responded Harry, who, however, had but a very vague idea as to what his reward was to be.

" You shall say nothing, goot boy, nothing at all of that you haf said to me. No one shall know, and ze tief shall be caught. Goot boy, here is a schelling for you. Now go, and hold your tongue; if you cannot, give some oder boy sixpence, and he shall hold it for you."

Harry laughed at the kind-hearted professor as he hurried back to the college.

Then the boy bethought him of the dogs.

It would never do to go back and inform Mr. Marsham that he had lost them. Another effort must be made to find the truant animals.

Accordingly, he walked back to the wood, and after some little time discovered them half-buried in the earth, in a large hole they had pawed out, in a vain endeavour to unearth a rabbit.

So intent were they upon their occupation, that they did not notice Harry till he was close to them, and had slipped a string over their necks.

That done he led them back in triumph to the "Six Bells," and condemned them to imprisonment for the remainder of the day.

In the meantime Professor Moeritz had created no small sensation at Lexicon College.

He rushed at full speed into Doctor Whackley's study, where some twenty of the senior boys were assembled, and hurriedly related his tale—purposely omitting to say from whom he received his information.

The principal of the college, though as sound a scholar as one could wish to meet, was slightly informed in the ways of the world, and felt as Charlie Fitzgerald expressed it, "no end of bothered."

"What is to be done, Herr Moeritz, what is to be done, boys?" he asked. "This is a big house, and it is impossible to say where they will make their entrance."

"Send for ze police," suggested Professor Moeritz. "They shall protect you."

"That is the best thing to be done, I fancy, sir," said Fitzgerald, who was one of the company in the study.

"And if the thieves should, by any chance, effect an entrance, we shall be able to give a good account of them," added Egerton. "As we are forewarned we shall be in readiness."

"I almost wish they would do so," said Marsham.

"It would be a delightful sensation— the capture of a gang of housebreakers by Dr. Whackley's pupils," continued Frank.

"But from whom did you get your information, Mr. Moeritz?" the principal at length asked.

The question being thus directly put, of course the worthy German could do nothing less than give an equally direct answer.

"Do you think this London street boy's information is correct?" was Whackley's next question. "Or is it not quite possible that he may have been in league with the thieves, and at the last moment, fearing detection, has preferred to betray his comrades rather than share their punishment.

"I think he is perfectly honest," said Egerton.

"And I!" "And I!" "And I!" echoed Fitzgerald, the Earl of Pembridge, and several others.

"Very good; your opinion may be well-founded, but until this matter is settled, the boy must not set foot on my premises."

"You shall be obeyed, Doctor Whackley; but as you have given no instructions to the contrary, I shall continue to employ him—beyond the boundaries of the school," said the young earl.

"As you please," was the doctor's polite response, and the interview terminated.

A messenger was sent to the police office, and, consequently, a couple of extra constables were detailed to keep guard over the school premises.

After some talk with these men, Egerton and Fitzgerald decided upon constructing a patent alarum.

They procured a long kite string belonging to one of the smaller boys, and passed it quite round the building, keeping it about six inches above the ground by means of forked sticks.

Half-a-dozen old bells were fastened at various parts of this cordon.

The result, of course, would be that any one unaware of this trap, would, in approaching the house, kick his foot against the string and set the bells ringing.

Baynes who was still compelled to keep his bed, was informed by Crawley of all these preparations, and expressed the greatest concern.

He wrote a note and bribed one of the servants to take it down to the billiard-rooms, and deliver it to Captain Robinson.

The servant took it, but, to Baynes's great disgust, returned with the information that the captain had not been there during the day, and was not expected.

Such news as this did not give Baynes any very great pleasure : he tossed about on his bed and the feverish symptoms became considerably aggravated.

The senior boys (the juniors had not been told anything about the expected visit) remained in their rooms ready dressed.

All the lights were extinguished, but it would be only the work of a moment to re-kindle them.

For a long time all was quiet.

At length the great bell of the cathedral tolled the hour of midnight.

Then a few minutes afterwards was heard the faint tinkling of one of the alarum bells.

At the first sound of the bell, Egerton and Fitzgerald left their room, joining Pembridge, Marsham, and half-a-dozen others in the passage.

They all wore slippers, and moved along noiselessly towards one of the side doors, near which the tinkling of the bell had been heard.

All in a body they rushed out of the doorway towards a spot where, in the murky darkness, two figures could be seen struggling.

"Help, help, help!" screamed a shrill, boyish voice.

"There spoke 'the Heir of a Noble House!'" exclaimed Webber, who although he had not received any official information of the intended burglary, had managed to find his way out as soon as any of the seniors.

"To the rescue, then !" said Egerton.

The small boy, anxious to distinguish himself, and win golden opinions from his superiors, darted off, and found that the two struggling figures were—

Harry the London waif,

And,

A black-whiskered individual, respectable as regards costume, but disreputable in respect to facial expression.

"Surrender, villain !" said Webber, seizing the black-whiskered gentleman(?) by the coat collar.

"Get out of this, you muff !" was the

response, and young Webber received a blow which set all his teeth rattling, and landed him some six or eight feet from the scene of conflict.

"What an uncivil brigand," muttered Webber, as Frank Egerton, the Earl of Pembridge, and Doctor Moeritz collared his assailant.

The struggle that ensued was brief.

The black - whiskered gentleman yielded to superior numbers, and the two extra policemen (who, of course, were not on the spot when most wanted) handcuffed him and led him off to the station.

"Don't worry yourselves, I'll go quietly enough," the boys heard him say. "I can produce several very respectable townspeople to speak as to my character."

"Delighted to hear it," responded the police, who, however, kept a tight hold, the prisoner not being known to them.

Then the *King of the School* and his companions went back to their beds, well satisfied with their night's work ; but, of course, the news quickly spread through the building.

In a very few minutes every one in the place knew what had taken place.

Most of them sleep well, but there was one to whom the hours of darkness were a terror. *His* sleep was haunted by dreams of the most fearful kind.

*   *   *   *   *   *

In the morning all those who had assisted in the capture of the supposed burglar, attended at the magistrates' office.

The sapient landed gentry who dispensed justice in Ballsbury, sat only three times a week, but it so happened that this was one of the days.

Doctor Whackley was there, with Professor Moeritz, and half-a-dozen pupils from Lexicon College ; and after one or two cases of turnip-stealing had received their just punishment, in the shape of six months imprisonment for each offence, the great prisoner of the day was placed in the dock.

The charge was, being found loitering about the premises of Doctor John

Whackley with intent to commit a felony.

Having heard the statements of the witnesses who captured him, the senior magistrate said—

"Have you any defence to make, prisoner?"

"Certainly."

"Well, then, let's hear it."

"I wish, in the first place, to say that I had not the slightest intention of committing any felony, either at Doctor Whackley's school or elsewhere. I am a commercial traveller; the police hold papers showing who I am, and the name of the firm I represent."

"Is that so?" demanded the magistrate, appealing to the superintendent of constabulary.

"We certainly found these papers on him, sir," replied the officer, handing in a variety of accounts against several tradespeople of the town, price lists, letters, and other commercial items.

"Have you not been to the 'Red Lion' to inspect my luggage?'" asked the prisoner.

"Yes."

"What did you find there more than my samples, books, and wearing apparel?"

"Nothing."

"You did not find any skeleton keys or house-breaking implements of any kind?"

"No."

"Did you find any about me when I was brought to the station-house?"

"No."

"Then I have not much more to say except that I, being a commercial traveller, am well-known to the landlord of the 'Red Lion' and several other tradesmen of the town. I don't see them in court, although I asked the police to request them to attend."

"Did you go to the people mentioned by the prisoner?" asked the magistrate, turning to the police-sergeant who had been on duty the previous night.

"No, sir, I had no time—three drunken cases brought in this morning."

"I also requested you to telegraph to London to my employers. Was that done?" inquired the prisoner.

"Yes; the message was sent two hours ago."

At that moment a boy from the telegraph office elbowed his way into the court, and handed a paper to the sergeant, who, after reading it, said,

"This is the answer, your worship."

"Read it aloud."

"From Wilkins and Co., Cheapside, to Police-sergeant Jenkins, Ballsbury. —Mr. Wilkins, junior, will be at Ballsbury, 3.15 P.M."

"Then," said the senior magistrate, "the prisoner had better be brought up again at half-past three."

"Perhaps your worship will instruct the police to call upon certain tradesmen I named to them, and request their attendance?"

"Certainly; the police will see to it."

The prisoner was then removed, and Doctor Whackley's pupils returned to Lexicon College, delighted at the idea of escaping for a whole day from lessons.

They were required to attend at the second examination of the prisoner.

At half-past three in the afternoon the court-room in the little town hall was thronged with people anxious to know how this strange case would terminate.

Just as the magistrates took their seats, a sharp-featured, sharp-eyed gentleman sat down at the table appropriated to the legal profession.

"Mr. Ferret, solicitor to the firm of Wilkins and Co. Mr. Wilkins, junior, is in court," he replied, in answer to the whispered interrogation of the magistrates' clerk.

The superintendent overheard the words and began to tremble for his reputation as an active, intelligent officer.

A dozen witnesses then came forward to prove that the prisoner was Mr. Hall, and that he had been for years traveller for the firm of Wilkins and Company, the junior partner of that firm giving evidence to the same effect.

"I think, sir, there is no reason for detaining the prisoner in the dock, where he would never have been placed, but for the gross stupidity of certain persons," observed Ferret, glancing at the little group of police.

"Certainly not—that is, if the prisoner can give any satisfactory reason for his being in the College grounds at that late hour."

Superintendent and sergeant gave each other knowing looks, as much as to say—"Ah, our magistrate, if he is a country gentleman, won't allow this pert London lawyer to have it all his own way. I wonder how he'll explain it."

They were not kept many seconds in suspense, for Mr. Hall immediately replied—

"I had been to the 'Six Bells,' to see the landlord, who is a very old friend. I stayed at his house till midnight, and was returning to the 'Red Lion' when I missed my way, and found that I was wandering about the cathedral grounds. I was trying to find the roadway when some one seized me, then a lot of boys came up, and last of all two policemen."

The host of the "Six Bells" was then called by Mr. Ferret, and testified that Mr. Hall left his house only about twenty minutes before he was captured.

"Quite sufficient," said the presiding magistrate. "The prisoner is dismissed, without a stain upon his character. At the same time I must caution him —ah—hump—not to do it again."

"Not to do what, may I ask, sir?" demanded Mr. Ferret.

The magistrate frowned, and the schoolboys tittered, but the London lawyer pressed his question.

"Not to be found in the grounds of Lexicon College after midnight. That's what I mean, sir."

And then the prisoner was dismissed; it having been established beyond doubt that he was a respectable commercial traveller and not a burglar.

The next day Baynes received a letter. He turned deadly pale as he read it, and then, having struck a lucifer match, burned it with the greatest care.

CHAPTER VI.

A NOBLE ACTION.

ABOUT a hundred yards from Lexicon College was a river, where, in the summer months, the young collegians bathed, and held their rowing matches.

The stream was very curved in form, and one of its bends was the natural boundary of three-fourths of the circumference of the ancient city of Ballsbury.

It should be mentioned, however, that only those who could swim well were allowed to bathe in, or row on this river: those who could not, being restricted to a tributary stream, whose greatest depth was about four feet.

Of course Frank Egerton could swim like an otter, and, of course, was allowed to use the big stream.

One afternoon he happened to be walking along its banks alone.

Lord Pembridge had gone for a long ride. Fitzgerald was deeply engaged in the study of Julius Cæsar, having been pronounced deficient in knowledge of that noble Roman; Marsham had gone up to the "Six Bells" to prove, by actual experiment, how many rats his terriers could kill in twenty minutes; Crawley was known to be engaged with Captain Robinson at the billiard-rooms, and others were engaged in amusements for which Egerton had not much taste.

So he resolved to walk down to the boat-house, row to Brightford (a village about three miles up stream), and persuade on old boatman there to give the Lexicon eight some professional training for their annual match.

He started across the meadow, sauntering along very slowly.

Suddenly a loud scream caused him to lift up his head and stare round.

The cry was repeated.

Apparently it proceeded from a part of the river, a couple of hundred yards above the boat-house.

Frank instantly changed his course, and hurried towards that part of the river from which the cries seemed to come.

As soon as he reached the brink of the stream the cause of the commotion became apparent.

In the middle of the water was a boat, keel upwards, to which clung an old man.

A few yards from him, and being gradually carried away by the current, was a young girl struggling violently to reach the bank, and uttering from time to time the piercing shrieks that had alarmed him.

One glance was sufficient to enable him to comprehend the state of affairs.

In an instant Frank threw off his jacket.

"Keep yourself afloat a minute longer," said he.

Then in he plunged.

It was easy enough to reach the girl, but to rescue her was a more difficult matter.

The poor creature, in her extreme terror, grasped wildly at his arms as he approached.

"If you do that, we shall both be drowned," he said. "You must wait till I turn my back towards you; then put a hand on each shoulder; but if you cling close to me I shall not be able to swim."

The girl made no reply, but it was evident from her look that she understood.

Five seconds afterwards, Frank was swimming with her towards shore, a matter of some difficulty, as, in spite of his exhortations, she kept so close as to greatly impede his movements.

At length, however, he had the satisfaction of landing her upon the bank.

Though much exhausted, the girl was not unconscious.

"My father!" she exclaimed, pointing piteously towards the old man, who still clung to the boat. "Oh, save him,

sir! Save him if you can! Pray save him!"

"I mean to," was Frank's simple response, as he again dashed into the stream.

"Hold fast!" he exclaimed, and commenced pushing the boat before him towards shore.

The gallant deed was done.

Two lives had been rescued by the King of the School!

As the weather was tolerably warm, neither the man nor his daughter received much injury from their immersion, beyond the fright, and in a few minutes they were able to walk away towards the town.

Frank cut short the profuse thanks they showered upon him, and hurried off to Lexicon College to change his clothes.

The Rev. John Whackley was walking up and down in front of the building as our hero approached.

"Why, Egerton," he exclaimed, "what have you been doing?"

"I—I have been in the water, sir," replied Frank.

"So I perceive. But why bathe with your clothes on."

Frank blushed, but did not reply for a few seconds.

"I always look upon hesitation as a symptom of fear or guilt. You have been doing something I should not approve of, I suppose?"

"No, sir, indeed! I——"

Again Frank hesitated, feeling bashful at having to tell the story of his own heroic actions.

"I must insist upon an explanation," continued the doctor, growing stern. "What have you been doing?"

"Well, sir, I was walking by the river, when I heard a scream, and saw that a boat had been overturned, and that a little girl was being carried away by the stream; so I swam out and brought her to shore."

"Bravo, Egerton! that was indeed an heroic action. But how came this little girl to be in a boat by herself?"

"Her father was with her, sir."

"What! then he is drowned?"

"No, sir; I managed to get him to land."

"Egerton, I am proud to number you among my pupils. But now hasten away and change your clothes, or you will be laid up with colds, rheumatism, and all sorts of ailments."

Although Frank resolved not to tell his companions anything of the adventure, and kept his resolution, his exploit soon became noised about over the school, and he became more of a hero than before.

CHAPTER VII.

PLANNING AN EXPEDITION.

"AND how are your dogs, Marsham?"

The speaker was Earl Pembridge; the company consisted, in addition to to the above-named, of Egerton, Fitzgerald, young Webber, and Harry, the general servant of all.

The place of meeting was an elm tree in the cathedral grounds; the time some three days after our hero's exploit as recorded in the last chapter.

"Stunning!" was the dog-fancier's proud response.

"Let's go out to the 'Six Bells' and get a lot of rats and see the beauties kill them," suggested Webber.

"That's a rather low occupation," suggested our hero.

"I'll tell you what would be fun," said Pembridge. "We'll take them up in the spinney and catch a lot of rabbits."

"We should want a ferret," Fitzgerald said.

"You had one at the court the other day," retorted Webber. "He was a trifle too sharp for you."

"No joking, Freddy; poaching and burglary are too very serious subjects."

"Some people can't see a good joke," replied the younger of the two boys.

"Silence! you fellows. What are you quarrelling about?"

"Freddy has cut up because I declined to burst myself through laughing at his attempts at wit."

"Well, now, attention all. It is agreed that we will go and catch some rabbits, if we can get a ferret; it would be useless to attempt it without."

"Yes; all agree."

"Then who knows where the ferret is to be procured?"

"Chancery Lane, London," chimed in Freddy, who could not help returning to the old subject of mirth.

"Be quiet."

"I know where to find one, sir," said poor "Harry the Heir," poor, however, no longer.

"Where?" asked all the boys at once.

"At the house I live in. The man keeps one in a box in his back garden; it bit me one day when I went to stroke its back.

"I should think it did, you little muff," observed Marsham; "the only way to be safe with a ferret is to grip it round the neck. However, you go and fetch it."

"Supposing the man won't lend it me, sir?"

"Then, all you have to do, is to take the animal, put him in your pocket handkerchief, and trot back here as soon as possible."

"But that would be stealing, sir!"

"You young stupid, don't you see—"

"The boy is quite right," interposed Egerton. "It would be stealing, and neither you nor I have any right to en-

courage him in so doing. The predatory instinct is quite strong enough in
all classes of society without needing
any encouragement."

"Do you hear that?" said Freddy
Webber; "you must learn to distinguish
between *meum* and *tuum*, and subdue
your predatory instincts, for remember,

"He who prigs what is'nt his'n,
  When he's caught is sent to prison!"

Young Harry who had not understood a word of the commencement of
Webber's oration, laughed most heartily
at its concluding couplet.

"Hold your tongue, Freddy," said
Egerton.

"Sir," replied Webber, endeavouring
to put on a look of fierce indignation,
"I desire you will not address me with
such coarse familiarity."

"Hold your tongue, I tell you."

"Have at ye, villain!" exclaimed
Freddy, in melo-dramatic tones, as he
sprang forward, aiming a playful blow,
which fell about six inches short of
Egerton's nose.

The next instant he was seized, and
lifted high above Frank's head.

Being thus captured, Freddy's great
idea was to escape; and, being rather
quick-witted, soon hit upon a plan.

He seized a bough of the elm tree,
about eight or nine feet from the
ground, and kicked himself free from
Egerton's grasp.

"How are you going to get down,
Freddy?" asked the Earl of Pembridge,
who knew that Webber was very timid
at jumping.

"Yes, that's what puzzles me."

"You'll have to roost there, Freddy."

"Nonsense. Here, you young Harry,
go and fetch me the garden ladder."

Harry was on his way to purchase or
hire the ferret, having been supplied
by the young earl with sufficient money
to purchase half-a-dozen of the vicious
animals.

More by way of joke than from in-
tentional desire to frighten him, the
others ther walked away. leaving poor
Webber perched up.

"Like a sparrow, by Jupiter!"

muttered he, after he had seen them
depart. "Well, my perch is not very
comfortable."

Immediately he began to chant—

"Of all the birds that seek the tree,
  Which is the wittiest fowl?
'Tis the cuckoo—the cuckoo—for he
  Is wiser than the owl.

"He dressed himself in his Sunday's best
  When breeding time began;
Then sent his children out to nurse
  In the house of another man."

Now it so happened that the reverend
principal was on his way to the cathedral, and, crossing the close, heard the
above lines carolled in no very gentle
voice.

He looked round, but none of the
pupils were visible.

"My ears must have deceived me,"
thought he, but at that moment again
came the refrain, louder and more
melodious than ever—

"'Tis the cuckoo—the cuckoo—for he
  Is wiser than the owl."

Seeing no one upon the ground, the
worthy doctor thought that the air was
the next best element to search, and,
not perceiving any human being soaring
in the sky, cast a glance up into one of
the venerable elm trees with which the
cathedral close abounded.

First of all he became aware of a pair
of boots attached to legs, dangling from
one of the lower branches of the tree,
and, looking more closely, perceived
that they belonged to Master Fred.
Webber.

"Why, Webber, what on earth are
you doing there?" demanded the much
amazed doctor.

"Trying to discover some way of
getting down, sir."

"How did you get there?"

"Why, sir, I was put up; and, as I
did not find my *nest* very comfortable,
I thought I would try a *lay*," replied
Freddy, who was as great a favourite
with the doctor as with his fellow
pupils.

"Ha, ha, ha! punning again, Webber;
bad habit. But you must get down;
how will you manage?"

"I think, sir, if you were to send

some one with the garden ladder it would be much more convenient than jumping."

"I'll send some one; but you musn't sing that curious song of yours so near the cathedral. Promise me that."

"I promise, sir."

The doctor hurried away, and soon afterwards Freddy was released.

When he rejoined his companions he pretended to be very much hurt at the joke played him.

"But, Freddy," said Egerton, "I believe it was you who placed the water jug over my door the first night I was here. You are good at playing practical jokes, so you must not object to having them practised upon yourself."

"Good argument, but it won't save you."

"Won't save me from what?"

"From my vengeance. I have meditated long on the subject, and I am determined that viewless beings from the innermost recesses of the earth shall nightly disturb your rest. Yes; I swear that in punishment for your enormities, Lexicon College shall be haunted!"

A loud laugh followed this bombastic speech.

"Laugh away, but remember my words when you pass sleepless nights, in endeavouring to discover what will be hidden—till I choose to reveal it."

"I fancy I shall be able to lay any ghosts you can raise, Freddy," said the Earl of Pembridge. "Why, I have lived in a haunted castle the best part of my life—I am not the least bit afraid of supernatural visitations."

The conversation ceased, and the boy Harry having returned with information that the ferret could be had on the following day, an arrangement was made by six or eight of the youths to meet at the "Six Bells" after school hours in the afternoon, and from thence proceed to the wood above the chalk-pit, where rabbit holes were known to be numerous.

CHAPTER VIII.

A LITTLE BIT OF SINGLE-STICK.

ACCORDINGLY, at the time and place appointed, they met.

"A werry good ferret, gents," observed mine host of the "Six Bells." "But surely you ain't a going to take them dawgs of yourn, Mr. Marsham? Why, they'd be just about as likely to kill the ferret as a rabbit."

So the "dawgs" were ordered back to their stable, and the jolly landlord produced half-a-dozen nets shaped something like bags, a string being threaded through the outside meshes of the mouth of each.

He explained to them that these bags were to be put down over the holes in which the rabbits resided. They, when disturbed by the ferret, would jump out, and become entangled in the bag-nets.

Thus equipped, the young heroes sallied out, and soon reached the wood.

Lord Pembridge had that day applied for and received permission from the proprietor of the wood to take rabbits there; the same privilege being accorded to any schoolfellows his lordship might choose to accompany him.

It was not necessary to search long ere a rabbit colony was discovered—a series of holes about five or six feet apart.

A net was put over each hole, the greatest silence being observed.

Then the long-bodied, pink-eyed

ferret was put down at the mouth of one of the holes, into which he very deliberately walked.

Marsham held up his hand to enforce silence.

A minute elapsed, then a rattling noise was heard under foot.

"Hush!"

Then, with a bound, a fine white-tailed rabbit leaped right into one of the bag nets, and rolled over, a kicking, struggling prisoner.

Marsham put his foot upon the hole to prevent the ferret from following.

Then he took out the prisoner and threw it, still alive, into a large sack.

A few seconds afterwards another net contained a captive, then another.

Then the ferret came out, and the earl suggested that they should try another locality.

They did so with equal success.

But suddenly came an interruption.

Four or five burly-looking men suddenly appeared upon the scene, and, in no very gentle terms, demanded—

"What are you young poaching rascals doing here?"

"Come, that's good," exclaimed Egerton. "I should advise you to keep a civil tongue in your head, or you may find yourself receiving a lesson."

"Who is going to give the lesson?" demanded one of the keepers.

"I will."

"Ah, you sall no fight!" exclaimed the well-known voice of Dr. Moeritz, and a minute afterwards the professor stepped forward.

"You had best get out of the way, old Frenchy," the keeper rudely said.

"I do not allow that you may threaten me," was the firm response of the German.

The keeper raised his stick in a threatening manner, and Herr Moeritz instantly prepared a trusty cudgel he had with him.

"Well, if you want your head broke, have it then. You Frenchers think yourselves good at fencing; let us see how you can manage a stick. Bill, Jim, see the youngsters don't get away."

"We are not going you may depend on it, till we have had the pleasure of seeing you receive a good beating," responded Charlie Fitzgerald.

The keeper, who was noted as a single-stick player, smiled, and assumed his guard, holding the stick at about half-arm's length before him, the top slightly pointing upwards.

Professor Moeritz assumed a hanging guard, sorely puzzling the keeper, who had never seen such a thing before.

Then they began.

Leatherlegs, the keeper, relying on his prowess, aimed a blow at the German's head, but it was cleverly stopped. However, he could not recover his own guard in time to save his hat—a new one, by-the-bye—from being sent spinning up among the trees.

"Capital! glorious!" exclaimed Webber, dancing about in his excitement. Then he began to sing the chorus of the old poaching song—

"For we can wrestle and fight, my boys,
   Jump over anywhere;
And its our delight on a shiny night,
   In the season of the year—"

"Freddy, I really think you must have been one of the singing birds, before you came to our side of the college," observed Egerton. "But would either of you gentlemen in corduroy like a little stick-practice? I should be very pleased to accommodate any one of you."

"Make it a four-handed game, and I'll be your partner," said Pembridge.

The under-keepers did not seem to see it though, and informed our hero that their chief's orders were to avoid fighting on all occasions.

All this time the two combatants were rattling away merrily, the blows sounding almost as rapidly as the clattering of an Ethiopian minstrel's "bones."

Occasionally a dull thud would be heard as the professor's stick paid a severe visit to the keeper's arm or shoulder.

Leatherlegs was perfectly astonished to find that no matter how he showered his blows, no matter how artfully he feinted, not one blow reached his antagonist.

Leatherlegs could not make it out.

His own right arm had been well punished from the wrist right up to the shoulder.

He grew wild and desperate, and, consequently, received more punishment than before. Still, he managed to guard his head pretty well, and trusted to his strength of limb and lung to weary Professor Moeritz, and at last break through his guard.

But Leatherlegs, on this occasion, reckoned without his host.

Professor Moeritz was far too experienced a swordsman to allow anything of the kind to take place.

He only waited for a safe opportunity, which soon came; then his stick descended with terrible force upon the keeper's head.

Leatherlegs, half stunned, dropped upon one knee, and held up his hands in token of defeat.

"Now you shall explain why you insult these young gentlemen!" said the professor.

"They are poachers; they have no right to come here and catch rabbits."

"You are wrong, my friend," replied the earl, "I received a letter from Squire Ousely this morning giving me permission to do so, and bring any of my schoolfellows. Can you read, Leatherlegs?"

"Yes."

"Then read that."

The earl handed him a letter.

Leatherlegs started rather as he perceived the address—"To the Right Honourable the Earl of Pembridge, &c."

After a glance at the contents of the note, he handed it back, saying—

"I begs your lordship's pardon, and yours, gentlemen, but the squire didn't tell me anything about this, and it was my duty——"

"All right; now show us the best part of the wood for this kind of sport, and I'll give you five shillings."

"Certainly, my lord."

"I say, isn't that giving a sound crown to heal a cracked one?" asked Webber.

"Now, Freddy, you really must not behave in this outrageous style," observed Fitzgerald. "Egerton was obliged to check you yesterday, remember."

"How kind of him."

"Freddy rather liked being stuck up a tree, I fancy," said Marsham.

"Not at all; I should be very sorry to put Frank to any inconvenience. But I can assure you that, although I was *stuck up* yesterday, I did not feel the least bit *proud* at occupying such an exalted position."

By this time they had reached another rabbit colony, where, after following the experienced advice of Leatherlegs, they managed to procure six more live rabbits.

Well pleased with their afternoon's sport, they then returned to the schoolhouse, the rabbits having been left at the "Six Bells," excepting three which Webber thought fit to carry home with him to help him in carrying out a scheme his fertile brain had invented.

"DR. WHACKLEY SUDDENLY STOOD BEFORE THEM."

No. 3.

CHAPTER IX.

A LITTLE BIT OF MYSTERY.

THAT evening, between the supper hour and bed-time, story-telling was the order of the day.

Some of the smaller boys commenced by relating to each other scenes from the "Arabian Nights," and when the hour came at which they were all compelled to retire, half-a-dozen groups might have been seen eagerly listening to some wonderful yarn.

Even our special and particular friends did not escape the mania, for young Webber came up and treated them to a ghost story, which, for accumulated horrors, could not be equalled.

As he proceeded with it deserters came in from other groups, till at last nearly half the inhabitants of Lexicon College were gathered round him.

When he had finished, many a boy went away to bed shuddering; but, as a finishing touch, Freddy intimated that a barbarous murder had been committed by one of the masters of Lexicon College many years ago.

"Tell us about it," said some of those who lingered about him.

"I don't know how it was done, but the story goes that a boy was one day called into the doctor's study — this happened more than two hundred years ago, mind—and he was never seen afterwards, till, during the holidays, some boys who did not go home were assembled in the box-room, when they noticed the missing fellow's box.

"Some one suggested that it should be opened to see what it contained. It was opened, and so horrible was the sight it presented, that three boys at once went into convulsions and died on the spot.

"What was in the box?" asked a small boy.

"The head and arms of the missing boy. The head opened its mouth, and said—'I was placed here by the head-master. Avenge me!' The boys promised to do so, and then the head became silent for ever. Nothing was ever known of the real facts of the case, but it was conjectured that the master locked the poor fellow up in his own box, where, rather than die of starvation, he gradually devoured himself!"

Egerton, Fitzgerald, and one or two others laughed heartily at this, but the majority of Freddy's hearers were evidently inclined to receive the story as gospel.

"You don't expect us to swallow that?" said Frank.

"It would not be so difficult a task as the poor fellow I have been telling about had—to swallow his own leg bones."

"What was done to the master?" inquired a junior.

"Why, it happened that at the time his horrible crime was detected he was away in London. It is supposed that he heard of the discovery and thought proper to abscond to Central Africa, where he lived for a time in a most magnificent style upon the interest of the pocket-money he took from his innocent victim. But during one week in the year the ghost of the poor fellow who died in the box is permitted to visit the old house. Let me see, it first comes on the—the——"

Freddy pulled out his pocket-book and pretended to refer to some entries in it.

"It begins its visits on the last night in July."

"Why, that is to-night," whispered one of the youngsters.

"Yes," said Fred, solemnly; "and I remember last year about this time some very strange noises were heard all over the house long after we had gone to bed. Don't you remember, Charlie? Don't you, Marsham?"

The two youths addressed, having a recollection of the uproar caused by a bolstering match, assented, and the hour having struck, they all retired.

At Lexicon College the bed-rooms were arranged on each side of two long corridors, one on the first floor and one above.

Some were occupied by parties of four, six, or even eight small boys; but the seniors slept two in a room.

The Earl of Pembridge in consideration of his rank, had an apartment to himself; and so did Webber, his companion, having been sent to that part of the building devoted to the sick.

The boy had caught a violent influenza and inflammation of the throat through not wrapping himself up properly after taking violent exercise on the water.

Half-an-hour was allowed them to disrobe, then a bell sounded, and all candles were extinguished.

On this particular night, a few minutes after the lights were out, a little party assembled in the earl's bed-room to partake of a second supper of cold chicken, cherry pie, and sherry.

The youngsters did not trouble about a candle, for the window was wide open, the moon was half-full, and the road to the mouth is never very difficult to discover.

Frank Egerton, Fitzgerald, Marsham, and Lascelles were there, but they still waited for Freddy Webber.

Egerton, as KING OF THE SCHOOL, occupied the post of honour at the head of the table, the host being on his right hand.

The feast was spread, and the boys felt hungry.

"What can keep Freddy, I wonder?" said Fitzgerald.

"Perhaps he has frightened himself with his own ghost story, and dares not venture along the corridor," suggested Lascelles

"I should like to bet two to one that Freddy does not believe in the supernatural more than any of the rest of us," said Marsham.

Just then the door quietly opened, and Webber entered.

The others could just see by the dim light in the room that his face seemed brimful of suppressed mirth; but he offered no explanation, and the feast commenced.

Dr. Whackley was well aware that the boys were in the habit of meeting in each other's rooms after hours, but so long as no disturbance was made he closed his eyes to this breach of the rules.

For some time they enjoyed themselves quietly enough, conversing in low tones, and pledging each other in tumblers of sherry and waters.

Suddenly they heard a very, very slight tap at the door.

"Come in," said the host, thinking that perhaps some other boy had heard of the feast and wished to join them.

There was no answer to this invitation, but a few seconds afterwards they again heard the sounds—tap, tap—followed by a slight scratching sound.

Lascelles, who happened to be sitting nearest the door, looked out immediately, fancying that some practical joke was being played.

Not a living being to be seen! He heard a rattling, pattering noise, though, towards the end of the corridor.

"Some of the fellows are getting up a spree," said the boy, as reseating himself at the table he reported what he had (or rather, had not) seen.

"They had better mind what they are about," observed the Earl of Pembridge.

Frank Egerton said nothing, but placed the water jug on the floor beside his chair, in evident readiness for a raid on the disturbers.

For some time all was silent, except that sundry sounds from the rooms beneath told them that others had been similarly disturbed.

Webber's face, as seen by the moon light, was a picture of delight.

The boy seemed brimful of mirth, and could scarcely refrain from indulging in a hearty peal of laughter.

About a quarter of an hour after the first disturbance, another slight tap was heard.

Frank dashed open the door in an instant, and threw half the contents of the water jug down the passage.

The same pattering sound as of some one scudding away at full speed was heard, but nothing could be seen.

"I tell you what, Freddy, you know something about this," said Marsham.

"I! How could I know anything about the noise in the passage when I am sitting quietly in the room. ?"

"It's one of your confounded ghost tricks."

"I said you should be haunted," replied Freddy, mysteriously.

"More likely it is the cat," observed Frank.

All his companions laughed at this.

"Don't you know old Whackley's weakness?" demanded Marsham; "he goes into fits at the sight of a cat. There isn't one in the house."

"But tell us what all this noise is about, Freddy. Hark! the fellows below are having a fine time of it."

As the boys listened, they could hear doors in the lower corridor opened, and boots, books, bolsters, and various other missiles hurled at the unseen foe.

Then another sound was heard.

A martial footstep was heard pacing along the passage beneath, doors were opened, and a voice was heard demanding what was the matter.

"The doctor, by everything that is scholastic!" exclaimed Freddy.

"A nice mess you have got us into, youngster," observed Lascelles, with a sigh.

"Pooh! he won't come here; and if he does, we can all very truthfully affirm that we have made no noise."

As if to give Freddy a direct contradiction, the next moment a knock was heard at the door, and, without waiting to be invited to enter, Doctor Whackley suddenly stood before them.

"So, young gentlemen, you seem to be enjoying yourselves. You should all by this time know that such proceedings are most decidedly against the rules."

"Certainly, sir, we were all well aware that, strictly speaking, we were breaking the letter of the law; but I appeal to you, sir, whether it has not been customary to allow a certain amount of licence to the upper forms of the school?"

"It has generally been so, I am willing to allow, nor should I have interfered on the present occasion had you not, by the perpetration of some practical joke, disturbed all the school."

During all this time Freddy Webber, struck with the brilliant idea that it would be as well to conceal as much of the feast as possible from the doctor, had carefully concealed the cherry-pie, or rather its remains, between the sheets of the Earl of Pembridge's bed.

Having done so he turned round and observed—

"I am sure, sir, we have been too busy eating and drinking to wish to disturb any one. We have heard strange noises in the corridor——"

"And I looked out once to see what it was," interrupted Lascelles.

"You will each translate fifty lines from Virgil before seven o'clock to-morrow evening. Oh!—what was that?"

The boys eagerly inquired what was the matter, while Doctor Whackley turned about sharply, striking wildly with his stick at something in the passage.

"I received a blow which I am convinced could not have been dealt by any of you, it came from behind."

Egerton immediately rushed to the door, and walked from one end of the corridor to the other.

"There certainly is no human being here, save ourselves," said he, on returning from his peregrinations. "Yet I certainly heard the sound of some one breathing. There! I received a pat on the calf of the leg."

"Light a candle," cried Egerton.

A candle was lighted immediately, but though the doctor looked about him in every direction nothing could be seen.

"This is certainly very strange," observed the doctor. "I can't make it out. However, I should advise all you young gentlemen to retire to your respective rooms. Good-night."

"Good-night, sir. But how about the fifty lines?" asked Marsham.

"Humph! Well, as it seems you were not so much in fault as I supposed, you may do only twenty lines each. Now go to bed."

"But, sir, if these noises are repeated another night may we not try to discover the cause?"

"Well, yes; I should have no objection. But if you discover the offender you must give him up to me."

With these words the doctor departed.

"Come, Freddy, enlighten us as to the nature of this little joke," said Lascelles.

"What little joke? How is it possible I could strike the doctor and Egerton while I was sitting here? It is very absurd, indeed, to ask me to enlighten you; I shall take the doctor's advice, and go to bed."

"Don't go yet, Freddy," said the earl.

"Yes, I must; the thought of having twenty lines to do has completely spoilt my appetite. Good-night."

Webber took his departure, and in a few minutes afterwards the strange noises ceased.

Having recommenced their interrupted feast, the others began to look for the cherry-pie.

It was not to be seen.

"Another of Freddy's games," observed Egerton. "I suppose he has taken it with him. However, there is plenty of chicken left."

It was at least half an hour after the doctor's departure ere the guests took their departure from the young earl's room, and dispersed to their own apartments.

"Twenty lines of Virgil! heigho!" yawned the young peer, as he began to disrobe. "And I wonder what became of the pie."

He was not left to wonder long, for, having attempted to step into bed, he put his foot right into the very midst of the very piece of pastry that had so mysteriously disappeared, and succeeded in overturning the dish.

"Here's a pretty mess!" he ejaculated, gazing at the sheets, stained a bright red, as was his own foot and leg. I shall have to speak seriously to Master Freddy on the subject. However, as the night is warm, it will be no great hardship to sleep upon the sofa."

Which he did.

⚜

CHAPTER X.

BOYISH COURTSHIP, RESULTING IN DISGRACE.

BAYNES had recovered from the effects of the severe beating given him by the King of the School.

He kept very much to himself, however, seldom mixing in the sports and pastimes of his schoolfellows.

Crawley was his inseparable companion and toady.

Baynes's chief amusement was fishing.

It reminded him so much of real life, he said; the simple being always caught by the cunning.

To this Crawley assented, little thinking that Baynes looked upon him as a gudgeon that, having been long since caught, was now being used as a bait for others.

"I don't think you'll catch young Egerton though."

"I can see plainly enough that he is destined to be a thorn in my side. Either he must fall or I shall. The game has commenced, the question is, WHO WILL WIN?"

This conversation took place in the playing field.

The speakers were seated beneath a tree not far from the river; Crawley engaged in tying some flies for his friend; Baynes, with hands thrust deep in his trousers pockets, was meditating.

Other groups of the pupils of Lexicon College were scattered about the field.

One of these groups was headed by Frank Egerton, who was most anxious to try the driving powers of a new cricket-bat he had that morning purchased.

At that moment a small boy made his appearance at the gate of the field, shouting—

"Egerton, Egerton!"

"Here!"

"A letter for you."

"Bring it over, you lazy little beggar!" exclaimed Marsham.

"Just walk round quietly, Crawley," said Baynes, "and see if you can find out anything about that letter. It must be from the town; for London mid-day mail was delivered two hours ago."

Crawley did not like the job very much, but he had not the strength of mind to disobey his imperious friend.

After prowling about for some minutes, he returned with his report.

"It is from that old man he saved—or rather from the daughter."

"Ha!"

"I couldn't hear all, but there was a lot of bosh about eternal gratitude, and so forth, winding up with an invitation to visit the humble roof of the writer to-morrow afternoon."

"Good! And what said Egerton?"

"Why, he invited Fitzgerald and Pembridge to go with him, much to the disgust of Marsham, who fancies himself a lady-killer. It seems the girl has one or two sisters—milliners' work-girls."

"Ah!" exclaimed Baynes. "We shall see what the doctor will think of it if this self-styled King of the School degrades himself by visiting a lot of low people."

"But I heard Pembridge say that he knew the father, a most respectable old buffer."

"So he may be, but we must make it appear to the contrary."

"Why?" asked Crawley, who was not quite such an adept in plotting as his friend, not from want of disposition, but from lack of ability to form a crafty scheme and carry it out boldly

*   *   *   *   *

The next afternoon, when school hours were over, Frank Egerton, the young Earl of Pembridge, and Charlie Fitzgerald, started from Lexicon College, and walked briskly away towards Fishingham, one of the suburbs of the old city of Ballsbury.

"Who knows the way to Mr. Conway's house?" asked Fitzgerald.

"I know the street," responded the Earl of Pembridge.

"And I know the number," said Egerton.

In a few minutes they had reached the house from which the invitation was dated.

It was a pleasant-looking little place, though, as the Earl of Pembridge afterwards observed, the whole house could very well have been placed in the entrance hall of the home of his ancestors.

Mr. Conway, as the old gentleman was called, whom Frank Egerton has rescued from destruction, was standing at the door, evidently waiting for them.

He stepped forward, and grasped Frank's hand, exclaiming—

"You are most heartily welcome

Mr. Egerton, and your friends too. But, come in; Kate is anxious to thank you!"

So saying, he ushered them into the small parlour where Kate Conway was sitting, busy with her needle.

As soon as she saw who it was she dropped her work, ran forward, and grasped him by the hand.

"Oh, Mr. Egerton!" she said, "this is kind of you."

"The kindness is on your side rather in inviting me, Miss Conway."

"We were obliged to do so, or else we should never have had an opportunity of thanking you for your bravery in rescuing us. I am indeed grateful, Mr. Egerton, more so than I can find words to express."

"Pray say no more about this, Miss Conway. I only did as any one else would have done."

Frank then introduced his companions, Charlie Fitzgerald and the Earl of Pembridge.

Kate Conway opened her blue eyes a little wider than usual when the young peer held out his hand, and was a moment, in doubt whether she ought not to go down on one knee, and kiss the fingers he extended, or do something equally ridiculous.

In a moment, however, he gave her hand a hearty shake, and shortly afterwards found herself on such friendly terms as to be boldly asking him whether he got flogged the same as other boys when his conduct was not quite in accordance with the laws of Lexicon College.

The young earl laughingly explained that no distinction was made, and that his title was no protection to his person.

After little conversation the young lady began to busy herself about the tea table, observing that her sister, Lizzie, would soon be home from work.

"Is Lizzie dark or fair?" asked the impudent young earl.

"Dark," responded Kate.

"Is she pretty?"

"Yes."

I'm so glad."

"Why?"

"Because I like dark beauties. How old is she?"

"A year younger than myself. But, if you are not very good I shall not give you any tea; so, be kind enough not to frighten the poor girl, for she is very timid and nervous."

A few seconds afterward Mr. Conway entered with his youngest daughter, a piquante brunette of nearly fifteen, who certainly appeared quite as bashful and nervous as she had been represented.

Then came the tea.

Kate Conway presided, and a merry meal it was.

There was so much laughing and chatting, when the brunette had vanquished her shyness, that it is wonderful how they found time to eat and drink; yet the brown bread and butter, shrimps, watercresses, seed-cake and toast certainly did disappear most rapidly.

Mr. Conway at first watched rather anxiously to see how the young fellows treated his daughters, but finding that they knew how to behave as gentlemen he gradually became lost in his own meditations, which seemed to be of a rather sorrowful nature.

Tea being finished the two girls rapidly cleared away the fragments of the meal.

Fitzgerald perceiving an old cottage piano in one corner of the room began to play a melancholy air.

"Come let us have something a little more lively," said Pembridge.

Charlie instantly struck up a merry polka.

By some strange instinct Frank Egerton's arm immediately founds its way round Kate's waist, the young earl quickly secured Lizzie as a partner, and the two couples began dancing.

Fitzgerald was a pretty fair musician, but the feet of his companion seemed destined to tire his fingers.

After about a dozen polkas and waltzes had been performed, he gave up or rather rested for a time.

Frank and Kate were seated near the window.

The King of the School still kept his arm round her waist, and, unable to resist the sudden temptation, he bent over and kissed her bright red lips.

The fair girl blushed, but did not look very displeased, and Frank felt compelled to repeat the salute, a peculiar noise close at hand informing him that his friend Pembridge was similarly engaged.

At that moment a look of intense surprise and alarm crossed Kate Conway's face.

"Look!" said she, glancing timidly at the window.

Frank did so, and beheld the face of the Reverend John Whackley.

If the truth must be confessed, Frank Egerton was not a little astonished to see that stern face at the window.

However, he had sufficient presence of mind to bow, and then, in obedience to a signal from the head master, he went to the door.

"You and your companions will return to college within the hour. On your arrival there I expect to see you in my study."

With these words the doctor stalked away.

"What's in the wind now, I wonder?" asked Frank, as he returned and reported his interview to the others.

"I don't know—can't imagine? responded Pembridge.

"However, as he has given us an hour to return, I shall take advantage of it. We can walk back in ten minutes, so we have forty left for enjoyment.

"Will you be flogged?" asked Lizzie, staring with her great black eyes in the Earl of Pembridge's face, and making a terrible hole in the young peer's heart.

"No; I don't think so," was the response. "Not that I care much for a whipping."

"Come, don't talk in that doleful style," said Frank. "I am the chief offender; but I want another waltz before I go to be executed."

Charlie Fitzgerald re-commenced playing, nor was he allowed to stop till the forty-minutes had expired, and it was time to hurry back to Lexicon College.

After bidding Kate and Lizzie a hurried farewell, they hastened away, and shortly afterwards stood in the presence of the irate pedagogue.

"Well, young gentlemen, and what have you to say in excuse for such infamous conduct?" he asked.

"Sir!" exclaimed all the three boys, immensely surprised.

"I say what excuse can you make for such infamous conduct?"

"I am not aware that I have been guilty of anything to which the term infamous can be applied," responded Frank.

"But I myself saw you in that house with those people.

"Certainly, sir; but there is nothing very infamous in that."

"Poor boy! are you so misguided, blinded, then? Could you not perceive the character of the neighbourhood, the house, and the people? Yet, stay; you, of course are too young and inexperienced to know.

"I certainly do not clearly understand you, sir," said Pembridge.

"Then I will tell you in plain words. That house and the people in it should never be seen by pupils of mine. See, here is a letter I received only this afternoon, warning me of the place, and that pupils of mine were in the habit of going there.

The doctor handed a letter to Egerton, whose face flushed as he read it.

"The writer of this is most guilty of foul slander," said the King of the School, as he handed the paper to his friend and relative, Charlie Fitzgerald.

"So say I," observed the latter.

"And I," said Pembridge, who had been looking over the other's shoulder.

"Since you have formed that opinion, it will be necessary to convince you that I think to the contrary. You will all remain within the school premises for three weeks, copying each day one of the odes of Horace. You will also take place below all the other boys in your form. Away with you; I consider you have disgraced the college."

"But, sir——"

"No excuses will avail now. To your rooms and never go near that house again.

Our three friends marched off to the schoolroom, looking rather crestfallen.

Knowing very well that it would be useless to attempt to conceal the disgrace into which they had fallen, Frank Egerton, after brief consultation with his companions in tribulation, deemed it best that they should relate their own story before any garbled statements were set afloat.

Most of the boys were sincerely sorry to hear it, though about half-a-dozen of the Baynes and Crawley stamp did not attempt to conceal their joy and exultation.

As they were retiring to bed that night, the Earl of Pembridge whispered to Frank—

"Come into my room presently, Egerton; I want to have a long chat with you."

As invited, Frank went.

After some little preliminary talk, the young earl plunged boldly into the subject.

"What do you think of those girls, Frank?" he asked.

"They are both charming creatures, and far better educated than most people in their position."

"They are lovely—divine! Do you know, Frank, I have fallen over-head-and-ears in love with that delicious little Lizzie."

"That's wrong, old fellow."

"Wrong! Why?"

"Because you cannot think of marrying her."

"But I do think of doing so—in a year a two, of course. I'll try and wait till I've been down to Oxford."

"You will not be allowed to marry her till you are twenty-one, at any rate. Do you forget that you are a ward in chancery?"

Earl Pembridge sat in silence for some few minutes, then he said—

"Frank, when you hear, in a few years' time, that I am married, come and see me, and you will find that Lizzie will be my wife, I love her; and the Court of Chancery, the House of Peers, both spiritual and temporal, backed up by a few committees of the House of Commons, won't induce me to alter my resolution."

"I wish you success and happiness."

"Of course, I know," continued the earl, "there will be some tremendous difficulties with my mother, who, though she is the jolliest, nicest woman out, is awfully stuck up about family dignity, maintaining the honour of an ancient house, and all that kind of stuff; but I'll find some means of quieting her."

"We will hope so."

"But tell me, Egerton, how do you stand with the fair-haired Kate?"

The question made the KING OF THE SCHOOL start and change colour; he was not prepared for such a direct thrust.

After a few moments' hesitation and confusion, Frank commenced his reply.

"Well, you see——"

"I saw, certainly."

"What did you see?"

"I saw you kiss her just as old Whackley looked through the window. That's what put him in such a rage."

"She's a nice girl—very nice," observed Frank, contemplatively.

"And the truth is, you are about as fond of her as I am of Lizzie."

"I suppose that is about the case, old fellow."

"Now what will your mamma say, you naughty boy? Of course you old country families are quite as particular about anything that lowers your dignity as any wearer of a coronet could be."

"Of course there will be difficulties; but I should like to know who wrote that letter."

" So would I. But, Frank, I am not going to stay in bounds for three weeks."

"I don't think I shall. But, good-night, old fellow; I am most awfully sleepy."

The two boys then sought their respective couches, to dream of the pretty creatures they had been dancing with.

Hope whispered in their ears that time might and would remove many of the obstacles that stood in the way of the attainment of their wishes.

CHAPTER XI.

CHANGED PROSPECTS.

A WEEK passed away.

Neither Frank Egerton nor the Earl of Pembridge had as yet gone beyond the boundary prescribed. Charlie Fitzgerald, not being in love, took his punishment more calmly, though the confinement was very irksome even to him.

One morning Frank received a letter.

" It was in his mother's handwriting, but Egerton was compelled to read it through twice ere he could thoroughly comprehend it.

" My darling Frank," it said. " You must ask doctor Whackley to allow you to return home immediately. Your father is very, very ill, and I fear for the result. His unfortunate city speculations have been the ruin of his health. So come home at once, dear Frank, to your affectionate, grieving mother.

"ADA EGERTON."

Frank at once rushed off to Doctor Whackley's study, showed him the letter, and was told that he might start immediately.

Two or three of his friends assisted him to pack up his portmanteau, and then saw him off to the railway station.

How long the journey seemed compared with that *to* school, and how different everything appeared.

At length he reached London.

Calling a cab, he jump into it, and was speedily driven to his father's town residence.

His mamma was waiting for him in the hall, and as Frank leaped from the vehicle, he could see that she had been weeping.

In an instant he clasped her in his arms and kissed her.

" You must not worry yourself, my dear mamma," said he. " All will be well in a few days."

Mrs. Egerton's only answer was a sob.

" And how is papa ?"

The sobs increased, but in the midst of them Frank fancied he heard the solemn word, " DEAD ! "

So sudden, so solemn and fearful was the news that it proved too much for even the healthy nerves of the boldest boy of Lexicon College.

He swooned.

On his recovery, he found himself lying upon a couch, by the side of which knelt his mother imploring the powers above to grant the widow and the orphan strength to bear the great trial that had befallen them.

* * * * *

Three days elapsed.

All that was mortal of poor Frank's father had been consigned to the tomb, and a little party had assembled in the library to hear the will read.

It was very short.

Everything the testator possessed was bequeathed to his son,—Mrs. Egerton and Mr. Throckmorton, the family solicitor, being executors.

The ceremony had scarcely been concluded, when the butler entered with a large official-looking letter, addressed to Mrs. Egerton.

"Read it for me, please," said the widow, handing it to Mr. Throckmorton.

The legal gentleman did so.

"I must speak to you and Mr. Frank alone," said he, when he had looked through the letter.

Mrs. Egerton wearily rose, and led the way to another apartment.

"This letter," said Mr. Throckmorton, when he had closed the door, "is from a solicitor, and is to inform you that his client, Thorfield Hilton Baynes, holds a mortgage on all the estates of the late Mr. Egerton, and that if the sum of £9,475, 16s. 8s. is not paid within three days from the date of this letter, the mortgagee will be compelled to foreclose without delay."

"Then, pray, settle with him without delay, Mr. Throckmorton."

"I am sorry to be obliged to inform you, madam, that the matter is too serious to be disposed of in so easy a manner. There is not an eighth part of that sum standing to your credit in the bank."

"Oh, why did you not advise him against such a step?"

"I assure you, on my word of honour, madam, that I never, till this day, heard of such a mortgage. He once spoke to me on the subject, but I fancied I had persuaded him to abandon the scheme."

"Then, what is to be done?" sighed the poor widow.

"That requires consideration, madam. Your husband borrowed all the available cash I possessed some three months since, or I could have offered to relieve your difficulties."

"Only three days! that is cruel!" exclaimed Frank. Surely, this must be the father of the boy I thrashed!"

"What!"

"There is a boy named Hilton Baynes at Lexicon College. I gave him a very severe beating the first day I was there. Perhaps this is his revenge."

"My son, why did you fight to bring all this trouble upon me?"

"I would not have done so, mamma, had I guessed what it would result in; but I could not stand by and see him ill-treat one much smaller and weaker than himself."

"It cannot be helped now, Frank, dear," said Mrs. Egerton, throwing her arms round her son's neck. "The only thing we have to consider is how to get rid of this mortgage."

"I will see this solicitor at once, and get an interview with Mr. Baynes, if possible," said Throckmorton. "Perhaps we may be able to come to some amicable arrangement."

Mr. Throckmorton did manage an interview with Mr. Baynes's solicitor the next day, and Mr. Baynes himself happened to come in while the two were conversing.

But no good resulted from the meeting, and he was compelled to return to Mrs. Egerton, and inform her that, according to the terms of the letter, the money must be forthcoming within the specified time.

The remainder of the term of grace granted was spent by Mr. Throckmorton in endeavouring to raise sufficient money to pay off the encumbrance.

In that too he was unsuccessful, though he tried in every direction.

* * * * * *

Heartrending was the scene when the widow and orphan were compelled to quit the home which, for so many years, had been one of happiness to them.

On examination it was found that Mrs. Egerton, after setting aside a sum for Frank's education, would be in receipt of an income of nearly two hundred a-year.

"That's enough to live on till I can retrieve our fortunes," said Frank, endeavouring to put a gay face upon the matter.

Eventually a small house was taken in the southern suburbs, to which the widow lady removed.

Frank returned to school, it having been determined that he should remain there for another year at least.

<hr />

CHAPTER XII.

A CONSULTATION.

At Lexicon College Frank found things going on much as they had been previous to his father's death.

The boys had heard from the Earl of Pembridge and Charlie Fitzgerald that it was Baynes's father who had held the fatal mortgage; accordingly Baynes himself was for a few days shunned more than before.

Gradually however, he was re-establishing himself in the good opinion of some.

"How can it be my fault? What blame can attach to me?" he would ask. "I am not responsible for my father's business transactions. And, if Egerton had written to me when notice was first given, I might have helped to make some arrangement."

This argument was accepted by many of the boys; but it was quite evident to some of the more observing ones that Baynes was in reality very pleased at the misfortune that had come upon our hero.

For a day or two after his return Frank was permitted to do as he pleased, but he very soon settled down into the regular routine of the school.

*　*　*　*　*　*

Egerton very soon found that the mysterious sounds in the corridor were still heard at nights.

No one had been able to discover now they were caused.

Watching was useless.

Frank had a notion that Webber had something to do with it.

By way of proving the correctness of his idea he took an opportunity of quietly turning the key in the lock one night when leaving Freddy's room after a friendly chat, thus making that ingenious youth a prisoner.

The trick was so far successful that no strange noises were heard that night.

It would be impossible, however, to always keep Freddy under lock-and-key, so Frank set his wits to work to find out in what manner the peculiar sounds were produced.

The next night, as soon as all the boys were in their rooms, he strewed the whole of the floor of the corridor and staircase with fine sand, upon which would appear the footprints of any one who walked about in the night.

Next morning after the sounds had been louder than usual, Frank, and one or two others to whom he had entrusted his secret, looked out.

The sand upon the flooring was marked with the most peculiar kind of scratches imaginable, but no footmarks could be seen.

The boys were more puzzled than ever, and the younger ones were confirmed in their belief that Lexicon College was haunted by unquiet spirits.

Frank Egerton, Marsham, the Earl of Pembridge, and Charlie Fitzgerald, held a consultation.

Each of them had thoroughly examined the floor of the corridor before the sand was swept away.

"Those marks could not have been caused by any human being," observed Fitzgerald.

"Yet how could a phantom—a thing of air, a mere shadow—do anything of the kind?" asked Frank.

"Perhaps neither a human being nor a spirit is the moving cause of these strange noises observed the earl.

"In which case we must suppose some vegetable substance to be endowed with powers of locomotion. How absurd!" sneered Marsham.

"Not at all," replied Pembridge.

"Then how could the noises be made?"

"By animals of the inferior order."

"Ah, that is possible," said Frank.

"But where do the animals come from? There are no cats or dogs in the house," said Marsham.

"That's what we have to find out.'

"Then if they are animals, my animals, my pets, shall have a look at them."

"What do you mean?"

"I mean to bring my two terriers into school to-night, and take them up to my room. As soon as the noise is heard open goes the door, and out goes Pincher. The result is, of course, that any living thing not big enough to run away with the dog is stopped."

"Very good. But what will be the consequence?"

"We discover the ghost."

"And the Doctor discovers that your dogs have been brought into the school-house, contrary to his express orders."

"I don't think he would be very angry. At all events, I'll risk it for the sake of unearthing Freddy's ghosts."

The little group then separated. Marsham went to the "Six Bells" to visit his ghost hounds, as he now styled the terriers.

He had the satisfaction of finding them in a very lively condition and evidently well fitted for the task he desired them to perform.

Fitzgerald, who had taken a very studious turn of late, went back to the school-house to thumb the pages Homer.

"I must imitate his example," Frank Egerton remarked to his companion, the Earl of Pembridge.

"I hope not. Charlie is getting quite ill."

"It is necessary for me to study now more than ever. My prospects are very much changed, and I shall have to work hard to make myself a name and position when I leave school."

"What profession do you intend to adopt?"

"It is my father's wish that I should become a barrister, and I now feel more than ever compelled to respect his wishes."

"Frank, I have, or shall have much influence. It shall be exerted to the utmost to promote your welfare."

"For which promise I sincerely thank your lordship."

"Oh, bother! and drop the title please, Frank."

"Certainly if you wish it. And now I want you to tell me if you have seen or heard anything of those girls?"

"No; I wrote to Lizzie though, and had an answer. She and her sister were extremely sorry to hear of your misfortune. I wish I could find out who sent that note to the doctor.

"So do I. 'Sorry to inform you that your pupils frequently visit a house inhabited by people whose moral character will not bear examination—a house well known to the police.' By Heaven! a good idea strikes me. The police shall tell the doctor what they know about old Conway and his daughters."

"That would be best."

"I will write to the inspector this evening, and ask him to call upon the doctor to-morrow!"

Acting upon this idea, the two boys returned to the school, and concocted an epistle which they dispatched by the hands of their general servant, Harry, to the inspector of the Ballsbury police.

In half-an-hour the messenger returned.

" Well?" demanded frank.

" That's his answer, sir," said Harry, handing a letter.

Eagerly tearing open the envelope, he read that the inspector knew nothing whatever against the people mentioned, believed them to be very respectable, and would be happy to serve Mr. Egerton and his friend, the Earl of Pembridge, by stating as much to the principal of Lexicon College.

" That's all right," said he, most joyously.

～～ᴂᴄᴏ

CHAPTER XIII.

LAYING THE GHOSTS.

THAT evening at supper-time there was a general buzz of whispered conversation going on.

Somehow or other the secret had leaked out that Egerton and Marsham had bid defiance to the ghosts, and that the secret would most probably be divulged during the night.

As they trooped off to bed Frank and his companions stood at the bottom of the staircase, and cautioned them all to keep in their rooms.

They were the last to retire.

Doctor Whackley had been informed that his senior pupils intended to trap the midnight disturbers, but had not been told how it was to be done.

He promised them that no one should be permitted to interfere with their arrangements, then went to his study.

For about an hour after retiring all was quiet.

The four boys had met in Marsham's room, which happened to be close to the head of the stairs.

Of course the dogs were there (Freddy had not been told of this): and the owner of the apartment had also provided a policeman's lantern.

" Freddy is frightened; he won't let his ghosts loose to-night," said Fitzgerald.

" Hark ! here it is," observed Pembridge, holding up his finger in a listening attitude.

" I don't hear it," said Frank rising softly.

" Nor I," said Marsham. " Besides I know these two beauties would soon give the alarm if any one walked along that corridor."

" Well, I fancy I shall go to bed," observed Fitzgerald after a pause.

" Don't go yet," was the general response.

" I can hear the spirits moving now," said Frank.

At that moment one of the dogs, Pincher, half rose, and, looking towards the door, gave a low growl.

" Be quiet," muttered Marsham, stooping down and placing a hand over each dog's mouth.

The pattering noise was now plainly heard on the staircase.

At last there came the gentle scratching sound at the door of the room they were in.

That was the signal for action.

Fitzgerald immediately turned on the bull's-eye, while Frank Egerton threw open the door.

" At them, good dogs ! Kill them !" exclaimed Marsham, and with a succession of shrill barks the two terriers dashed out.

One boldly scampered down the stairs, its feet making a noise something like that they had previously heard, while the other dashed up the corridor.

By the time Fitzgerald could get to the door with the light a succession of shrill voices were heard.

The next moment they saw that Pincher had secured a fine rabbit.

The other dog had rushed down stairs: and, as soon as captive number one had been killed, the boys prepared to see what was going on below.

Of course many of the other boys had kept awake in anticipation, and more than one door was thrown open as they passed to see what had happened.

Freddy Webber peeped out.

"Sold, my boy!" exclaimed Marsham, playfully striking him on the head with the dead rabbit.

"What a shame to kill the poor rabbit," replied Freddy, retiring into his room to hide his vexation at the discovery of his trick, and the death of his pet.

Egerton and his friends hurried away towards the lower part of the house.

On arriving at a large room in which the pupils were allowed to keep boxes to contain their bats, balls, cricket shoes, &c., they found the dogs making desperate exertions to reach two or three more rabbits.

The animals had retreated to a kind of hutch, and were safe.

"At all events we know how the noise is made," said Frank; "that is one great satisfaction."

"But we must punish Freddy in some way or other," replied the proprietor of the dogs.

"We had better wait till to-morrow," said Frank. "Let us see how the doctor takes it."

At that moment the gentleman spoken of made his appearance.

"Well, young gentlemen, have you discovered——Ah, what is this?" he exclaimed, as one of the dogs took a sniff at his leg.

"Two dogs, sir," said Marsham.

"Is it these animals that have caused this disturbance for some weeks past?"

"No, sir."

"Then how came they here?"

"They are mine, sir; I brought them into the college to assist in detecting the offenders."

"Against the rules. Remind me of this circumstance in the morning, Fitzgerald."

"I assure you, sir, this is the first time they have been in the building. I should not have brought them in now, had it not been suggested that they would find out the nocturnal prowlers."

"Humph! Well, don't let it occur again. What did you find?"

"Some rabbits, sir. Here is one of them."

"Killed the ghost, eh? ha, ha! But now we must find out to whom these four-footed animals belong. Do you know, Fitzgerald?"

"Yes, sir," responded Charlie, after a moment's hesitation.

"Who is the owner?"

Fitzgerald hesitated more than before, and the doctor repeated his question, adding—

"If you know, you may as well tell me. If you refuse, you only draw down punishment upon yourself; and I shall be pretty certain to find out from some one else."

"They belong to Webber, sir."

"Very good. Now then to your beds, boys. These dogs, I suppose, must remain here all night? I hope they won't bark or howl."

"I'll take care of that, sir," replied Marsham.

"'MURDER!' BELLOWED FREDDY, HOLDING UP HIS HAND WITH THE CRAB."

CHAPTER XIV.

FREDDY IS DOUBLY PUNISHED.

THE next morning, when the names were called over, Doctor Whackley ordered Freddy to come to the front.

He then harangued the whole school on the sin of practical joking generally, and of Freddy's joke in particular.

The worthy doctor detailed every circumstance; how the rabbits were originally captured in the woods, how Webber had brought them home and confined them in this hutch, always taking care to leave the door open at night, a circumstance which the instinct of the animals led them to take advantage of, for the purpose of indulging in a scamper over the premises; the same instinct inducing them to return to their lair at daybreak.

Having been thus solemnly reproved, poor Freddy was well birched, an operation which brought the water into his eyes.

However, he soon recovered his natural good spirits, and an hour after school, had, in all probability, forgotten his whipping.

The King of the School and those who aided in the detection of the rabbit trick, had, after another consultation, come to the conclusion that the dozen strokes Freddy received were not a sufficient punishment for his offence.

So, in spite of the doctor's warning against practical joking, they resolved to victimise poor Webber.

How to do it though was the great question.

Stale dodges would be simply a waste of time, for Freddy would naturally be on the look out, and, therefore, would not be very easily trapped.

Several plans were suggested, but all were found fault with.

"Let us take a stroll through the town," said the earl. "We may see something or other that will give us an idea."

The proposal was agreed to, and they set out.

A shoemaker's shop very naturally suggested wax, but that was over-ruled.

"See!" exclaimed Frank, pausing before a fish-stall, on which some crabs were exhibited. "If we could only get some of those alive!"

"What would you do with them?"

"Put them in his bed."

"You can have some live ones this evening, sir," said the proprietor of the fish establishment.

"That's jolly. What time?"

"About eight o'clock."

A bargain was immediately concluded.

* * * * *

Evening came, and poor Freddy little knew what was in store for him.

After supper, the Earl of Pembridge slipped away without being observed, and placed the live crabs beneath the covering of Freddy's bed.

Webber feared that something was intended, and hastened away soon after.

His room, however, appeared not to have been entered by any one.

He waited for the boy who occupied the other bed, and who had returned from the sick department, and saw Hutchinson fairly beneath the sheets ere he himself attempted to undress.

When he did commence to disrobe, it was not many seconds before he had divested himself of his clothing.

Then he sprang into bed, leaving the light burning.

He felt some *foreign substance*, and immediately put down his hand to feel what it was.

This, of course, was a fine opportunity for crab number one, who immediately seized Freddy's finger in its powerful claws, while at the same moment crab number two made a desperate onslaught on his toes.

"Murder!" bellowed Freddy, holding up the hand from which dangled the crab, and——"Murder!" he shouted a second time, as he kicked aside the bed-clothes, exhibiting the foot that was being attacked by the other animal.

Hutchinson raised himself up on his elbow, and gave a quiet chuckle at the strange scene.

"What's the matter, Freddy?" inquired Egerton, opening the door. He and his companions had been waiting outside in expectation of some such scene.

"Matter enough! This is a very shabby way of serving a fellow."

"Serves you right, Freddy," said Marsham.

"Does it? Well, I wish you had one of these brutes dangling to each ear, then you would be served right."

"Freddy is out of temper to-night," said the earl. "His birching has soured that naturally sweet disposition of his."

"He is in a *crabbed* humour," observed Fitzgerald.

"Come, none of that, Charlie," said Webber, joining in the general laugh. "It is quite bad enough to be eaten by these beasts, without being compelled to listen to such fearful attempts at jocularity."

Having succeeded in loosening the crabb's hold on his fingers, Webber threw it among the group.

On turning round to see what had become of it, Egerton saw the broad placid features of Professor Moeritz.

"What is dis? You haf play some joke! Bad poys."

"Please don't say anything to Doctor Whackley, professor. We won't do it again."

"Mein Gott! what shall this beast be?"

"It is a crab."

The professor stooped, took it up, and immediately received a sharp nip.

He dropped it much more hastily than he had picked it up, to the great delight of the boys.

"I shall say nothing; but if ze doctor shall observe this noise I must flog you," said he, wiping the damaged finger.

"The doctor won't know, sir."

"Won't he," said Freddy. "I can't get this beast off, so I shall be obliged to go down to school to-morrow with it dangling to my foot."

Thinking that poor Freddy had been sufficiently punished, Frank Egerton exerted all his strength, and released his friend from torture.

"I want to speak mit you, Egerton," said the professor.

"Certainly, sir," said Frank, following him out.

"I haf told you of ze Englander mit whom I fight. Ze same name as you?"

"Yes."

"I haf seen him in town. You must watch and see if it is your uncle."

"But, sir, I should not know my uncle if I saw him."

"You will see if his features resemble those of your father."

"Well, I will try. Good night, sir."

* * * * * *

The next evening Frank and the professor were strolling about the town together looking for this mysterious individual who might, or might not be, the uncle of our hero.

Having perambulated the streets for some time, they walked towards the "Six Bells."

Professor Moeritz had resolved to taste some of the ale of that noted hostelry, which, as he averred, resembled in flavour the beer of his native land.

The beer was produced.

Some little time was spent in discussing it, then the professor and pupil rose to return.

They had just gained the street-door when a man passed.

His face turned away, so that they could not see it; but Professor Moeritz grew very excited and exclaimed—

"That is the man, mein young friend."

Frank gazed upon the figure with some astonishment.

"Why not go speak to him?" continued Moeritz.

"What possible excuse can I make? I am not a stranger in the town."

By this time the unknown individual had walked some distance up the road towards the wood.

"Do you watch him," said the professor; "see what he does in that wood. *Ich will warten bis er zurück kommt.*"*

He watched him pass along the crest of the hill, then descend, and enter the town by another route.

But our young hero could scarcely believe his eyes when he saw the individual he was watching enter the house in which sweet Kate Conway and her father lived!

Of course Frank imagined that the inmates of the house entered by the stranger must be well acquainted with the fact.

"Shall I go in?" thought he.

Then the strict commands of Doctor Whackley recurred to his mind, and, though careless as to personal punishment, he deemed it his duty to uphold the principle of obedience to the master.

He returned to the "Six Bells," and reported what had taken place to Professor Moeritz.

"The mystery must be solved," observed the German, as he very thoughtfully walked back to Lexicon College.

Frank was of the same opinion.

Professor Moeritz, on arriving at the college, at once retired to his own room to look once more at the scrip of paper he had found years before—a short time after the duel already spoken of.

Then he called Frank, and showed it to him.

"Is dis de writing of your oncle?" he asked.

"I do not know," replied Egerton. "I never saw my uncle's handwriting."

"How many years is it since that you have had news from him?"

"It must be nearly twenty years ago."

"In what land was he then?"

"In England. He wrote to my father to say that he was about to go

* I will wait till he returns.

to Australia, and since that time has not been heard of. The ship in which he should have sailed was lost with all on board, but the owners declared that no such person ever embarked."

"Then he could not have been drowned?"

"He might have shipped under an assumed name. I wish, indeed, he could be found, for now my mother is in such great trouble, it would be a great comfort to her to have some *relative* upon whose advice she could rely. It is a hard trial, sir, for both of us."

"Doubtless; but remember what was once said by a countryman of mine, named Meissner. 'In heavy tribulation let not discontent transport thee beyond thyself. *Look round, and thou wilt certainly find some with whose destiny thou wouldest not exchange.*'"

"Perfectly true, sir. But we must find out all about this stranger."

"Yes."

Frank then wished the professor good-night, and retired to his own room, where he sat down and wrote a letter to pretty Kate Conway.

"My dear Miss Conway,"—he said —"As you have already heard of my great misfortune, I shall not waste time and paper in telling it, when I have so many things of far greater importance to write about. First of all I must speak of myself:—I have been very disappointed at not being able to see you, but the doctor has forbidden us to go to your house, and I suppose you do not get out very much. But I hope that order will soon be revoked, and then I shall take the very first opportunity of seeing you, which will be a great pleasure indeed.

"Now, I want to ask you a question. Does an elderly gentleman, rather tall in height, with iron-grey hair and beard, visit at your house? I saw such a person enter your door this evening; but. of course, could not know whether he called on business or as a friend. I shall thank you very much indeed if you will answer me this question, as am extremely anxious to know what he is and his name.

"There is to be a little boat-race to-morrow. If you would like to see it, be in the field about four o'clock. *I* shall be *very pleased* to see you.

"Yours, very sincerely,
"FRANK EGERTON."

Having sent this epistle to the post, Frank retired to rest, and dreamt that his uncle was turned into a boat, in which he (the King of the School) was rowing Kate Conway to an uninhabited island, where they meant to live for the rest of their lives.

CHAPTER XV.

THE BOAT-RACE.

As soon as Frank knew that the doctor was in his study the next morning, he wrote another letter, in which he enclosed that which he had received from the inspector of the Ballsbury police, testifying to the respectability of the Conway household.

Half an hour afterwards Egerton, Fitzgerald, and the Earl of Pembridge were summoned to the doctor's presence.

Frank told his companions what he had done, and much speculation took place as the result.

"I have sent for you," said the doctor, "to inform you that I have now no objection to your visiting a house which, some time ago, I forbade you to enter. The police say it is a respectable place, so I presume I have been made the dupe of some anonymous individual who has a spite against one of you."

"Thank you, sir, for your kindness," said the three boys, who were then about to leave the study.

"One moment. You are all three of good family, and you are at the same time young and impulsive. As I hear there are some young girls there—good girls, no doubt, but in a very humble station in life, it is my duty to warn you against any foolish love-making!"

"There is not much danger of *my* falling in love with them, sir," said Charlie Fitzgerald.

"I will remember what you say, sir," observed the earl.

Frank Egerton said nothing, but, with a low bow to the doctor, walked out of the room.

I shall go down there as soon as the boat-race is over," said the Earl of Pembridge, as they walked together towards the school-room.

"So shall I, unless I see Kate in the meadow!"

"That was a bold plan of yours to write to the police!"

"Perfectly successful though."

"Yes."

"Upper fifth for mathematics," shouted a loud voice; and as our three friends happened to belong to that form, they walked off to the apartment in which Professor Moeritz lectured on angles, co-sines, tangents, and all kinds of mathematical abominations.

Frank Egerton had by this time regained his position as head of his form.

On this particular morning he experienced a severe attack in the mathematical class from Baynes, who had evidently been reading hard for the occasion.

At the conclusion of the lesson, Professor Moeritz gravely shook his head, and pronounced them equal, awarding both the same number of marks.

Baynes walked away to his friend

Crawley, who was much lower in the school—being, in fact, a great dunce.

"How did you get on?" asked the toady.

"Capital—the same number of marks as Egerton!"

"That's jolly! Equal in class—equal in the doctor's good opinion."

"Are you sure of that?"

"Yes. I heard him mention both your names yesterday in such terms as convinced me he thought quite as much of you as of this bouncing Egerton. You know he went down some degrees in the doctor's estimation when he was found at that place up town."

"True."

"Do you know who wrote the letter."

"What letter?"

"To the doctor, telling him where Egerton had gone."

"Yes."

"Tell me."

"I will; but mind, if you blab, I'll give you the greatest thrashing you ever had. I overheard them planning their tea-party, and I wrote that letter."

"What a jolly lark!"

At that moment a loud sneeze somewhere close by alarmed the boys, who had been under the impression that they were alone.

The conversation had been taking place in the box-room before-mentioned.

Both boys looked round, half expecting to find Egerton or one of his friends behind them.

Strange to say, however, no one could be seen.

The room appeared empty.

"It must be one of Webber's rabbits," said Crawley.

The aforesaid pet animal had since their identification with the strange noises been allowed to run about the box-room, to the great disgust of Marsham, whose dogs were banished.

"Let us hunt them out," suggested Baynes, who knew that the rabbits frequently curled themselves up behind the boxes, to enjoy a quiet sleep.

They moved nearly all the lumber in the place, but no rabbit could be found, and the two boys were just prepared to believe that their ears had deceived them when the noise was repeated.

It seemed this time to come from the floor close by their feet.

"Perhaps it is the spirit of that poor boy who was killed," suggested Crawley, turning pale.

"More likely one of the fellows down in Tiddy's den," replied Baynes. "Come away quietly."

It happened on this occasion that Baynes had made a correct guess.

Tiddy's den was not a very large or light cellar in which dwelt an elderly, blear-eyed individual called Tiddy, whose occupation was cleaning boots, knives and forks, &c., for the numerous inhabitants of Lexicon College.

It so happened that Tiddy being rather thirsty, had bribed our old friend, Harry, the heir of a noble house, to help him while he himself took a walk to the nearest beer-shop.

There Harry was, when he suddenly became aware of voices overhead, and heard the name of his kind patron, Egerton, mentioned.

He at once mounted on an old box which served Tiddy as a seat, and listened.

Not a word of the conversation escaped him, though he could not recognise the voices.

"This will be something to tell Mr. Egerton," thought he; "but perhaps he won't believe me unless I can tell him who it was."

In a moment he ran out of Tiddy's den, and took up a position where he could see any one who passed from the school-room into the playfield.

A moment afterwards Baynes and Crawley walked out, casting furtive glances over their shoulders.

"I was right," thought Harry, as he hurried away towards the boat-house by the river, where Egerton, Pembridge, Marsham, and Freddy Webber were preparing for a race in outriggers.

Egerton had not devoted much attention to boating before he entered Lexicon College, and in consequence was not considered such an adept at the oar as Marsham and the Earl of Pembridge.

The two last-named had rowed a tie previous day, and Egerton having criticised their rowing rather severely, had been jointly challenged by them, so that the race was really to decide who should be the champion oarsman, of the school.

Freddy Webber, hearing this, vowed he could beat them all; and after some good-natured chaff, was permitted to make one in the race.

Freddy was really not a bad rower, though, of course, he stood very little chance against such dashing fellows as his opponents.

Crawley and some of his set had tried to put Baynes forward as their champion; but that worthy declined the honour, and strolled down town to learn the latest betting on the Leger.

Having imparted the information he had acquired to those whom it most concerned, Harry stood by the river bank to watch the aquatic contest.

In his heart of hearts he hoped Egerton would win, for, though both Marsham and the young peer, had always treated him with the utmost kindness, Harry remembered who had first been his protector.

Having put on their boating costume, the four boys stepped into their outriggers, and slowly paddled down to the starting point, which was about a mile and a quarter below the boat-house, the winning-post being about a quarter of a mile above that building.

Charlie Fitzgerald had gone down to act as starter; Professor Moeritz being stationed at the winning-post to proclaim the winner.

Both points could be distinctly seen from the boat-house, where Dr. Whackley, his daughters, and some of the boys, were assembled, though by far the greater number of the pupils had accompanied the German professor.

A puff of white smoke announced that the signal had been given (they had agreed to start by pistol shot), and the next moment the boats were in motion.

About twenty strokes had been rowed in something like half-a-minute, then one of the rowers was seen to drop behind, and slowly bring his boat to shore.

"Freddy has soon been beaten," observed one of the spectators.

"It isn't Freddy," said Lascelles, who had been watching through a glass.

"Who is it, then?"

"Marsham. I can't understand why he should give up like that."

"You must be mistaken."

"No, you will see in a minute; they will soon be here. What a pace they are coming at!"

Egerton and Pembridge were rowing a fair thirty-six strokes per minute, and almost lifting their boats out of the water.

To the surprise of every one, Freddy Webber was not many yards behind them, struggling hard to distinguish himself.

"How splendidly the earl feathers his oar!" observed a boy named Seaton.

"Yes; but you see his stroke is flagging. He has not the same power of endurance as Egerton," said Lascelles.

"Of course you stick up for Frank."

"And I am right to do so. See, he puts on a spurt, and gradually draws a-head."

His remark was perfectly correct.

The King of the School was slowly yet surely creeping away.

"And see, Freddy puts on a spurt," remarked Seaton.

Webber, who was at least a dozen yards behind the others, though no one had fancied he would be able to gain or keep such a position, was seen to be working most violently in hopes of improving his chance of success.

But the race, however, was between Pembridge and Egerton.

The young earl had a vast amount of pluck in him, and would not see that

"THE RESULT WAS THAT FREDDY FELL OUT OF HIS BOAT."

he was beaten, though the boys on the banks already hailed Egerton as winner.

"Bravo, Frank! Hurrah for the King of the School!" shouted Lascelles.

"And hurrah for the earl of Pembridge!" bawled Seaton.

"Hurrah for the earl!" responded Lascelles, though not quite so heartily as he had cheered Egerton.

Yet he could not help admiring the indomitable pluck of the young peer.

"Egerton wins! Egerton wins!" was now the general shout.

"No! Pembridge for ever!"

The earl had actually managed to get his boat's nose at least a yard in front.

It seemed that things were to be entirely altered.

The boats were not more than twenty yards from the winning-post, Freddy still maintaining his post about twelve or fifteen yards behind, when suddenly the Joe Miller of the School, as Webber was sometimes called, managed to catch a crab.

Of course the immediate result was that he fell out of his boat, and circumstances seemed very much against his ever regaining *terra firma*, for the lookers on had entirely lost sight of him, and were watching with the most intense earnestness the struggle between the earl and Frank Egerton.

Freddy, it should be observed, was unable to swim, and therefore, strictly speaking, had no business upon the water.

"Egerton has won, hurrah!" he heard every one shout, and then he sank.

The King of the School had won, his boat being a yard in advance of the other, and loudly were he and his opponent cheered as they stepped ashore.

Both were very exhausted, and had to be helped home, followed at a little distance by Kate Conway.

"Who is that in the water?" sud-denly exclaimed Doctor Whackley, as his eye wandered over the late race-course.

"Why, it must be Freddy Webber, sir!" said Seaton.

"But who is that in after him?" cried Lascelles.

"Don't know," responded Seaton. "It is not one of our fellows."

Lascelles immediately stepped into one of the boats and rowed to the spot."

"Bravo, Harry!" he exclaimed, when he saw who was attempting to rescue Webber.

The rescuer was Harry, the poor lad who had been protected and helped by the pupils of Lexicon College.

Freddy Webber was quite as obstinate in the water as out of it, and insisted upon being saved in his own way.

His idea was to clasp Harry round the neck and cling to him; a proceeding that would certainly have drowned both.

Lascelles saw it, and, by a quick stroke, sent his boat between them, thus preventing Freddy from adding murder to suicide, as he afterwards observed.

"Cling on, one each side," said he, as soon as he had effectually parted them.

Fortunately, Freddy had sense enough to understand the command.

Not seeing Harry, he caught hold of the boat, and, the water not being very cold, had no great difficulty in supporting himself.

Poor Harry caught hold on the other side; Lascelles used the oars gently, and very soon had both of them on shore.

Loud applause greeted both, and so delighted was Doctor Whackley with Harry's courageous conduct, that he publicly expressed his intention of taking the poor boy under his own care and protection

CHAPTER XVI.

TWO SCOUNDRELS.

BAYNES having declined to have anything to do with the boat-race, went, as we have already hinted, to hear the latest news about betting.

He took his way towards a billiard-room, to which the reader has been already introduced, hoping there to see Captain Robinson, who had sent two or three very sharp letters lately respecting a certain debt of honour—or, as we imagine, dishonour.

He had not got very far on his journey before he met two girls whose faces he remembered.

They were Kate and Lizzie Conway.

As they passed he heard them speak of a boat-race.

"Ah," he muttered, "this King of the School, as they call him, cannot even row a friendly match but he must have some foolish milliner girl to look on and admire."

For some seconds he thought of going back to put the doctor on his guard.

"But that would betray me, though," he thought after a time. "Besides, if he speaks to these girls, the doctor will be safe to see."

On reaching the billiard-rooms, Baynes found the captain alone.

Chalkey, the marker, had gone out, and the gallant officer, being left in possession, was practising a wonderful *screw* of his own invention.

As soon as Baynes entered, he laid down his cue.

"So you have come at last, Mr. Baynes," he said.

"Yes, captain. I want to make my book all right, so I thought I would come down and ask if you had heard anything new."

"Cool, 'pon my word."

"Extremely. What is the use of exciting one's-self this hot weather?"

"Mr. Baynes, have you brought any money with you?"

"A few shillings!"

"Have you forgotten how much you owes me?"

The captain's grammar was, as we have already hinted, very defective.

"I have not."

"When do you mean to stump up?"

"As soon as I have the money to spare."

"Hell and furies! I shall be compelled to expose you!"

Baynes, who had been rehearsing a certain line of conduct to himself during his walk, simply gave another of his cool smiles.

"You may expose as much as you like, Captain Robinson!"

"If I let your father and Doctor Whackley know, the results won't fit you, not exactly, my boy!"

"Suppose I have already made my peace with them, have explained all, and have been forgiven!"

"Why then——"

"Why, then, Captain Robinson, if you behaved rudely in any way, I should be compelled to explain to the police that you are simply a discharged soldier, and that your business in Ballsbury is merely to swindle as many of the foolish inhabitants as possible!"

The captain grew pale even to the roots of his whiskers.

However, suddenly plucking up courage, he said—

"Since you have told so much, and know so much more, I may as well tell *all* I know."

Ringing the bell, he ordered pen, ink, paper, and envelopes.

Baynes stood looking on very coolly, while the captain commenced to write; but when he saw one letter finished and another half written, he began to wonder what it was all about.

The more he watched, the more curious did Baynes become.

At length he put the question—

" Are you making your will, captain, or writing composing letters to your creditors ?"

" I am now writing to your respected father, having just finished a letter to your master, the Reverend Doctor Whackley."

It was now Baynes's turn to change colour.

" Do you doubt me ?" asked the captain, holding up the first letter, which was addressed to Baynes, senior.

" I don't see what you can have to write about."

" Perhaps you will know in a day or two."

The captain then very coolly finished writing, sealed both letters, put stamps on them, and rang the bell.

" Take these to the post-office," said he to the waiter.

" Stay !" exclaimed Baynes, starting up. " Leave them on the table and go outside for a few minutes."

The waiter looked from one to the other, hardly knowing which to obey.

" You may do as the gentleman says," said Captain Robinson.

As soon as the waiter had retired Baynes spoke.

" What are you going to do ?"

" Send these letters, acquainting your father and the schoolmaster with the share you had in the attempted burglary at Lexicon College."

" You have no proof."

" I have a letter which I wrote to you. Really, Mr. Baynes, there would not be the slightest difficulty in getting the postman to prove that he delivered this at your school. You dropped it."

" Fiend, you have me in your power."

" I know it. But I ain't going to be 'arsh."

" Well ?"

" I must have the money."

" But how is it possible to get it ? You know pretty well how I am situated."

" Where are these rich swells as could be gulled so easy ? Why, Mr. Baynes, your school-fellows don't play billiards any more than if they were a lot of methodist parsons."

" I can't tell how it is. The Earl of Pembridge, I know, goes to Harris's rooms, but neither he, nor Marsham, nor Lascelles will play with me ; and Egerton isn't worth picking up, now."

" Couldn't you pick up a blank cheque out of the doctor's book ?" whispered the captain.

" What would be the use ?"

" You are a good hand at imitating signatures."

Baynes flushed, and then turned pale.

" You shall have the money to-morrow, captain," said he, in a hoarse, low whisper.

" That's right ; I knew you would act like a man of spirit."

Baynes buttoned up his coat and walked away, while the captain, with a fiend-like grin on his face, resumed his practice with the balls.

CHAPTER XVII.

A SERIOUS PIECE OF NEWS.

THE next morning Doctor Whackley came into school with a very serious look upon his face.

"He's been bitten by a member of the Norfolk Howard tribe," observed Webber.

"Take care he doesn't bite you, Freddy," replied Frank Egerton.

"Silence ;" exclaimed the doctor, sharply.

"As soon as they were all seated, he began thus—

"I little thought that ever I should be called upon to address my pupils on such a subject! In fact, so deeply do I feel the disgrace that has been brought upon the place, that I hardly know how to begin. It must be said, however, and I blush to say it, these walls enclose a thief!"

There was a general start at this announcement.

"There is a thief in the house! Last night three ten-pound notes were stolen from the table-drawer in my library! Of course it would be absurd for me to ask the thief to come forward and acknowledge his sin; but I publicly state that if the missing notes are restored within the next forty-eight hours nothing more will be said on the subject, though I most sincerely hope the culprit will take an early opportunity of leaving the school he has disgraced!"

Frank Egerton, Marsham, Pembridge and Fitzgerald, who had been whispering together during the latter part of this harangue, now sent a note to Professor Moeritz.

"It has been suggested by the senior boys, sir, that the notes should be stopped at the bank, and their numbers sent to the tradesmen of the town. Your pupils fear that the innocent may come under suspicion, as many of us have bank-notes of our own; for instance, I have several," said the earl.

"So have I," said Marsham.

"And I, and I, and I."

The speakers were Baynes, Fitzgerald, and Seaton, all of whose parents were known to be very rich and proportionately indulgent.

"Unfortunately I do not know them."

"You might get the information from the person who paid them to you, sir."

"Right. I will send at once, and, if the information can be gained, I will forward it to all the tradesmen with whom I think it likely you are in the habit of dealing."

The doctor then left the school-room.

An hour passed away, then came the news.

The numbers were known, but the three notes had been changed at different shops in the town by—

An elderly man, who was accompanied by two respectably-dressed girls, apparently about fifteen years of age.

"The notes are gone; but let the thief beware, for if I find him now I shall certainly prosecute him," said the doctor, in announcing the news to his scholars.

Deep was the gloom cast over the school by this event.

Boys looked at each other distrustfully, and never before was known such a locking of desks, boxes, and drawers.

A week passed away, during which time Frank Egerton had several very pleasing interviews with Kate Conway.

In one of these he told the artless tale of his love.

"Do you love me, Kate?" he then asked. "Will you be my wife in two or three years' time?"

No verbal response was given, but a pair of loving arms were thrown round his neck, and the sweet girl hid her face on his shoulder.

"That means yes, does it not, dear?" he asked, and gently raising her face, he gave and received the sweetest kiss of his life.

"I must ask your papa now, dear. I must not conceal anything from him."

"I am afraid, dear Frank, that your mamma will never allow it," whispered Kate, whose tender little heart was beating at a most rapid rate.

"I am not afraid. I shall be a poor man, and have to work my way in the world. No rich heiress would look at me, so I am sure my dear mother won't object to my marrying you."

Then they began to talk a lot of nonsense that could not possibly be interesting to any of our readers.

After a time Mr. Conway came in, and Frank, in a very straightforward manner, told him all.

The old gentleman listened gravely while the young lover pleaded.

When Frank paused, he replied—

"If you are of the same opinion when you reach the age of twenty I shall not object. But let there be no engagement between you, for youth is fickle; you may be parted for a time, and possibly one or the other might find some other object of affection."

"No!" exclaimed Frank. "It is impossible!"

And sweet Kate faintly echoed his words.

"You think so; but wait till you have seen as much of the world as I have, then you will alter your opinion. Therefore, I will not hear of any formal engagement between you, but both shall remain free to choose elsewhere, if fancy should lead you to do so. There need be no difficulty about your coming here, for I shall always be most happy to see you."

That was all Frank could extract from Mr. Conway, and with it he had to be satisfied.

He then asked some questions about the stranger who had been seen to enter the house.

"Describe him," said Mr. Conway.

Frank did so.

"I have no very distinct recollection of such a man, but as I am secretary to my trade society, it is quite possible that such a man may have called to get helped on to the next town."

"Then you think he is a working man?"

"Yes, if he came here."

"It can't be my uncle, then," observed Frank, *sotto voce*, and he looked towards Mr. Conway.

That gentleman's face, however, happened to be turned away.

* * * * * *

Blissful beyond comparison was Frank's walk home from school that night, with Kate Conway's arm linked in his.

Equally blissful were the dreams which visited his sleeping hours.

But painful was the scene in the school-room next morning.

Doctor Whackley again appeared angry and grieved.

When silence had been proclaimed, he addressed another speech to the expectant boys.

"I thought," said he, "when I told you a week ago I had lost some bank notes, that some boy had yielded to a momentary temptation, and had committed a single act of dishonesty. But now I find that there is a confirmed thief in the house!"

"Is it possible?" exclaimed several.

"It is possible. I have not lost any more notes, but some blank leaves have been taken out of my cheque-book. Let the thief beware how he adds forgery to his other crimes."

Now, this was not pleasant for the boys.

The innocent members of the school, of course, could not tell who was guilty, so that the suspicion was redoubled.

A strict watch was kept at the bank; but then country institutions of that kind are not quite so wide-a-wake as large London houses.

The doctor had to be continually writing cheques for one and the other, and the bank clerks, after stopping at least half-a-dozen innocent people who had presented genuine cheques, began to relax their vigilance.

At length they were rudely roused from their lethargy.

A cheque for forty-seven pounds some odd shillings was presented by a middle-aged man one day, and, after a careful examination, cashed.

The next day a youth about fourteen, well dressed, and representing himself as one of the boys of Lexicon College, called for the doctor's pass-book, which was at once given up to him.

A few hours afterwards the reverend gentleman received it, and a note to the effect that a forged cheque for forty-seven pounds, &c., had been presented, cashed, and the cancelled cheque abstracted from the pocket in the cover of the book.

This time the doctor did not make any public announcement of the fact, but sent for an experienced detective.

As soon as Dr. Whackley had related the case, a grave shake of the head showed him plainly that the experienced officer saw great difficulties.

"Very poor chance, sir, of finding out anything."

"How so?"

"Why, don't you see, sir, even if I knew pretty well who did it, I ain't certain that it would be safe to arrest him. He's a cute chap, whoever he may be."

"You are not afraid of one of my boys?"

"I fear no living human being, if it comes to a fight."

"Then what do you mean by saying that it would not be safe to arrest him?"

"If I arrested a man or boy and placed him in the dock on a charge of forging a cheque, I might be asked—'Where is the cheque you say he forged?' He has destroyed the evidence against himself by that artful dodge of getting hold of the pass-book; there's nothing to prove the forgery but that anonymous letter, and you are man of the world enough to know how much that would be worth in a court of law."

"Then what can be done?"

"Nothing at present."

"Nothing!"

"When I say nothing, I mean nothing openly."

"But you will endeavour to make some discovery?"

"Of course, sir."

"And when you have found the culprit you will tell me?"

"I am not so certain of that; I must learn a little more about you before I promise. I don't know whether you can keep a secret."

"Let me know if I can do anything to help you."

"Yes. Let me have a specimen of every boy's handwriting, and the letter that was sent back with the pass-book. It will be something to find out who wrote that."

Doctor Whackley immediately gave up possession of the letter that had accompanied the pass-book, and, a few hours later, furnished the detective with specimens of the handwriting of most of his pupils.

The officer then made inquiries about the assistant-masters. His thief-hunting mind regarded every man as a rogue till the real culprit could be found.

Having thus obtained all the evidence he could, Mr. Sharp walked down into the town, and put himself in communication with the chief of the Ballsbury police.

From him he learnt that the pupils of Lexicon College were rather a daredevil set of youths, addicted to practical jokes, field and in-door sports, and rather fond than otherwise of a jolly row with the apprentices and other young men about the town.

"Are they allowed to visit any of the taverns?" asked Sharp.

"I believe it is against the regulations, but they do so openly," replied the inspector, who then gave a catalogue of the places most resorted to by the senior pupils—our friends.

"HE HELD IN HIS HAND A PIECE OF PAPER LIKE A CHEQUE OR BANK-NOTE."

" Don't see any harm in that," the detective said, musingly. " Are there any shady places—cribs you would not like to see your son in?"

" There is one—a billiard-room. I have watched the house for a long time, but they are too knowing for me." .

" Do any of the Lexicon pupils go there?"

" A few; but the greater number of them prefer the ' Six Bells,' which is really a most respectable house."

Some other talk took place, and then the detective walked off to have a look at the billiard-rooms.

" Very shady," was his inward remark, as he looked round, and took a mental measurement of the place and the players. Then, recognising an old acquaintance, he said,

" Ha! Moss, how are you? What are you doing here?"

" I am pretty well, thank you, Mr.— sir."

" Come over here, man; I want to have a talk with you."

Captain Robinson, for he was the person addressed, obeyed most humbly.

" I thought I hadn't seen you about the Strand lately," Sharp continued. " Perhaps it's a good thing for you. How are you getting your living?"

" Why, billiards, of course, Mr. Sharp."

" Ha! do you know any of the college boys?"

" I have seen one or two of them here sometimes."

" Their names?"

" One of them is named Bruton, another is De Vere, and another Fitzroy. Those are all I know by name."

" You lie," the detective thought to himself. " But I'll find you out."

" If you don't like me to be here, Mr. Sharp, I'll move on to Westhampton."

" Hum—no—in fact, you had better remain here, in this room, for an hour or two. Don't speak a word about me, or I may chance to remember something you would not like to have brought up."

The poor, trembling billiard-sharper promised obedience, but his play was spoilt for the day. The sight of the detective had unnerved his arm; he missed nearly every stroke, and rendered himself the laughing-stock of the room.

After a time he threw down his cue, and retired in disgust to the remotest corner of the room.

In the meantime, Mr. Sharp had returned towards Lexicon College.

He asked the doctor about the three youths who had been mentioned as frequenters of the billiard-room, and found that they bore very good characters.

" Moss is deceiving me," he thought. " However, I must let him have plenty of rope, and he will be safe to tie himself up after a time."

* * * * * *

By that evening's post Frank Egerton received a letter from his mother.

The widow lady had not much news to impart, but seemed to have written for the purpose of enclosing a five-pound note which Frank found in the envelope.

She could not bear to think that her handsome boy, who had been accustomed to have plenty of money at his disposal, might, perhaps, be unable to keep up his position.

" This is kind!" exclaimed Frank, to a little knot of friends, as he read the letter aloud. " But I won't keep it; I'll send it back to her to-morrow."

He consigned it to his pocket-book, resolved to diminish his own expenditure rather than narrow his mother's means.

Among those who were near him when he received the letter was Crawley.

By him the intelligence that Frank's mamma had sent money was quickly conveyed to Baynes.

" Wish him luck," was the surly reply. " Come out into the field."

It so happened that Mr. Sharp, the detective, was strolling about the neighbourhood at the time.

Seeing two boys apart from the others he took it into his head to watch them from beneath one of the great elm trees in the field, Crawley and Baynes being beneath another.

As he watched he saw the elder of the two (Baynes) draw from his pocket an oblong slip of paper, which he held out to the view of his companion.

"It looks like a bank-note or a cheque," Mr. Sharp muttered to himself, making a step forward.

Then he resisted the impulse that urged him forward.

"On the other hand, it may be only an ordinary letter or a school exercise; in which case I should be very wrong to interfere, for the news would instantly spread over the school, and then I should never catch this artful one."

So he resolved to wait and carefully watch.

The next day he saw them enter the billiard-rooms together.

"Moss is at the bottom of all this," Mr. Sharp thought to himself. "I was wrong to say anything to him about the boys. Never mind, I've lost one trick, but I'll win the game."

CHAPTER XVIII.

A NIGHT CHASE.

FIVE or six days passed away, and nothing had been discovered, except that a few of the pupils of Lexicon College were in the habit of going to the billiard-room in Catherine Street.

Dr. Whackley, after grave deliberation, resolved to prohibit the place; not that he had any objection to the game, but because it was frequented by a queer set of people, and his pupils were sometimes induced to play for higher stakes than they could afford.

Baynes and Crawley grumbled loudly.

"Why, what is the matter with you two sore-headed bears?" Marsham asked.

"Its too bad to stop our billiards."

"The doctor has not stopped them. He has only prohibited a certain house; and there is quite as good a table at the 'Six Bells.' "

"That's an awful slow place."

"How so?"

"You don't meet the fellows there who go to Catherine Street."

"So much for everybody—except the fellows you speak of."

"It may suit you to sneer at them, but I have met some jolly good men at Smith's, in Catherine Street."

Marsham, not being inclined to argue the point, walked away, though he saw no harm in repeating the conversation to his more immediate friends; consequently the matter was discussed throughout the school.

Mr. Sharp, the detective, heard of it, and his opinion of Baynes was not heightened.

He watched that young gentleman more strictly than ever.

Baynes was, to say the truth, in an awkward fix.

He was, as we know, for some reason or other, afraid of the sham Captain Robinson, alias Moss, and wished to conciliate him.

How that was to be done was more than the youth could say, for he dared not go to the billiard-rooms, and a letter to Robinson only resulted in a reply to the effect that Captain Robinson was too busy to be able to go to Lexicon College, and if Mr. Baynes wished to see him, he was to be found at the rooms in Catherine Street. Mr. Baynes had not hesitated to break the college regulations on other occasions, and might do so now for the sake of seeing an old friend.

Not one word about the detective.

Two days afterwards Baynes wrote another letter, the contents of which we must not at present divulge.

Egerton had by this time regained his position as King of the School.

Baynes was not far behind him as regarded scholarship, and evidently intended to compete with him for the classical and mathematical honours of the college.

Frank knew this, and, although pretty confident that in the end he would be the victor, wisely resolved to work a little harder than he had done.

Late at night he would sit up; after every one else had retired, he would sit up reading in the little study occupied during the day by Professor Moeritz; having, of course, obtained the consent of that worthy.

About ten days after the detective first made his appearance on the scene, Frank had been so engaged till a very late hour.

He was just thinking of retiring, when he heard a slight noise in the direction of Dr. Whackley's study.

The next moment came a loud shout for help in the doctor's voice!

"Help! Mur——"

There was a sound like the fall of a heavy body.

Then all was silent.

Frank immediately rushed towards the apartment from which the sounds seemed to proceed.

At the door of the study he encountered a man whose face was entirely masked in black crape.

"Villain, I have you! Help! Thieves!" he shouted, springing up and catching the intruder by the collar, while with his left hand he endeavoured to tear away the mask.

"Let me go, you young whelp!" said the man.

"Help! help! Thieves!" shouted Frank.

"Let me go, I say, or it will be the worse for you."

The more the robber struggled and threatened the more firm did Frank keep his grip on the man's collar.

By this time the household had been alarmed by the shouts, and footsteps were heard approaching hurriedly.

"You won't! Then take that, you obstinate young fool!" the robber exclaimed, in a voice husky with passion.

He thrust one hand into his coat-pocket, drew out a small pistol, and fired.

Frank fell, and just at that moment Fitzgerald, Marsham, and the Earl of Pembridge, arrived, followed by Professor Moeritz, who had retired to his bed-room some time before.

The boys were just in time to see the midnight robber leap through the doctor's study-window. They called to the German to look after the two senseless bodies on the floor, and then jumped out in pursuit of the flying figure, which they could see dimly some yards ahead.

"You to the right, Marsham, you to the left, Pembridge," said Fitzgerald, as they raced across the playing-field. "Spread out; if he attempts to turn you can stop him. He is going straight for the river, and we must have him."

The pursued leaped the fence like a deer, but the pursuers were equally agile. Neither of the boys had any clothing on except shirt, trousers, and slippers, and all three were in splendid training.

It seemed as though the robber had some idea of his enemies' tactics, for he made several attempts to get off towards the town as they passed through the cathedral grounds; but the boys headed him back, and drove him on in the direction of the river.

He dared not stop and encounter them, for he knew, from the pertinacity with which they followed, that they would stick to him like bulldogs.

Apparently resolved as to his course, he kept straight on.

The river came in sight.

"We shall have him now," shouted Marsham.

"Will you!" muttered the robber, setting his teeth, and not relaxing his pace in the least.

On arriving at the brink of the water he plunged in, and without the least hesitation began to swim across.

The earl of Pembridge, who was about a yard in front of the others, followed suit, and Marsham and Fitzgerald did the same.

Four dark forms might have been seen crossing the water.

In spite of the chilliness of the water and the swiftness of the current, the man succeeded in getting across.

He stood a moment on the other bank, shook himself, and then looked for his pursuers.

Great was his astonishment when he saw the three boys in the water, swimming bravely, and rapidly nearing him.

"Curse the young whelps, they mean to hunt me down," he muttered.

Turning with a shiver, he made off at a long, swinging trot, for the wood on the hill beyond the chalk-pit.

"Tally-ho-ho-ho!" shouted Marsham, as he landed.

The hunting-cry was caught up by the others, and taken up by some of the boys who had followed, but preferred remaining on their own side of the river.

"Put the steam on, or we shall lose him!" said Marsham. "The villain means to make for the trees."

The three boys put on their best speed, but the robber had gained on them during the swim.

"You may as well surrender, scoundrel; I know you," the young earl shouted.

The only answer from the man was a low, mocking laugh.

"He is but twenty yards ahead; we must have him," exclaimed Charlie Fitzgerald. "If he does not stop I shall shoot."

The robber, who was close to the edge of the wood, overheard the words, and shouted back—

"You can't, your powder is damp."

"We'll see all about that," responded Charlie, who of course, had no pistol or powder about him.

He stooped down as he ran along, and caught up from the ground a flint stone something larger than his fist.

Taking as good aim as possible under the circumstances, he hurled it with all his force at the flying robber.

A dull thud, followed by a low muttered cry of pain, told that the missile had found its mark, but the man still continued his flight.

He leaped the fence surrounding the wood, and was heard for a few minutes crashing through the bushes.

Then, as the three breathless boys pulled up at the hedge, which they were too exhausted to jump, dead silence reigned around.

"Got away!" Marsham exclaimed in sorrowful tones.

"It would be useless to attempt to follow him in that copse," remarked Fitzgerald, whose words were echoed by Pembridge.

They waited a few minutes, listening attentively for any sound that might betray the path taken by the fugitive; but the wood seemed noiseless.

"Let us get back, I am beginning to feel cold," said Fitzgerald.

"Right; but we'll kick a few holes in the ground to mark the spot where we lost our game.

Marsham immediately produced a pocket-knife, and, kneeling down, cut three square pieces out of the turf, thus making a mark that could not be mistaken.

That done, they turned back towards school.

"Double!" exclaimed the earl. "It will never do to get cold in these wet things."

"Shall we go straight!" asked Marsham.

"Of course," replied Fitzgerald and the earl in a breath.

They ran down the hill at a pretty good pace, once more reached the river-bank, jumped in, and swam back, amid the loud cheers of half-a-dozen youngsters who had just brought an old punt and were about to go over.

"How is Egerton?" was the first question the three young heroes asked.

Of course the other boys had been waiting on the bank, and could not answer the question.

However, they all hurried back to the college, and learnt the news.

Egerton had received a pistol-shot wound of a very dangerous character.

The shot had grazed the head with sufficient force to fracture the skull, and the patient was consequently in great danger.

Doctor Whackley, who had received a blow from a life-preserver, had recovered sufficiently to be able to make a statement to the police.

He was sitting in his study, he said, when he became aware, from a stream of cold air on his back, that the window had been opened.

Turning round for the purpose of closing it, he was rather startled to see a tall man, whose face was hidden, standing behind him.

On demanding what he wanted, and calling for help, the robber struck him a heavy blow with a life-preserver, after which the doctor could remember nothing till he returned to conciousness in his own bed-room.

The dripping appearance of the three lads who had chased the robber attracted immediate attention.

"Go to your rooms, my dear boys, change everything, and jump into bed," said Mrs. Whackley. "I will send up some hot brandy-and-water in a few minutes."

"Can't I see Egerton?" asked Fitzgerald.

"No. Go to bed, or you will catch cold."

"I don't mind about that, only I wished we had caught the thief."

"Ah, well, never mind," and the kind-hearted lady bustled them out of the room.

The brandy-and-water was sent as promised; the three lads thoroughly dried themselves and jumped into bed.

With the exception that Fitzgerald had a slight cold the next day, neither of them was the worse for the night's adventure.

All night long the doctor and an experienced nurse remained in attendance on Egerton.

A telegram was sent to London requesting the most celebrated surgeon of the day to hasten down in the morning.

He came, and, after a brief examination of the wound, said—

"It would be advisable to let his parents know of this. He may not live twenty-four hours."

A messenger was sent immediately to inform Mrs. Egerton of her son's dangerous wound. In the meantime the great man from London brought all his professional skill to bear upon the case.

CHAPTER XIX.

THE SICK BED.

ABOUT eight hours after Doctor Whackley sent to Mrs. Egerton, a train, in which that lady was seated, was rapidly nearing the old city of Ballsbury.

Swiftly though it sped along the iron-track, its speed seemed a snail's pace to the widow lady, who pictured to herself her darling, daring, handsome boy, lying in the agonies of death. And at the thought of the utter desolation that would follow such a cruel bereavement, her spirits fairly gave way, and floods of tears flowed from her eyes.

Her watch was frequently consulted, and her head thrust from the window to see if they were approaching the town.

About half an hour's ride from Ballsbury, the sun, which had hitherto been concealed behind some clouds, shone out, lighting up the whole of the beautiful country.

"I accept the omen—there is hope!" she exclaimed, pressing her hands to her throbbing temples.

*   *   *   *   *   *

About that same moment Frank Egerton awoke from the long and death-like trance into which his wound had thrown him.

Doctor and nurse were both watching, and, from the first glance, knew that he was not delirious.

"How is the doctor? What has become of the burglar?" were the first questions he asked.

He would have sat up, but the nurse held him back.

"Doctor Whackley has quite recovered; but you must be very quiet, for you have received a dangerous wound."

"A wound! Ah, I feel weak, my head throbs."

"Lie still and be quiet."

"I want to see Pembridge—and Fitzgerald—and—"

Before he could complete the sentence he swooned again, and was unconscious when his mother arrived.

The medical gentleman had at first some fears for Mrs. Egerton, so excited was she.

At length she calmed down and took up her position by the bed-side, prepared to act as nurse.

Several hours elapsed, however, before any necessity for her services arose.

The flame of life had been so nearly extinguished that the surgeons feared it would die out entirely.

During the continuance of this second swoon, the Earl of Pembridge and Charlie Fitzgerald were permitted to come into the sick-room, which was not that in which Frank usually slept, but at the back of the house, the window overlooking the doctor's garden.

It was quite dark, and the night being somewhat sultry, the casement had been thrown up to admit as much of the night air as possible. The light was shaded, and the boys being at supper, everything was perfectly quiet.

After some whispered conversation with Mrs. Egerton, the young earl gallantly proposed to fetch her a glass or wine.

Fitzgerald remained in the room, and in a very low tone of voice related to the lady all he knew of the manner in which Frank met his wound, and also the chase Marsham and the earl had after the would-be assassin, modestly forgetting to mention that he himself had taken part in that chase.

"FRANK WAITED AN OPPORTUNITY. AT LAST IT CAME."

During this time Frank once more opened his eyes.

The two swoons had, to a certain extent, weakened his brain; he had no recollection of where he was or how he had come there.

Being far too weak to turn his body, or even his head, he could only look straight before him, and there, to his great surprise, he saw his mother.

In a vague way he began to speculate how she could possibly have come there.

"I didn't send. She didn't write. Where am I?" he thought. "It's a strange place, I can't remember coming here. I recollect collaring the robber, and then——Ah! I have it! I am dead, and in the next world!"

His mother sat still, her face was turned towards Fitzgerald, whose well-known voice he could distinctly hear relating the principal incidents of the chase.

Another whimsical idea entered the sick boy's mind.

"My mother is a visible spirit. Why should Charlie be invisible because he, like myself, was killed by a robber. *I must be invisible,* or else my mother would speak to me."

At that moment the earl returned with a decanter and three wine glasses.

Fitzgerald was relating the finish of the chase, and expressing his regret that the stone he threw did not stop the robber.

"It's a good job you did not kill him, Charlie; it would be very inconvenient to have to get out of my very comfortable bed here in Hades, to punch the head of the ghost of that confounded robber fellow who killed me," said Frank, in a very weak voice.

"My darling boy," exclaimed Mrs. Egerton, delighted beyond measure to hear his voice again; "thank Heaven he did not kill you."

The words were accompanied by a shower of kisses upon his pale cheeks and brow.

"I thought I was dead," said he, "and we were all phantoms."

Frank made a feeble attempt to put his arm round his mother's neck, but not having sufficient strength to do so was quite content to lie still and be caressed by her, while she whispered to him that having heard he was ill she had come from London to be his nurse.

"And now you must keep perfectly quiet and still, Frank. The doctor says that is the only way by which you can regain your health and strength."

Frank promised to be perfectly passive, but returning consciousness brought with it great pain.

Although he made no complaint, it was evident, from the twitching of the lips and the spasmodic working of the muscles of his face, that the wound was torturing him.

CHAPTER XX.

KATE CONWAY'S CONFESSION.

It was quite a week before Frank's medical attendants could pronounce a decided opinion that his life was out of danger. His safety they then attributed to the constant and careful nursing of his mother.

But Mrs. Egerton began to look pale and weary. Constant watching, night and day, was a thing to which she was little accustomed.

As soon as it was known that Frank might safely be left for a time to the care of a professional nurse, the widow lady was persuaded to take first a little rest, then a little exercise.

In the first of her walks round the outskirts of the old town, the Earl of Pembridge, who, though barely sixteen years of age, fancied himself quite a man, gallantly offered to be her companion and escort.

As they approached the gate leading from the school-field they noticed a very pretty girl, very neatly dressed, loitering about as though waiting for some one.

The instant this fair maiden caught sight of the earl, she ran forward, and eagerly asked—

"How is he to-day?"

"Much better, I am happy to say," replied he. "The doctors pronounce his recovery certain."

"I am so glad," was the earnest remark that followed.

"You are speaking of my son, I presume?" said Mrs. Egerton, very much astonished at what she saw and heard. "May I ask who this young lady is who seems to take such an interest in his health?"

"Mrs. Egerton—Miss Conway," said the earl.

"Miss Conway must explain a little more about herself. How came you to make my son's acquaintance?"

"He saved my life when I was in the river," said Kate, who had inquired at least twice a day as to Frank's health ever since he received his wound.

"Well, once thanking would have been sufficient. What is your father, girl?"

"He is copying-clerk for a lawyer. I and my sister are milliners," Kate replied, in a very hesitating manner, alternately blushing and turning pale.

"Does your father know of the friendship existing between my son and yourself?"

"Yes; he saved my father's life as well as my own, and—"

"And what?"

For some time there was no reply. The question had to be repeated.

"I—I love him," at last came slowly from her lips.

Then, as if astonished at the enormity of the confession, the fair girl began to cry.

"Love my son! how dare you, a milliner girl, do such a thing?" said Mrs. Egerton, in angry tones.

Kate Conway's tears came faster than before.

"I knew it," she murmured, speaking more to herself than either of the persons in front of her. "I told him she would never allow us to marry."

"I would see him in his grave first?" was the reply of the angry mother.

The fair girl's face grew paler than ever, her limbs sank beneath her, and she would have fallen to the ground had not the Earl of Pembridge's arm sustained her.

"You are too severe," said the young peer

"Not a bit. She must be brought to a sense of her proper position in life."

"Her position does her credit, madam."

"Credit! A milliner girl who has to stitch for her living! What a prospect."

The earl looked very angry, but was prevented from replying by poor Kate, who, at that moment, opened her large blue eyes, and looked up.

"My dear Miss Conway, you must return home; you are ill," said he.

"I—am ill—yes."

As she spoke, she turned her face full towards Mrs. Egerton, who could not help acknowledging to herself that the girl was very beautiful. But, then, how could she permit her son to marry a common girl who had to work for a living?

The fact is, Mrs. Egerton had forgotten for the time that her own and her son's prospects in life had very much altered for the worse lately, and that unless Frank married money *he* would be compelled to work.

With a little more kindness in her manner than before, the widow said—

"Now, run home, child, and forget that you have ever seen my son, for I cannot allow you to see him any more."

"Yes, home," poor Kate repeated. "Never see him any more in this world," and tears again began to stream down the poor, white face.

"Do you go a little way with her, my lord, as you seem to be acquainted with her," Mrs. Egerton whispered to the earl. "She will get better when she has walked a little distance."

"I fear you have killed her, broken her heart," was the reply of Earl Pembridge, as he walked off slowly with his fair charge.

Not a word said poor Kate all the way home till they reached the door of the little cottage in which she resided.

"You had better not come down to the college again, Miss Conway," said her escort. "I will bring you news every day, and that will be a fine excuse for coming to see Lizzie."

"No, no, no; you must not see her again, my lord. She must never feel the pain I have suffered to-day."

"She has promised to be my wife in a few years' time. When I am twenty-one I will marry her, if my guardians do not allow it before; that is, unless she prefers another."

"Write to me, my lord, and tell me how he is. I may not see him, but she cannot hinder me from loving him."

So saying, she entered the house, proceeded straight to her bed-room, threw herself on the bed, and sobbed herself to sleep.

The earl walked back to where he had left Mrs. Egerton.

"Has she gone home?" that lady asked.

"She has, madam."

"I am glad of that. How absurd to think of marrying my son! they are but children, both."

"I am not so old as Frank, but I shall marry her sister."

Mrs. Egerton looked perfectly astounded.

"Nonsense!"

"It is a fact. If my guardians do not consent, I shall wait till I am twenty-one, and celebrate my coming of age by marrying a milliner girl, *who has to stitch for a living.*"

"Marry a milliner! Impossible!"

"Nevertheless such an event will take place within the next six years, unless death interferes. *My* prospects in life does not so much depend upon what matrimonial alliance I make as Frank's."

Poor Mrs. Egerton was completely dumbfounded.

CHAPTER XXI.

ANOTHER COMBAT.

IT certainly was rather hard hitting on the part of the earl; but then he thought, felt, and spoke on behalf of his friend.

Mrs. Egerton could not understand it, and maintained a perfect silence as they walked back to the school. Then she said, as she parted from the earl—

"You had best say nothing about this for a few days. In his present state of health it might have an injurious effect."

"I shall be silent on the subject till he has quite recovered.

*   *   *   *   *   *

Several days passed away, and no one in the school but Pembridge and Charlie Fitzgerald had heard of the scene we have just described.

Every day one or other of the last-named personages took a stroll in the direction of old Conway's cottage, and left word how the invalid was progressing; but Frank himself did not know that his mother had discovered his little love affair.

At length the invalid was able to rise from his bed and walk from one room to the other: and a few days after he showed himself in the schoolroom for half-an-hour, though he took no part in the lessons that were going on.

An enthusiastic cheer greeted him, and Olympian Jove (*Doctor Whackley*) descended from his throne to salute the King of the School.

"I am delighted to see you here again, Egerton," said he, "It would nave grieved me much hau you lost your life in saving mine."

"Sir, I only did what I hope and believe any other of your pupils would have done, replied our hero.'

Professor Moeritz came up beaming at Egerton through his spectacles, and shook him by the hand, muttering,

"Zo glad, zo glad dat der Rauber—ze tief have not killed you. Goot poy."

"Thank you, Doctor Moeritz. I am sorry we did not catch the thief."

There was one person in the school, and not far from the head of it, too, who took no share in these congratulations. Our readers will have no difficulty in guessing that we allude to Baynes.

During all the time Frank had been an invalid, this youth had been endeavouring to keep the chief seat in the form, but in vain. Charlie Fitzgerald and the Earl of Pembridge studied to prevent him from so doing. Never before had the earl such an incentive to study.

At length Frank Egerton fell into accustomed routine of school life again, and his mother, having no longer an excuse for remaining with her darling, returned to London.

She had not said a word to him about the pretty milliner, for she considered him still to be too weak to be worried.

"I will speak to him when he comes home for the holidays," she said to herself, and so she left him.

Since the death of Frank's fatner and seizure of his property by Baynes, Senior, Baynes himself had been very unpopular in Lexicon College.

Few of the boys cared to speak to him, and those who did so condescend, were very cold and abrupt in their conversation. This was certainly very annoying.

"Now," thought the bully, "now is the time to be revenged. He pretends to be quite recovered, but I don't think he is. I'll pick a quarrel with him, and risk the results."

But, as you must all be aware, when one boy studiously avoids another it is a difficult matter for either to disagree with the other.

Baynes saw this difficulty, and well knowing the chivalrous nature of the King of the School, resolved upon a course of action which he well knew would excite Egerton's anger.

For a whole day the smaller fry of the college trembled when Baynes was seen approaching, or his voice was heard.

Freddy Webber ventured to remonstrate with the tyrant, but was roughly told to mind his own business.

" I am doing so," was the reply.

" Then don't interfere with me, or I shall be obliged to lick you."

" You are a coward, Baynes. You know you are longer in the arms and stronger than I, therefore you say such rude things. But we both know how to use a stick."

"What say you; shall we have a trial?"

" With all my heart."

" No," exclaimed Egerton, who had overheard the conversation; " leave him for me, for I know he is too clever for you, Freddy. Baynes, you are a cowardly bully to threaten and insult those who are so much younger and smaller than yourself. You shall not fight Webber; but if you wish to have a bout with the sticks I will not disappoint you."

" Of course, I will. Do you think I am going to let you bully me always? Under the elm at four o'clock this afternoon, and take care of your sore head, for I hit hard."

" As hard as you like. I shall not play gently, I assure you."

That day, after school hours, a group of boys might have been seen under the elm trees that formed one of the principal ornaments of the play-field.

In the centre of the group stood Frank Egerton and his second, Charlie Fitzgerald; facing them Baynes and Crawley.

Presently the earl of Pembridge made his appearance, attended by Harry, the waif Egerton had picked up. The boy carried half-a-dozen sound ashen sticks with basket hilts.

These he threw on the ground, and the seconds immediately began to select weapons for their principals.

Crawley made his selection for Baynes first, choosing a rather heavy stick.

Fitzgerald, in looking out a weapon for Egerton, selected one possessing more pliability than the others, and handed it to him.

The King of the School, after a critical examination, signified his approval of it by a nod.

Both combatants then took off their coats, rolled up their shirt-sleeves, and placed themselves opposite each other.

" Guard!" exclaimed the earl, who acted as referee.

The sticks cracked together as the combatants assumed attitudes of defence.

" Commence," was the next word and Baynes at once began to shower down his blows as rapidly as possible.

He calculated on the reduction of strength Frank had suffered through his illness, and hoped to break through his guard.

He had resolved, if possible, to strike on the old wound.

The result would, probably, be death—or at least another long and severe illness for Frank; but Baynes had gone on so far in sin that he was not inclined to stop at murder, especially as he knew the law well enough to be aware that, *legally*, it would only be termed manslaughter.

It was not so easily done, though.

Frank held up a good guard, and carefully protected his head, without attempting to return the blows.

" I must alter my tactics," thought Baynes, and immediately he began to direct all his attention to his opponent's body and legs, a mode of attack which he kept up for some time.

Suddenly changing, however, he delivered a blow which, had it taken effect, would have entirely stopped all poor Frank's fencing, for it was directed at the scar left by the robber's pistol-bullet.

Egerton felt it impossible to ward it off with his stick, so he raised his left hand, and received the stroke on the wrist.

With such force it was delivered, that Frank's arm was nearly paralyzed.

"I claim that as foul play!" said Crawley.

"No," said the referee; you ought to know that, according to the rules we formed last half, for regulating serious fights, it is not foul play unless he holds the stick."

The combat then recommenced.

In the second bout, Frank assumed the offensive, for he saw that his opponent was out of breath.

He managed to get a blow home on Baynes's head, almost staggering that youth.

Fierce fighting was the order of the day, and it was evident that one or the other would get severely damaged.

Scientific attitudes were neglected; the combatants only thought of hitting hard.

Frank's blows began to tell.

More than once he beat down Baynes's guard, and gave him severe visits on leg, body, and head.

All this made Baynes more savage than ever.

In proportion as his anger increased his caution decreased.

Frank Egerton noted it, and watched for an opportunity.

At length it came.

Crack, crack, crack! went the sticks, then there was a dull, heavy thud.

Baynes, whose head had received the full force of the blow, grinned a ghastly grin, turned very pale, dropped his stick, and then fell to the ground.

"Egerton wins! Hurrah!" burst from a dozen throats, and caps were thrown into the air by delighted youngsters who had witnessed the defeat of their tyrant.

"Ha, you haf kill Baynes vith ein Schlag mit dem Stocke," (a blow of a stick), said Professor Moeritz, who had been surveying the scene and had come forward as soon as he saw the vanquished youth fall.

"Ich habe ihm nichts zu Leide gethan (I have not done him any harm)" replied Frank, who was learning to talk with the professor in the language of Vaterland.

"Take him up," said the professor, addressing the bystanders.

But some water having been sprinkled on Baynes's face, he was able to rise and walk away, sorely lamenting that ever he had been tempted to take up the stick against Frank Egerton.

Of course his friend Crawley accompanied him.

CHAPTER XXII.

NOBLE HORSEMANSHIP.

FROM the time of the combat we have just described, a month passed away without any renewal of open hostilities between Baynes and Egerton.

Not that Baynes had forgiven; no, his longing for revenge was stronger than ever, but circumstances, as we have already seen, had convinced him that he could not obtain that gratification by his own right arm in fair and open

"HURRAH! THE GAME IS OURS!" SHOUTED FRANK.

No. 6,

combat; so he waited for an opportunity of striking some unseen blow.

He even condescended to speak to Egerton on matters connected with school discipline; but, beyond that, there was no communication between them.

Doctor Whackley saw all this with much grief, but it was hardly a case that called for his interference.

So each youth went his own way without interfering with the other.

Frank, not having been forbidden by his mother, still continued to visit the pretty milliner, whose pale cheeks began to grow rosy again.

I dare say the four young people, Egerton, Pembridge, Kate Conway, and Lizzie, used to talk a great deal of nonsense during their afternoon and evening walks; but this I know, they were supremely happy, although sometimes the poor girls would think, with something like dread, upon the many obstacles that had to be overcome before they could be happily united to those they so truly loved.

Frank and his friend did not spend all their leisure time in love-making, however, but took a fair share in the boyish sports and pastimes of the school.

The weather was now getting a little too cold for cricket or boating, so football and paper hare and hounds became the favourite sports.

Earl Pembridge, Marsham, and one or two of their friends took long rides in the country occasionally on horses which could be hired at some stables in the town. Of course there was no occasion for the earl to hire horseflesh, as he possessed his own Arab steed.

Frank Egerton, the King of the School, seldom took part in these equestrian excursions. His finances were not in a sufficiently flourishing condition; for, although his mother frequently sent him money, Frank rarely omitted to return it, being well-assured that she could ill afford to spare it.

There was hardly a boy in the school who would not have felt much pleasure in being permitted to pay the horse hire for him; but they knew that Frank was very proud, and that such a proposition would have been hurtful to his feelings.

So Frank generally remained behind on such occasions, and either took a walk with Kate Conway, or had an interview with the detective, who had attached himself to the local police force, but had hitherto failed to discover the perpetrators of the several robberies at Lexicon College.

Egerton had been made aware of the secret that the school and its inmates were watched, and was endeavouring to aid the detective in hunting down the scoundrels.

From the circumstance that the villain who assaulted Doctor Whackley in his study, and then so nearly terminated our hero's existence, was a man who evidently could not have been an inmate of the college, the detective had been induced rather to relax the vigilant watch he had kept over Baynes, after seeing him beneath the trees with Crawley holding something in his hand like a bank-note.

A careful examination of that young gentleman's pockets and desk a short time afterwards resulted in the discovery of a letter, from which it appeared that he actually had received five pounds from his father that very morning.

Frank Egerton, though unable to say why, felt convinced that Baynes, if not the thief, was at least an accomplice, and kept a very sharp eye upon him.

All their watchings had been of no use, however; it seemed as though the thief would have the good fortune to escape detection.

Baynes seemed to be tolerably free from duns.

He was unable to go to his favourite billiard-rooms on account of the doctor's strict orders to the contrary; and the big boys of the college, who sometimes met at the hostelry known as the "Six Bells," had not enough of the true spirit of gambling in them to make it very pleasant or profitable for him.

Captain Robinson, so far as could be learnt, had left the town; at all events nothing was seen of him.

To the great surprise of every one, Baynes took to riding, and was, with his friend Crawley, frequently seen cantering across the open downs in the neighbourhood of Ballsbury. One thing, however, was soon discovered, they did not get their steeds at the same place as the other boys—at the " Red Lion."

Freddy Webber, too, took to the same kind of exercise, though in a mild way, for he had first of all to master the rudiments of riding, while the others were tolerably practised horsemen.

To all this Doctor Whackley could not, and did not, object.

Though anything but a ' muscular Christian " himself, he always encouraged his pupils in athletic sports of all kinds during the hours allotted to recreation, and very much disliked to see boys reading when they ought to have been playing.

One day, when Marsham, the Earl of Pembridge, Charlie Fitzgerald, and one or two others, had gone out for their customary canter, Freddy Webber approached the King of the School.

" Don't you like riding, Egerton?" he asked.

" Very much indeed, Webber. There is hardly anything I like better."

" I think I shall like it; but, you know, I was never on a horse's back till this half, whereas you, I dare say, have had a pony ever since you were too heavy to ride the house dog."

" You are right, Freddy. But as I can't see any prospect of being able to keep a horse for some years to come, I mean to give up riding; it only makes me long for what I cannot possess."

" But you can hire a horse."

" Yes—for a half-a-guinea. Really, Freddy, I cannot afford to pay ten and sixpence for an afternoon's amusement. I am poor now you must remember."

" I wish you would come out, old fellow. I know a place where we can get very good horses indeed for about half the ' Red Lion ' price."

Egerton did not require much coaxing, but speedily was on his way to the stables patronized by Freddy.

They were situated in rather an out-of-the-way back street, but that was their only fault; so far as horseflesh was concerned, Freddy vowed they were quite equal to the " Red Lion."

During the walk, the conversation turned upon Baynes, who had that morning shown some symptoms of a disposition to make another attempt to raise himself to the supremacy.

" I shall have to take the conceit out of him again," said Frank. I will not allow him to illtreat smaller boys."

Just as he had spoken, they turned into the stable-yard, and were very much surprised to find Baynes standing close to the gate.

From the grim, satirical sneer, on his countenance it was quite evident that he had overheard the last words of Egerton's speech.

He noticed the new comers with a slight nod, and then began speaking to one of the grooms.

Frank Egerton and Freddy Webber at once went up to Mr. Martingale, the proprietor.

" Good morning; can I have a horse to day?" said Freddy.

" Yes, sir; I've got your favourite in."

" My friend here requires a mount."

" Hem, that's rather awkward. I'm rather short of 'osses to-day, and that gentleman," he pointed to Baynes, " has just picked out the best bit o' stuff I had. I'll go and see though."

He entered the stables, and just at the door Baynes joined.

" So this is where Baynes comes?" observed Frank.

" I wonder how much he is in debt here?" queried Freddy. " I feel pretty certain he is not very regular in paying."

At this moment the stable-keeper re-appeared, and Frank heard him say—

"Well, I'll do it; but if anything happens—"

Now, as the intelligent reader well knows, such words will admit of a variety of constructions, and Frank, not being very suspicious, thought nothing of them.

"You can have a horse, sir; but she's rather fresh."

"That doesn't matter. I like a little spirit in a horse."

"Saddle Brown Bess," shouted the stable-keeper.

"Brown Bess, sir!" said the man, scratching his head.

"Yes, Brown Bess! Don't you hear what I say, you great gaping idiot?"

"*Mad* Bess she ought to be called," muttered the man, as he walked away to do as ordered.

"Don't you ride that mare, Frank," said Freddy, "She is a most vicious brute."

"Only a little spirit, I suppose."

In a minute Brown Bess made her appearance, and a wild-looking creature she was, though extremely handsome.

"Brown Bess is a soldier's musket, Frank. If you load that Brown Bess, it is you who will *go off*," observed Freddy, who could not resist the temptation to make a bad pun.

"She is certainly a vicious-looking brute."

At this moment Baynes, who was some little distance away, spoke ostensibly to the ostler by whose side he was standing, but evidently with the intention that his words should be heard by every one present.

"Pretty fellows to go out for a ride!" he exclaimed in a sneering manner. "They are afraid to mount the mare because she happens to be a little bit skittish."

"I must show them that I am not afraid," whispered Frank. "Keep her steady a moment, my man."

During a momentary pause in the antics her ladyship had been indulging in, Egerton lightly vaulted into the saddle.

"Let go!" he shouted, to the groom, at the same time gathering up the reins.

The groom instantly released his hold of the bridle, and Brown Bess commenced a series of the most extraordinary kicks and leaps.

Frank kept his seat well, and soon convinced the mad animal that he was not to be trifled with.

After riding her two or three times round the yard, she became tolerably quiet, and then Freddy, who was mounted on a very quiet and rather ancient steed, led the way out into the street.

A restless twitching of the ears convinced the rider of Brown Bess that she would require very careful riding.

Two or three streets were traversed safely, and Frank began to fancy that the animal was not quite so mad as was generally believed.

The market-place was at length reached.

A drove of pigs being conducted to the slaughter-house (the market was nearly over) attracted the mare's attention; but she showed no signs of fear till one of them, having felt the lash of the drover's whip, set up a loud squealing.

Brown Bess immediately managed to get the bit between her teeth, and began to leap over the railings which divided the various cattle pens in the market-place.

The few people about hastily got out of the way, and Frank, finding he could not control the mare, began to think of throwing himself off.

But the flagstones with which the market-place was paved looked so hard and uninviting that he resisted the temptation.

"What can the beast mean to do?" thought Frank, as Brown Bess made straight for the open portals of the town-hall which graced one side of the market-place, while Freddy, on his Rosinante, yelled to the people to help to stop it.

The intention of the animal was soon evident.

She would take refuge from the squalling, grunting tribe in the justice-room.

Well it was for the beadle that he fled from his post, and took refuge in the neighbouring hostelry, known as the "Wheatsheaf," for had Brown Bess come in contact with him, as she dashed beneath the portico, his portly carcass would have received many a dire bruise, even if, haply, no bones had been broken.

Frank, to tell the truth, began to grow alarmed, as he found his steed wildly careering through the entrance of the town-hall, and up the broad stone staircase that led to the offices of the corporation.

He began to calculate the chances of broken limbs; and the thought swiftly flashed through his mind that Baynes had persuaded the stable-keeper to mount him on this mad animal in the hope that a broken limb might be the result.

All things must have an end, however. Bess, on arriving at the top of the grand staircase, stopped so suddenly that our hero nearly went flying over her head.

By a great effort, however, he managed to keep his seat.

Had either of the office-doors been open, the chances are that the mare would have entered one or other of the rooms.

As it was, she half-turned her head, and seeing the difficulties of the position to which she had brought herself, began to tremble violently.

A slight relaxation of the jaws enabled Frank once more to get a firm pull at the bit.

"She has brought me up here, she shall carry me down," said he to himself.

A gentle pull at the near rein, and she turned as carefully and quietly as possible, still slightly trembling.

It was necessary to give her the slightest possible touch with the heel to induce her to commence the descent; then she began to pick her way down the stone steps as gingerly as a farmer's wife treading among new-laid eggs.

He reached the door, and was greeted with a terrific cheer from the people who had assembled to witness the dénouément of this strange performance.

The noise was listened to with the greatest calmness by Bess, who seemed in the perpetration of that one wild freak to have completely changed her nature.

Disregarding the cries of the beadle, who emerged from his retreat, and shouted to our hero to surrender himself to his custody for contempt of the corporation, Frank trotted quietly away, and rejoined Freddy Webber, who was waiting on the other side of the market-place, expecting each moment to see his friend appear, either flying through one of the upper windows or borne out on a shutter.

His delight when he saw Frank quietly riding towards him unharmed can be better imagined than described.

"For Heaven's sake, let us get back to the stables," he said, as soon as the first congratulations were over.

"Why go back?" asked Frank.

"To leave that horrid brute with her owner."

"I came out for a ride, Freddy, and I mean to have a ride. Come along."

"No, no; not on that beast."

"Yes, on this beast, as you rudely call her. She is a splendid animal, and when we get out on Oddman's Downs you shall see how she can go."

And despite all Freddy's entreaties to the contrary, Frank trotted off through the streets, and soon gained the large open space he had alluded to.

Looking round, he saw Freddy coming along at as good a canter as he could screw out of his somewhat antiquated specimen of a horse.

"Freddy, you see those three fir trees yonder?" he asked, as soon as his companion came up.

"Yes, I see them," said Freddy.

"They are quite a mile away, are they not?"

"More; a mile and a half, I should say."

"Then lend me your riding-whip."

"What for? Surely you are not going to touch the mad beast with anything like a whip?"

"Certainly; I mean to give her both whip and spur in moderation, and go out to those trees and back at racing speed."

So saying, Frank buttoned his coat, fixed his hat firmly on his head, and snatched the riding-whip from Freddy's hand.

"Don't do it, Frank. I know the brute will be the death of you."

"I am bound to bring Brown Bess to her senses, after Baynes's sneer," was the reply, and away he started.

Bess was more than three-parts thorough-bred, and Frank, though a fine, well-grown youth, did not carry over eight stone of flesh, blood, and bone.

The mare sped along like the wind.

The fir trees were reached and passed, but at such a headlong pace were they going, that ere he could pull up, he became aware of a ditch or gully before him, some eighteen or twenty feet wide —how deep he could not say.

Any attempt to check the mare's speed would certainly result in rolling both horse and rider in the ditch, when most probably both would be severally damaged.

So with a dig of the spurs and a cut of the whip, he put her to it.

The mare, however, was rather blown, and though her fore-legs cleared the chasm she had a hard struggle to fairly gain the opposite side, falling with her fore legs and body on the turf, while the hind legs hung down in the chasm.

Frank was obliged to jump off quick as lightning, and give a hard pull at the halter to get her out of the ditch.

"I think you are pretty well subdued now, my beauty," said the young equestrian, as he brushed the dirt off her legs and flanks, an operation she submitted to very quietly; "but you'll have to carry me back over that ditch."

He led her about a hundred yards, turned, remounted, and rode her at the dyke, which this time she cleared splendidly.

Then Frank rejoined Webber, and, after a quiet trot across the downs, the two youths re-entered the good old town of Ballsbury by another road.

Baynes was having a solitary ride out.

As Frank and his friend were returning they met him.

A slight nod was the only acknowledgment of acquaintance, but Baynes's flushed face betokened his mortification at the frustration of his schemes.

He had heard of the affair in the market-place and town-hall, and, while hearing, muttered curses upon the good fortune which seemed to attend every action of our hero.

Frank, on appearing with the tamed steed at the stable-yard, received a perfect ovation, which he took very coolly, not knowing how far the horsey people there assembled were sincere in their congratulations.

The master of the establishment was profuse in his apologies for the inconvenience to which Frank had been put, adding—

"I never knew the mare do such a thing before."

Frank thought that very possible, and accepted the apology, especially as the owner of Brown Bess offered him the free use of the quadruped two days a-week for a month.

CHAPTER XXIII.

FIRST PIC-NIC.

THE boys, when they heard of their king's adventures, were enthusiastic in his praise.

But some of them, when they heard the whole of the matter, were justly indignant with Baynes, who, by his taunts and sneers, incited Frank Egerton to mount the mad mare.

Bully Baynes was cut by many of them in consequence.

After tea that evening Frank and the Earl of Pembridge prepared their lessons for the next day in a very hasty manner, and then left the school-room for the purpose of taking a walk in the town.

Marsham, Lascelles, and two or three others volunteered to accompany them; but the offers were coldly received, as the KING OF THE SCHOOL and his friend were " going on important business."

The intelligent reader will at once guess that they intended to see two young ladies whom we have already introduced upon the scene.

We call them young ladies, because, though their surviving parent was poor, they had been well educated, and on all occasions spoke and acted as ladies.

Frank and his friend had hardly left the school-grounds when they saw Kate and Lizzie coming towards them.

The girl's had heard of Frank's equestrian feat at the town-hall, and had been told that he afterwards rode out of town.

They, especially Kate, felt anxious to know how the mad ride had terminated, and were walking down towards the school in the hopes of hearing something.

Right glad were they both to see our hero and his friend.

Dear reader, you really have no right to know all the tender nonsense that was said during the ten minutes immediately after the meeting of the young couples, so, with your permission, we will pick up the thread of their discourse from the time when they arrived at a certain green field, the proprietor of which had placed rustic seats by the pathway.

Having seated themselves, in the course of a very loving conversation the day of the month happened to be called in question.

" It's the third of September," observed the earl.

" Then next Wednesday is the holiday. How shall we spend it ?" asked Frank.

Now this was a very important question, and while they are considering—the girls waiting *very* anxiously for the decision—let me explain things.

From time immemorial it had been the custom to observe the first Wednesday in every month as a holiday.

The reason for such a custom no one could tell, the origin being lost in the clouds of antiquity.

On that day the pupils rose half-an-hour earlier than usual, lines were repeated before breakfast, and after that meal they had two hours class; the proceedings terminated at eleven in the forenoon, after which the boys were allowed to do as they pleased till ten o'clock at night, when names were called in the school-room.

" I know what we'll do," said Pembridge.

" What ?"

" We'll have a pic-nic; such jolly fun."

" Yes, that's jolly. These young ladies will like it, I know, won't you, Kate ?" Frank observed.

"Very much indeed. Oh, it is so kind of you!"

"What say you, Lizzie?" inquired the earl.

"I should like it above all things, dear Gordon (Gordon was the earl's Christian name). I have never been to a pic-nic yet."

"But we must get a few others," suggested Frank. "We'll bring three or four of our fellows, and you must invite some ladies."

These young people, not thinking any harm in a day's innocent amusement themselves, of course did not for a moment imagine that a cold and suspicious world would perhaps hint that it was improper for young people to enjoy the pleasure of a pic-nic without having a lot of old people to look after them.

So they made all their arrangements. It was agreed that two vehicles, each capable of holding about six people, should be in readiness at the "Red Lion," at half-past eleven on Wednesday morning, to convey the whole party to Knitton Folly, a most delightful wood, about six miles distant.

The earl of Pembridge undertook to make arrangements with White, the best pastrycook in the town, for a couple of hampers of refreshments.

* * * * *

Imagine that it is Wednesday, 11.30 A.M.

The scene is the court-yard of the "Red Lion" hotel.

In addition to the four people who arranged the affair, Marsham, Lascelles, and Freddy Webber are present, also two young ladies named Griffiths, with their mamma, who, on learning the manner in which the expedition was organised, volunteered to accompany it, as a sort of body-guard and defence against all kinds of scandal and evil speaking.

Frank Egerton, of course, drives one of the vehicles, which also contains Kate Conway, her sister, the Earl of Pembridge, and Mrs. Griffiths, the remainder of the party being in vehicle number two, tooled by Albert Marsham, who was a far better hand at driving than parsing.

A most pleasant drive was it.

First over the old stone bridge, then by the side of some fertile meadows; but, gradually ascending, they reached a range of glorious downs, covered with golden-blossomed furze.

Four hundred and odd feet above the level of Lexicon College playfield, where the summer breezes, though gentle and soft, sang weird songs in their ears, and nothing else could be heard on the now deserted race-course save the shrill cry of the lapwing, and the hum of the bee.

On one side of the road that famous region of fir and beach, known as the Warren (my lord's keepers would not allow pic-nics there); and on the other hand an expanse of some miles of open and cultivated land, in one part descending into a valley where the villages of Coombe, Stratford, Bishopsstone, and Chalk lay, hidden from the gaze of our young excursionists

At length they reached Knitton Folly, and turned aside out of the old, grass-grown, Roman road they had been travelling.

The earl was pilot, and told Frank to keep on down the central ride or avenue, which he did till they reached a vast cavity in the hill-side, commonly known as the Devil's Punch-bowl; popular tradition asserting that his satanic majesty was formerly in the habit of mixing his strong potations there.

Not far from the Punch-bowl was a little cottage, inhabited by one of the keepers, whose son, an uncouth urchin of ten, readily agreed to take charge of the horses and provisions.

It was not long past noon when our friends reached their destination; a slight luncheon was partaken of, and then the party dispersed, intending to meet again at four for a more substantial meal.

Of course Frank and Kate Conway walked away together, and equally, of course, the Earl of Pembridge placed himself beside Lizzie.

Marsham and Lascelles took charge of the other young ladies, leaving Freddy Webber to escort Mrs. Griffiths.

From the "Punch-bowl" to Buscombe Ivers, where nuts were plentiful, was not far, and thither they all flocked.

Kate Conway had never been in such a wild-looking wood before, and at first was rather afraid of meeting a wolf or a bear.

However, nothing worse than a weasel was seen, and she soon overcame her timidity.

It was at least half-an-hour after the appointed time when they returned to the spot where the vehicles had been left.

The keeper's son had collected a quantity of dry wood and made a fire, over which he had fixed a tripod of large sticks, from which a kettle was slung.

But while the tea was being made a most unfortunate accident took place.

Kate Conway had gone by herself to a bank where a quantity of large feathery grass grew, for the purpose of collecting a quantity of it.

While so engaged she felt a sharp sting on the palm, and hastily lifting up her hand, found a reptile about two feet and a half long hanging from it and endeavouring to twine round her arm.

She gave a loud scream, and in an instant Egerton appeared at her side.

"Oh, Frank, Frank!" exclaimed the frightened girl.

"It's an adder!" cried Frank, and seizing the venomous beast by the tail he jerked it away, throwing it very nearly in Freddy Webber's face, as that youth and Marsham were coming up to see what was the matter.

Frank was too busy, however, to notice what became of it.

"Turn your head aside, my darling, that you may not see what I am going to do," said he, taking the bitten hand in his own.

Kate, who had the most implicit confidence in her young lover, immediately looked away.

Frank instantly opened his penknife, made a deep cut where the poison fangs had pierced the skin, and sucked the wound.

"Oh, Frank dear, you will poison yourself," said the fair girl, as soon as she knew what he was doing.

"I think not, my love; I am trying to save your life, and if I fail I have no wish to live. Now, then, let me tie this round."

This was a pocket-handkerchief torn in strips which he bound round Kate's wrists so tightly that the circulation of the blood was stopped, the venom being thus prevented from spreading.

Freddy Webber and Marsham had killed the adder, which was certainly a very ugly-looking reptile, nearly three feet long.

Lascelles had busied himself from the time of the first alarm in getting the horses attached to the vehicles.

Kate Conway was handed into one of them, with her sister, the Earl of Pembridge, and Mrs. Griffiths; Frank seized the reins and drove off as sharply as possible towards Ballsbury, leaving the others to pack up the hampers and follow.

The surgery of Doctor Roberts was one of the first houses they came to after reaching the town.

Frank pulled up, lifted out Kate, and carried her into the place; the poor girl was almost fainting with fright, pain, and excitement.

The case having been explained to him, Doctor Roberts proceeded to make a very careful examination of the wound.

"You have had a very narrow escape," said he. "If this young gentleman had not acted with such promptitude you would by this time have been past recovery, for the wounds made by the adder's fangs were deep, and touched an important vein."

He then prescribed a variety of poultices, lotions and draughts, and recommended Kate to go home to bed at once, promising to call later in the evening and see how she progressed.

Frank would not leave her till she was safe at her father's door.

As they were about to part the fair girl threw her unbandaged arm about her lover's neck, and, while holding up her rosy mouth to be kissed, whispered—

"My Frank, you have twice saved me from death; my life shall be devoted to your happiness."

⌘

CHAPTER XXIV.

A MYSTERY CLEARED UP.

BEFORE he retired to rest that night, Frank sent his messenger and henchman, Harry, to Mr. Conway's house to inquire after Miss Kate's health.

To his great satisfaction the boy returned with the pleasing intelligence that the doctor had said all danger was over.

After that Frank was able to go to bed and sleep well, a thing he had previously despaired of being able to do.

The next morning the messenger was sent again, and this time Harry returned with the following news.

Miss Conway was not likely to suffer any ill effects from the adder's bite, but the surgeon had advised her to remain in all that day, that she might recover from the severe shock her nervous system had sustained.

Next day she was quite well, with the exception of a slight wound on the hand where Frank's knife had left its trace.

* * * * * *

A week after the pic-nic, which had come to so unpleasant a conclusion, a grand foot-ball match took place.

Thirty boys selected nominally by Crawley, but in reality by Baynes, who assumed the management of affairs from the time the challenge was given, undertook to play twenty selected by

Frank Egerton, the King of the School, king in sports and pastimes as well as in scholastic studies.

Crawley, artful fellow, had quietly enlisted all the big boys under his banner, except some half-dozen of our friends, who declined to take service with such a captain, so that when Frank began to look up his side he found he must content himself with smaller chaps.

He, of course, had Marsham, Fitzgerald, Lascelles, and Webber on his side, but the others were puny-looking compared with those attached to Baynes and Crawley.

But his fellows were full of pluck, and all looked up to him as their undisputed leader.

Every command of his was obeyed without the slightest hesitation, and each player did the work assigned to him without grumbling.

With the opposition it was different. Many of them knew quite as much about football as their reputed leader, and could play as well, if not better, there was much jealousy at and resistance to the authority assumed by Baynes.

Consequently, while they should have been practising, they were debating as to who should be their captain.

The all-important hour arrived.

"To the goals! To the goals!" shouted Egerton.

Small fry and non-players were unceremoniously bundled out of the way, and the two bodies of players took up their positions at their respective posts.

Foot-ball is a game so well-known and practised, that it would be unnecessary to here enter into a learned disquisition on the merits of the game, and its rules; so having separated the bodies of antagonists, let us commence playing.

Egerton, with his usual good-luck, had won the choice of goals and the kick off.

Having arranged his little army, some to keep the goals, and some to play up, he shouted out.

"Are you ready?"

"Yes," was the reply from the opposite side.

Without more ado, he took a short run of half-a-dozen steps, and sent the ball whizzing away towards the opposite goal, a fair flight of at least fifty yards before it touched the ground.

A loud cheer, and the opposite side rushed forward to drive it back; the two sides closed, and—

"When Greek joined Greek then was the tug of war."

There was a furious struggle, a dense mass of human beings struggling towards a central point, where hard kicks were plentiful, and where Frank Egerton might have been seen exerting all his strength to drive the ball towards the adversary's goal.

"Donner and bitzen! you haf break my legs!" exclaimed a guttural voice.

And Professor Moeritz, who played with Egerton's side, limped out of the crowd, but in a few seconds returned, again to receive something more than a share of the hard knocks of the battle.

At length the crowd suddenly separated.

The ball was driven back to Egerton's side, and a determined rush of Baynes's party carried it nearly up to the goal.

"Look out there," shouts Frank; but the warning was unnecessary. *His* players were all on the watch.

Back comes the ball, and with a well-directed drop-kick the King of the School sends it flying about two feet over the cross-bar between the goal posts.

Loud cheers from Frank's side, from the non-players, and from two young ladies, who had been very anxiously watching the game from the roadway near the gate.

Baynes and Crawley, who had not done much of the hard fighting, by-the-bye, bullied their men awfully, and an immense amount of grumbling ensued during the ten minutes that were devoted to changing goals, and preparing for the next kick off.

Glenny, one of Baynes's best players, roundly declared that he would not be ruled by an ass, who shirked his own share of the work; and being loudly applauded by the others, proceeded to make his own preparations for continuing the game.

He sent his leaders to keep goal, an arrangement they sulkily acquiesced in.

It was his kick off, and being rather an artful customer, he sent it into the air as high as possible, so that his own side might rush forward and catch it.

Frank saw the dodge, and led his own fighting brigade on to the charge.

Professor Moeritz, valuable for his weight rather than for scientific play, was in the front, and luckily for his own side, got tripped up in the thick of the scrimmage, just in time to prevent Glenny from giving a kick which must have sent the ball flying well into Frank's goal, if it had not fallen upon the professor's shoulder instead.

The King of the School, whose keen eye saw everything, at once noted his opportunity.

"Hurrah! The game is ours!" he shouted, and with a splendid drop-kick the ball was sent again flying between Baynes's goal posts.

Two goals had been gained in a very little over an hour, a thing not done every day, and of which Frank had great reason to be proud.

"You are too well drilled for us," said Glenny.

And that was in reality the secret of the other side's success.

So captains of cricket and foot-ball clubs bear this in mind—first of all make your men respect you, and then get them to move in strict obedience to your instructions.

What use is a general if his troops disobey orders, or act according to their own inclinations?

The game being ended, they picked up the German professor, who was rather severely bruised, though perhaps more frightened than hurt.

He had never before taken part in so fiercely contested a game.

* * * * * *

"Who has moved my coat?" said Glenny, as he proceeded to array himself in those portions of his attire which he had cast aside during the game.

"I did not leave my jacket here, I know," said another. "I placed it upon this bough."

Several others of Baynes's party also complained that their garments had been interfered with, but no one could give any explanation.

Every one had been so intently watching the play that they had not noticed a man who had stealthily been examining their pockets during the game.

This man was the detective, of whom we have already spoken as being employed to discover the perpetrators of the several robberies that had taken place in Lexicon College.

Hitherto he had not been successful.

While the boys were at their game, the man had quietly examined the pockets of all Baynes's side, apparently taking great interest in letters and papers of all kind.

Having satisfied his curiosity, the man retired from the trees on and beneath which the coats and vests had been placed, without having been noticed by any one of the players.

A great deal of confused grumbling went on among the boys as they dressed themselves, for the good beating they had received at foot-ball had not improved their tempers, and the interference with their clothes was an additional injury.

It would have gone hard with the offender had they known where to find him.

"I say, boys, look to your pockets," Glenny suddenly exclaimed.

"What's the matter?"

"Anything missing—lost some bank-notes?"

"No," replied Glenny, in answer to these inquiries; "but I am ready to swear these letters were in my right-hand pocket when I took my coat off, now I find them in the left."

The other boys at once began to examine into the state of their own possessions.

No one seemed to have lost anything but Baynes.

He turned suddenly pale.

"Some one has been looking over a lot of letters and things I had. One of them has been put in the wrong envelope, and——"

He paused, and had another search, after which he continued with increased paleness—

"One of them is gone. I would not have lost it for the world."

Hurriedly leaving his companions, Baynes went back to the house, and had a good search in his own boxes and his desk, hoping, though without much ground for hope, that he might have left the missing letter behind, though he perfectly remembered taking it from his pocket that very morning.

It could not be found.

That evening Baynes informed Doctor Whackley of his loss, and described the general appearance of the missing document, though he declined to state the subject of the epistle.

"Is this letter of any very great importance to you, Baynes?" asked the doctor.

"It is, indeed, sir."

"But you decline to give the writer's name, and to say what it is all about?"

"Certainly, sir. The thief, whoever he may be"—here he looked full at Egerton, who met his gaze so unflinchingly that the bully was compelled to turn away—"knows very well that the letter belongs to me. If he will not return it, I hope he will have a sufficient sense of honour to keep the secret he has discovered."

"It is a strange affair. However, I can only promise you that if the culprit is detected he shall be expelled. Boys," he continued, addressing the whole school, "I appeal to all to put a stop to this disgraceful state of affairs."

"I beg pardon for interrupting, sir," said a strange voice near the door.

Every head was turned.

A man, who had frequently been seen lounging about near the school, was standing there.

"That young gentleman has lost a letter, I believe?" continued the intruder.

"Yes," said Baynes, rising hastily and changing colour.

"I took it from your pocket, and I beg pardon of the other young gentlemen whose clothes I disturbed."

"Give it me instantly!" exclaimed Baynes, as he made a step forward.

"Sit down, sir!" replied the man, sternly, in tones so authoritative that Baynes immediately slunk back to his seat like a whipped cur.

"I should like to have a few words with you in private, if you please, sir," continued the man.

"Yes," replied the doctor.

"And while we are together let none of them get away."

"The heads of forms will see that no boy leaves the school-room under any pretext," said the doctor, who then gathered his robes round him and stalked out.

Let us follow them.

On entering his private study, the doctor threw himself into an easy chair and motioned his visitor to a seat.

That visitor, it is hardly necessary to explain, was the detective.

"You have discovered something of importance," said Doctor Whackley.

"I have sir."

"Pray Heaven it is not as I suspect. Well, let me know all about it!"

"The thief who stole your bank-notes, the forger who forged your cheque, is Baynes!"

"Thank Heaven! I almost feared it might be my pet pupil, the King of the School."

"This letter, which I took from his pocket while he was playing foot-ball, is from a billiard swindler who formerly haunted the rooms you have since prohibited your pupils from going to."

"But this is no proof. The writer only accuses Baynes of certain misdeeds."

"True; but as soon as I had read the letter I went to this Captain Robinson. I knew were to find him, and extorted from him a confession which gave me full proof of Baynes's guilt."

"Can it be possible?—A pupil of mine a common thief!"

"Yes; and a dangerous one, for he steals in such a way that the first appearances of guilt fall on others."

"What is to be done?"

"You must prosecute."

"What!"

"I say you must prosecute the offender."

"I cannot."

The detective merely smiled.

After a long silence the doctor again spoke.

"You, being a member of the police force, of course know the routine of the law in such cases. I do not; but I certainly shall not appear either as prosecutor or witness against one of my pupils."

"Then, sir, my mission is fulfilled. I have pointed out the offender; and if you refuse the remedy offered by the law I can only wash my hands of the case."

"Very good."

"And, of course, I shall be compelled,

to release the burglar, the man who made a savage attack on you, and nearly killed young Egerton."

The doctor winced at this rather, but replied, boldly—

"Yes. I cannot think that he will remain in the town long, knowing that he is detected."

"Very well. Good evening, sir."

"Good evening. Yet wait a moment."

The doctor wrote out a cheque for fifty pounds, and handed it to the detective, who quickly transferred it to his pocket-book.

He then walked away, and Doctor Whackley returned to the big schoolroom.

A row of no ordinary kind had been going on during his absence.

A few minutes after the detective called away the doctor, Baynes rose from his seat and walked towards the door.

"Baynes, you shall sit as ze doctor have ordered," said Professor Moeritz, and Frank Egerton, as head of the form, at once re-echoed the command.

"That man has my letter. I mean to have it," was the reply.

"Quite right," said Crawley, and one or two others.

"You can't leave the school," said Frank, placing his back against the door.

"I will."

The rash youth, who was evidently very much excited, put out his hand, seized Egerton by the coat collar, and endeavoured to drag him from his post.

Frank, of course, replied by hitting out straight from the shoulder, and flooring his opponent.

In an instant the school was in an uproar.

Baynes rose to his feet, drew a clasp-knife from his pocket, and made a rush at Egerton, with the evident intention of stabbing him.

Marsham saw it, and immediately jerked the weapon from his hand, receiving, while so doing, a severe blow in the face from Crawley.

That young sneak fancied he would not be seen, but Freddy Webber had been watching the melée, and at once began to pitch into Master Crawley.

People did not look upon Freddy as much of a pugilist, but he proved himself quite a match for his antagonist.

In the meantime, Frank Egerton was milling Baynes in splendid style, and very shortly reduced him to obedience, not before some desks had been overturned, and a few ink-bottles spilt upon the floor.

At this juncture entered Doctor Whackley.

"There has been some disturbance here?" said he, inquiringly.

"Yes, sir."

"What is it?"

"Baynes tried to go out against your orders, and I had a severe struggle to prevent him."

"Bring Baynes here."

Marsham, Lascelles, and Frank Egerton at once pounced upon him, and dragged him up to the steps of Doctor Whackley's desk.

"Hoist him!"

Marsham being the tallest of the party seized the struggling victim by the arms, and drew him up upon his shoulders.

Then followed the first public birching that had taken place that half, for the doctor was sparing of the rod, preferring to rule by love rather than by fear.

When the doctor's arm (and it was a strong one) began to descend with full force Baynes set up a most hideous yell for mercy.

But the pedagogue was relentless, and gave Baynes a fair four dozen.

"This is the thief,—" said he, when at last he threw down his birch, "the thief who for weeks past has been bringing disgrace upon the school."

The announcement was received with silent astonishment.

"Go to your bed-room, Baynes," continued the doctor, "and there remain till I send for you in the morning. You are no longer fit to associate with these gentlemen."

Baynes walked off, and Professor Moeritz followed, who, having locked him in, brought away the key of his bed-room.

There was an end to all study that night.

Books were thrown aside, and the boys broke up into little groups, speculating upon the strange affair.

Doubts were rife as to the ultimate result, for the boys did not know the resolution Doctor Whackley had formed, consequently there was some discussion as to whether Baynes would simply be expelled, or whether his expulsion would be followed by legal proceedings.

Frank Egerton and his friend, the Earl of Pembridge, thought so.

"It would be an insult to all of us to bring one of the old school into a police-court," said they.

After supper that night Doctor Whackley called two or three of the senior pupils into his study.

"I want to have a short talk with you about Baynes," said he, when they were all seated.

"I am very glad the thief has been found out, sir," said Frank.

"So am I, for there was a disgrace hanging over all the school."

"May I ask what you mean to do with him, sir," asked the Earl of Pembridge.

"He must leave in the morning, that is certain."

"No criminal proceedings I hope, sir?"

"Certainly not; I should be sorry to disgrace my good pupils by letting the world know they ever had such a bad companion. I also wish to know whether you think his expulsion should be public or private, as it is a matter concerning you all?"

"Private!" was the unanimous response.

"Let him be shown out by the back gate while the others are in school or at breakfast," suggested the earl, "I am quite sure we none of us wish to see him again."

"It shall be done so. I may add, for your satisfaction, that I have visited him once since this unhappy affair, and he has acknowledged his guilt. Good evening."

"Good evening, sir," responded they, and hurried back to the hall, all resolved to be silent as to the mode in which Baynes was to make his exit.

Nearly every one was abusing the detected rogue—none more loudly than his late friend, Crawley.

"Hullo, youngster, I thought you took his part?" said the earl, planting himself right before the sneak.

"So I did at first, for I did not think any one in the old place could be guilty of such a bad action."

"You are a bad lot yourself," said Webber, suddenly pushing himself to the front. "You struck Marsham when he was not looking, and then sat down so that he should not see you. I should like to give you a second edition of the punching I let you have—revised, corrected, and greatly enlarged."

"I don't think you could," was the sulky response.

"We'll see in the morning," said Webber.

At that moment the clock gave warning that it was time to retire, and they all hurried upstairs.

Frank Egerton and Fitzgerald had only recently been removed to an apartment adjoining that in which the captive slept.

While they were undressing, and for some time after the lights were extinguished, the two friends kept up an animated discussion on the events of the day.

In the course of time they came to speak of the challenge Freddy Webber had so boldly thrown down to Crawley.

Fitzgerald laughed loudly at the idea of a fight, Freddy being anything but a pugilist, though of undoubted courage, while Crawley was a notorious coward; and Frank joined in the merriment.

Suddenly the King of the School ceased, and motioned his also to be silent.

"THE PROFESSOR'S PIPE WAS SHIVERED BY THE EXPLOSION."

PRICE ONE HALFPENNY.

[Published Every Monday.]

"Our laughter must grate horribly upon the ears of the poor prisoner," said he. Let us not insult him now that he has been detected."

Fitzgerald assented, and, a few minutes after, both were asleep.

* * * * * *

The next morning Doctor Whackley ascended the steps of his desk and sternly commanded silence.

At once the whole school was hushed.

The boys guessed that they were to hear something of their late schoolfellow.

"Boys," said the doctor; it was my intention to have expelled Baynes from the school this morning for thieving, but he has saved me the pain of so doing by running away. He has gone, and I now have to request that you will cease to think or speak of him, so that the recollection of this very painful affair may die out as speedily as possible. Let it be forgotten that Baynes was ever a pupil at this establishment."

"I shall not mention his name again, sir, unless I am compelled to do so," said Frank.

"I hope the others will follow your example," observed the doctor, who then settled down to the regular business of the school.

CHAPTER XXV.

CRAWLEY TAKES BAYNES'S PLACE.

THAT evening the excitement was beginning to subside.

Boys could think of their games and their lessons, while Baynes was certainly not spoken of publicly.

Doctor Whackley was seconded well in his efforts to bring about oblivion (so far as Baynes and his misdeeds were concerned) by the under-masters, and notably by Professor Moeritz.

The worthy German told his drollest anecdotes in the drollest manner, and did all he possibly could to divert the attention of his pupils from the past.

He was sitting on a camp-stool, under a wide-spreading elm tree in the play-field, with a group of the boys round him, when he suddenly remembered that he had left his pipe in his study.

Professor Moeritz was a great consumer of the Indian Weed, and, as soon as he discovered that he was smokeless, called for a volunteer to fetch the missing pipe.

Three or four of the boys at once started on the errand, amongst whom was Freddy Webber.

A most exciting race across the field took place, but Freddy, being pretty swift of foot, managed to get in first.

Professor Moeritz had a variety of pipes in his study, all very much alike.

Freddy decided that it would be right to take that which appeared to have been most recently used, and accordingly secured it.

Then turning, in an unlucky moment, he caught sight of a case of duelling pistols, with their accompanying powder-flask and bullet mould.

Freddy's active mind immediately conceived a practical joke.

He seized the flask, and having enjoined silence on the part of the others, began to operate.

First of all he put a very small fragment of tobacco from the professor's pouch into the bottom of the pipe and pressed it down.

Then about half-a-pistol charge of powder was screwed up tightly in paper, and placed in the painted porcelain bowl, with more tobacco on the top, so that it appeared to be properly filled.

Our mischievous urchins then composed their features as well as possible, and conveyed the pipe to its proper owner, Professor Moeritz; Freddy having the task of presenting it to some one else.

The German gentleman was extremely pleased, and on finding that the bowl was filled, produced his patent tinder-box and applied a light to the tobacco.

Of course many of the boys who were gathered round the professor, listening to his wonderful story of the baron, who had a castle on an island of the Rhine, and was eaten by an invading army of rats during a famine, knew nothing of the trick that had been played.

Suddenly, however, they all started, while the professor nearly tumbled backwards with fright.

There was a loud explosion as soon as the fire reached the powder, and the pipe was shivered into fragments, one of which knocked the professor's hat off.

"Der teufel! der teufel ist in ze pipe!" he exclaimed as he looked at the stem, which still remained between his teeth.

At that moment a broad grin on the face of one of the conspirators—the boy who had handed him the pipe, and who intensely enjoyed the result of Freddy's stratagem—gave him an idea that the explosion was not the result of any supernatural visitation.

Professor Moeritz extended his right arm, caught the culprit by the collar, and gave him a stinging box on the ears.

"You young rascal, it ist you dat haf make my pipe into ein gun, a bombshell, and haf plown me oop like a Guy Faux. You shall write me two hundred lines from Virgil."

"I beg your pardon, sir," said Freddy stepping forward. "It was I who did it."

"You?"

"Yes, sir. I hope you have not been hurt by my very foolish practical joke."

"No; but you are a bad boy, and must write ze lines instead of Roberts."

"Very well, sir," said Freddy, and marched off towards the school-room to commence his task.

*   *   *   *   *

"I thought Webber was to have fought Crawley this morning," said Lascelles, some short time afterwards.

"Yes, so I thought," replied our hero; "and Freddy was really quite anxious to distinguish himself, but the other declined very wisely, I think, for Freddy would have given him a sound thrashing, you may depend on it."

Webber's task was completed early the next day, and he was once more at liberty to go beyond the school bounds.

So, in the evening, he took a stroll through the town by way of amusing himself.

He had got into a street which, though not prohibited, was not much frequented by the boys, when he became aware of a familiar figure before him.

It was none other than Crawley, who for some reason best known to himself, had chosen to walk that way.

And coming towards them was another old friend, Harry, the general scout and errand-boy to our young friends.

Harry was pretty heavily laden, having a big, brown-paper parcel under his left arm, while in his right hand he carried a basket of fruit, presents from Lord Pembridge to his little sweetheart, Lizzie Conway.

Crawley, who was walking in front of Webber, looked very hard at Harry as he came up.

"Stop, you youngster," said he roughly.

Harry obeyed.

"Don't your masters teach you manners, you unlicked young cub?"

"Yes, sir."

"Then why don't you touch your cap when you see a gentleman?"

"I can't very well, sir, while I am carrying these things," replied Harry.

"Can't you? Then you can take that."

At the same moment, suiting the action to the word, Crawley gave Harry a heavy blow on the face.

"Take that, you coward!" said Freddy, who had been gradually coming up all this time, and had overheard the latter part of the conversation.

The blow he gave Crawley sent that young bully, who was not prepared for it, sprawling in the gutter.

As soon as he looked up and saw who it was had struck the blow, he gathered himself up hastily, and ran off as fast as his legs could carry him.

Freddy, after saying a few words to Harry, was about to continue his walk, when suddenly he received a slap that prostrated him.

"You young ruffian!" exclaimed a gruff voice. I saw you ill-treating that poor boy. I am afraid your master won't whack you, so I'll take the liberty of doing it."

The speaker, a big, powerful man, then proceeded to give several severe punches about the head.

"Let him have it well," said another voice, the owner of which could not be seen.

Freddy started at the sound, for he thought he knew those tones.

During all this time, Harry had been shouting for the police, and at last a member of the blue coat force made his appearance.

The adversary then immediately left off beating Freddy, and bolted up one of the side-streets.

"What's the row?" asked the man in blue, as he came up.

Webber explained, and demanded that his assailant should instantly be pursued, and taken into custody.

"What's his name?" was the policeman's next question.

"I don't know. How should I?"

said Freddy, rather indignant at being thus cross-examined.

"You say a man's been beating of you, which is werry hevident, and you wants me to foller, and take him into custody. How can I do it, unless you tells me who he is?"

"He's a—a—big man, with black whiskers."

"Well dressed?"

"Rather seedy-looking."

"There's many like that about."

"What's to be done, then? Am I to have no redress?"

"You must wait till you sees him again, then collar him, and send for the perlice," said the member of the force, with a grin, as he walked away.

"Nice advice," exclaimed Freddy, as he continued his walk towards the school, where, in due course of time, he arrived with two black eyes and a cut on his cheek.

He was very quickly surrounded by a crowd of sympathising friends, who inquired how he had come by such disfigurements.

Freddy related his adventures.

Great indignation was expressed on all sides.

About half-an-hour afterwards, another boy came in who had been treated in much the same manner, near the same place.

Then came a third.

The boys were furious.

The seedy individual with black whiskers very evidently had some spite against the school, and was waylaying the boys whenever he had an opportunity.

"This must be stopped!" exclaimed Frank Egerton. "Who will go with me?"

"I will!" shouted a score of the biggest.

"Come, then," said Frank.

But at that moment the undermasters came round, and sent them all into the house.

CHAPTER XXVI.

A FREE FIGHT.

ANOTHER thing transpired that evening which only increased the anger of the boys.

Professor Moeritz, who, of course, was not bound down to any particular time of retiring, ventured out in the town at a late hour in the evening, a thing he was not in the habit of doing.

But the professor had heard that a countryman of his was in the town, sick, and in great distress.

Every recollection of Vaterland came back to his memory, and putting his purse in his pocket, he started out to relieve the wants of his fellow exile.

The boys were just retiring to bed when Professor Moeritz returned with torn, soiled clothes, and bruised features.

"I have been robbed," he muttered piteously.

Frank and some others took him into the dining-hall and gave him a glass of beer, for he was nearly fainting.

Then they persuaded him to give an account of the affair, from which it seemed that he had been set upon by the seedy black-whiskered individual before mentioned, who on this occasion, was aided by half-a-dozen other low-looking scoundrels.

Frank Egerton was more determined than ever to put a stop to these outrages.

He said nothing about the proposed expedition in the presence of Professor Moeritz, lest it should come to the ears of Dr. Whackley, who would be certain to forbid anything of the kind.

But when they had all gone upstairs, a meeting of the conspirators was held in Frank's room, to consider how and when the enemy's quarters were to be invaded.

"There must be no delay," observed Marsham.

"If we don't give this lesson at once, the cads will think we are afraid of them."

"We will teach them differently to-morrow after tea," said Frank, who was looked up to as the leader.

"How do you propose acting, Egerton?" asked Lascelles.

"Let me see; these affairs all take place in Church Street, where the ruffians seem to congregate. We can get at least forty fellows to go down."

"The cads will run as soon as they see us," suggested the earl of Pembridge.

"We must provide against that by cutting off their retreat. Marsham and Fitzgerald, you must head a portion of our troops and go round by St. Ann Street and get into Church Street by that way. Pembridge and Lascelles must lead the others down to the Milford Hill end of the street."

"And you?"

"I shall go first, by myself."

"Why?"

"They will be safe to make a rush at me, then you must come to the rescue."

A few more preliminaries were arranged, then the clock struck the hour at which all lights were to be extinguished, and the boys were very quickly in bed.

Very little was said about the proposed expedition the next morning, as the leaders judged it prudent to keep everything as quiet as possible.

Frank's lieutenants quietly went round and invited all those who seemed big enough to take part in a fight to be at the market-place at half-past four o'clock in the afternoon.

Only one boy declined the invitation, and that was young Crawley.

" You are a sneaking coward," said Lascelles.

" Why? How can I go out when I have fifty lines to write?"

" You are afraid of being hurt. I'll write your lines if you will go out with the others."

Crawley muttered something about the doctor recognising his handwriting, and avoided any further conversation.

As soon as the school was dismissed, at four o'clock, a great number of the boys might have been seen strolling down towards town, leaving the play-field entirely to the small fellows who wondered what their seniors meant by thus deserting them.

It might have been noticed, also, that most of those who went out of bounds carried sticks; not that it was a very un-common thing to do so—in fact, it was considered rather the correct thing to sport a walking-cane—but the sticks they carried on this occasion were thick and heavy.

All of them went towards the market-place, too; nor was that a circumstance to excite astonishment, for the best pastrycook's shops in the town were there, and thither did the pupils of Lexicon College much resort.

But neither to the pastrycook's, nor to any other of their many haunts did they flock on this occasion.

They gathered together in four groups, each party being composed of eight, or ten, or more boys.

" Out for hare-and-hounds, or some-thing of that sort?" observed the citizens to each other.

One of them tried to gain a little information on the subject from some of the boys, but was very sharply told that he had best mind his own business, unless he wanted to burn his fingers.

Upon which the man, very naturally, felt " shut up."

There was a great consultation of watches; then one boy (Frank Eger-ton) was seen to walk off alone.

Shortly afterwards two of the groups of boys walked off in one direction, and two in the other.

Let us follow Frank Egerton, who had so boldly volunteered to act as a bait to entice these very bad fish from their lurking-places and feeding-grounds.

Brave as he undoubtedly was, Frank's heart *would* beat a trifle faster than usual when he arrived at the bottom of the street which had, in so short a time, gained such an un-enviable notoriety.

Not that he thought of turning back.

He slackened his pace and just cast a glance behind.

Pembridge and Lascelles were not three hundred yards behind with their forces; and according to arrangement, the two bodies were to enter at oppo-site ends of the street precisely at the same minute.

So he fixed his hat firmly upon his head, and began to saunter up the street.

Apparently he took no notice of anything, but, in reality, his quick eye noticed everything.

Outside a low-looking public-house about half way up the street, was a party of some six or eight low-looking fellows.

" That is where the attack will be," thought Frank.

From this party came one—a seedy-looking, black-whiskered fellow—who walked past the King of the School, staring him full in the face.

Frank returned the stare with in-terest.

A minute afterwards the fellow re-turned towards his own party, and in so doing, brushed rudely against Frank's elbow.

" Mind where you are walking?" said the latter. " The pavement is quite wide enough."

" Mind how you are talking," re-sponded the other; and, clenching his fist, he made a blow at Frank.

The King of the School was prepared for this.

He stepped back and brought down the heavy end of his stick with all his force upon the ruffian's knuckles.

"Here, Bill, Mike!" shouted Black-whiskers, as he waved his hands.

Frank put his back to a lamp-post and prepared to resist a desperate attack, as he saw all the pack charging at him.

On they came.

Frank struck one to the earth and grappled with another, but the mob was being increased every second by fresh arrivals.

He was very soon thrown to the ground, and would no doubt have been severely handled had not his assailants at that moment heard a shout of—

"Forward, boys, at them."

Instinctively they all looked up.

Sixteen or eighteen boys were rushing towards them, armed with sticks, cricket-bats and other missiles.

The momentary pause enabled Frank to regain his legs and recover his stick, which had been wrested from him.

In another instant, the two opposing bodies met, and fierce was the conflict.

Sticks were used freely on both sides, and blood was seen trickling down many a face.

But the enemy had the advantage in numbers, as Frank soon found; and Marsham's body of reserve had not yet arrived on the scene.

The King of the School performed prodigies of valour; but he and his companions were being gradually driven back by the heavy masses of their foes, who were constantly being recruited by fresh forces from neighbouring courts and lanes.

"Where's Black-whiskers?" asked Frank of the earl, who was close by his side, in the thick of the fray.

"Here, to the right."

Frank immediately edged off to get at the ringleader of the roughs.

That individual was engaged in protecting his head from a succession of heavy blows aimed at it by Freddy Webber, who wielded a heavy stick, and was burning to avenge the injuries he had received the previous day.

"Stand aside, Freddy. Let me get at this chap!" said Frank, trying to push Webber away.

Having planted himself exactly opposite his man, Egerton threw down his stick, clenched his fists, and expressed a most decided determination to give Black-whiskers a good dressing.

Black-whiskers gave a contemptuous smile, and lunged out with his left.

The blow fell short, and Frank, diving under his foe's arms, delivered a sounding hit on the mouth, which made Black-whiskers' teeth rattle and his eyes water.

It also made him grow very savage, and rash in his fighting.

A minute and a half had sufficed to convince Black-whiskers, as we must call him till his name is divulged, that his opponent was a strong, well-built lad, and a capital boxer.

He began to funk, especially as his companions were getting very roughly handled. Besides, he was getting separated from them.

And what means that shout in the distance which is so loudly echoed by those who oppose him?

A muttered exclamation from a young costermonger informs him that—

There's another lot o' them young devils coming down the street behind us.

Black-whiskers growls an oath, and while so doing receives a blow in the throat, which knocks him backwards upon the costermonger, and both fall to the ground together.

The timely arrival of Marsham and his band turned the tide in favour of the school.

Still the roughs fought hard.

At the corner of a little lane, before-mentioned, in which most of them lived, they made a desperate stand, and began to throw stones at the school-boys, who immediately returned the compliment.

Suddenly a body of new rivals appeared on the scene of conflict.

Dr. Whackley had been walking in the town when he heard that a desperate fight was going on between

"NOTHING REMAINS BUT TO PRONOUNCE THE PUNISHMENT,' SAID THE MAGISTRATE."

some of his pupils and a number of town-roughs.

Fearing that his own authority would be insufficient to quell the riot, he at once hurried to the police office, and obtained the aid of half-a-dozen constables.

As soon as the roughs saw these gentlemen in blue, they fled, or tried to; but half-a-dozen of them fell into the hands of the police, Black-whiskers being among the number.

"Ah, Captain Robinson," said the man who collared him, "I had lost sight of you for some time. So, this is where you have been hiding recently."

"Hereabouts. But there's nothing against me."

"Rioting and breach of the peace. You must come to the station-house. You will kindly see that these young gentlemen attend in the morning, sir, if you please," continued the policeman, addressing Doctor Whackley.

"Yes," responded that gentleman, who had been jotting down the names of all those of his pupils who remained on the scene, in his note-book.

Having finished that task, he looked sternly at the delinquents for a moment.

"Back to college, all of you, instantly," he said, "and wait for me in the dining-hall."

The leaders, Egerton, Marsham, and the rest, touched their hats and walked away quietly.

Doctor Whackley then followed the police escort to the station-house, and had an interview with the magistrates' clerk, who had apartments there, for the police-station was in reality a portion of the town-hall, where the rioters were to appear in the morning and have justice dealt out to them.

When Doctor Whackley returned to Lexicon College, he found the culprits waiting rather anxiously for his appearance.

Some of the younger boys felt almost inclined to cry.

They expected nothing less than such a flogging as they had seen Baynes receive only a short time before; and, although they could make up their minds to endure the pain without flinching, yet the disgrace of being publicly flogged seemed something terrible to contemplate.

Frank and the bigger boys had no such fears.

They certainly did expect to be punished severely, but not flogged, thinking it very improbable that Doctor Whackley would undertake to birch from thirty to forty of his pupils in one batch.

Stern, indeed, was the pedagogue's aspect.

"Egerton," he said, "explain the meaning of this disgraceful riot, in which you seem to have been the ringleader."

"Several of the boys have been ill-used in that street, sir. I walked down there and was set upon by a gang of roughs; several others of ours were close by, and in a few minutes there was a general fight."

The doctor looked at him very fixedly.

"Answer me truthfully. Did you, or did you not, walk down that street with the intention, and for the purpose, of picking a quarrel, if possible, with these low fellows who had ill-treated Professor Moeritz and some of your schoolfellows?"

"We did, sir," boldly answered at least a dozen of the boys, promptly.

In spite of his severity, Doctor Whackley could not help admiring the candour with which they acknowledged their misdeeds.

"I am glad to find that lying and equivocation are vices that meet with no encouragement among my pupils," said he, after a pause, "Well, you must all appear at the town-hall, at eleven in the morning, until which time not a boy leaves the school premises under any pretext. I shall not inflict any punishment, but leave that in the hands of the justices, who, no doubt, will deal very impartially with you and your late adversaries."

A great many of the faces were considerably elongated at this announcement, which was so different from what they had expected to hear.

" May we not have legal advice, sir?" asked Freddy, after a pause.

There was a general titter, in which even the doctor joined, at this strange request.

" Yes, certainly, if you think your case requires it."

The doctor then left the hall, and the boys began a discussion.

It was voted that the best solicitor in the town, brother-in-law to the presiding magistrate, should be employed to defend them, and a messenger was sent to request him to attend at the school.

The legal gentleman very quickly obeyed the summons, and after an interview with his young clients, assured them that their fate would not be so very dreadful, not more than a month's imprisonment, at any rate.

The Earl of Pembridge and Frank then concocted an epistle, which was sent to the editor of the local paper, with a view to prevent any report from appearing, and soon after that supper was announced.

Several of the boys had completely lost their appetites, and when they retired to rest it was some hours before any of them went to sleep.

Breakfast was likewise disregarded by many of them, lessons were badly done, and, at last, with heavy hearts, they set out for the dreadful court of justice, to receive the punishment due to their sins.

CHAPTER XXVII.

JUSTICE.

EVEN Frank Egerton felt a slight sinking at the heart as, with the rest of the party, he neared the town-hall.

For he had never been in an English court of justice, either as witness, prosecutor, prisoner, plaintiff, or defendant, and the law, being to him a mystery, held forth certain terrors.

Great trepidation filled him as he passed up the staircase he had once ascended under such different circumstances—on the back of the mad horse; and earnestly did he hope that his exit might on this occasion be as triumphant.

" How many of you young gentlemen are there?" asked a very polite inspector, looking first at the boys and then at the doctor.

" I think there are sixteen," responded Mr. Whackley.

" Just the number. But I fancy there were more than these engaged in the riot."

" So I think. But these are all I could identify."

" Then, young gentlemen, it is my duty to take you all into custody, on a charge of rioting. Step this way, if you please."

Following the inspector, the boys found themselves in an official-looking apartment, furnished with a big desk and a leather-covered stool, while round the walls were wooden benches.

Doctor Whackley did not accompany them to this prison-cell, as Freddy Webber called it.

The worthy doctor had, the previous evening, arranged with the police authorities that, instead of going through the formality of issuing summonses against the boys, they should be induced to surrender themselves quietly.

and be nominally taken into custody as had just been done.

A police-constable was left in the room with them, while the inspector attended to other business.

"How long are we likely to remain here?" asked Frank, who was anxious to know the worst.

"Till the other charges are disposed of," said the officer.

"But how long will that be?"

"Can't say."

"Please, sir, what time shall we have our bread and water?" asked Freddy, who certainly kept up his spirits better than any of the others.

To this impertinent question "the myrmidon of the law" returned no answer; and Freddy, hiding behind some of his companions, resolved to distinguish himself after the manner of a certain very doubtful hero of romance, who

"Carved his name on Newgate stone."

Freddy, not being in Newgate, and having no chisel, contented himself with cutting his name on one of the wooden benches with a pocket-knife.

He had just completed it to his satisfaction when the inspector entered and opened another door, through which the boys were ushered into the presence of the magistrate.

One or two of the delinquents had expected to see an awful figure clothed in scarlet and ermine, and wearing a very large wig.

Therefore, they were very surprised to find only a rather mild-looking old gentleman, dressed in ordinary costume, with nothing to denote his authority except that his seat was raised a little higher than the others, while on the wall above it was a very badly carved representation of the lion and unicorn.

Frank cast a glance round the place and very soon saw that near him, but separated by a guard of police, stood the sham captain and some of those who had aided him in the riot.

Their names were then read over, and the inspector formally charged them with rioting and creating a disturbance against the peace of our sovereign lady the queen, &c., &c.

As soon as this was done, Mr. Peniston, the solicitor engaged by the Earl of Pembridge, rose and stated that his clients, the young gentlemen from Lexicon College, intended to make no defence, but threw themselves upon the mercy of the court, pleading in mitigation of punishment their youth and the great provocation they had suffered.

Captain Robinson and his companions were rather puzzled by this admission.

They had passed the night in the lock-up, being unable to find bail good enough to satisfy the police, and had arranged a plan of defence whereby they hoped to clear themselves.

All their schemes were now knocked upon the head.

Captain Robinson, therefore, pleaded guilty, urging that he had been attacked in the first instance by Egerton, and that his companions had only come to his assistance when they saw him surrounded by a crowd of school-boys.

The King of the School was about to contradict the latter part of this statement, but the magistrate interrupted him.

"As all the implicated parties have admitted the offence," said he, "nothing remains but to pronounce their punishment. You are fined five shillings each; and remember, if anything of this kind occurs again, I shall send you to prison."

Our young friends very quickly produced their money and paid the fines; but cash was not quite so plentiful with their late opponents.

It required all their funds to release part of the company, and one of them (not Captain Robinson, who took care to be treasurer) would certainly have been locked up in default, had not the Earl of Pembridge handed in the three shillings required to make up the amount of his ransom money.

But there's many a slip 'twixt the cup and the lip.

Just as Robinson was turning round

to leave the justice-room, he was confronted by Professor Moeritz.

"Not zo vast, mein goot vriend. Mister Boliceman, I sharges this man mit knocking me down, und stealing mein silber," said the German.

Mr. Policeman, who stood close by, at once collared the gallant captain.

"The case had better be heard at once, as the prisoner has already passed a night in the lock-up," said the magistrate. "Let the prisoner be put in the dock."

A very few seconds sufficed to place him in that ill-named, railed-off space, and Professor Moeritz was then sworn.

"Unt I vants you," said the professor, barring the progress of one of Robinson's bull-necked, beetle-browed companions, who was trying to slink out unobserved.

"Wot for? Git out of the way."

"You was mit dat big tief last night."

"I arrest you, also," said the policeman, interfering, and taking beetle-brows by the collar. "In with you."

Frank, who was now only a spectator, looked on with a considerable degree of pleasure.

He was able now to detect the local reporter, for that gentleman, who had hitherto kept his note-book in his pocket by editorial command, began to take a great interest in the proceedings of the court.

Montague Charles Robinson, captain on half-pay (regiment unknown), and William Smith *alias* Carrotty Bill, were then charged with assault and robbery.

Professor Moeritz being sworn, stated the circumstances under which he was robbed as already related, and made oath that the prisoners were his assailants, as well as two or three other persons not in custody.

Then came the inspector of police, who stated that when the prisoners were searched previous to being locked up, a purse was found upon Smith, and three German coins upon Robinson.

These articles Professor Moeritz swore were his property.

"How can you swear to coins?" asked Robinson.

"Because I did know dere vas tiefs, and I did mark 'em."

Captain Robinson's face looked considerably longer, and the magistrate, into whose hands the coin had been given, requested the professor to describe and point out the mark he alluded to, which Moeritz immediately did.

"The evidence seems very conclusive," observed the magistrate. "Have you anything to say in your defence, Smith?"

"No, nothink, only as how I vos put up to it by this ere cove; Captain Robinson he calls hisself. He's about as much a captain as my old moke."

Robinson looked as though he could have killed his friend.

"It is false!" he shouted. "Surely your worship won't take any notice of the ravings of that drunken fool?"

"I shall send you both for trial at the next assizes. Remove them, policeman."

"I can find bail, sir."

"I should not accept the security of the best householder in Ballsbury, which I fancy you would find some difficulty in procuring."

Two stalwart constables immediately came and walked the prisoners off, after which Frank and his companions returned to Lexicon College.

CHAPTER XXVIII.

AYNES, SENIOR, APPEARS.

OF course our young friends were looked upon by all their schoolfellows, except Crawley, as heroes covered with glory.

Not that we uphold the custom of fighting, but, when it becomes absolutely necessary to strike, we certainly do like to see boys go in and fight like Britons.

Crawley had fallen into a position somewhat similar to that lately occupied by his friend Baynes, only not being quite so big and strong, he was not so much feared.

Something, however, occurred that afternoon which, for a time, diverted the thoughts of the boys from the riot.

When they were in the playfield that afternoon, a well-dressed gentleman stalked into the enclosure.

"This is Lexicon College, I think?" said he.

"It is," replied Frank.

"Did any of you know Baynes?"

This question caused considerable excitement.

"Of course we all knew him," said Egerton, after a long pause.

"He ran away, did he not? What has become of him?"

"That is more than any of us can tell, or wish to know."

A dark frown passed over the man's features.

"I am his father, I would have you know."

"And I am Frank Egerton, the son of that widow whose property you took possession of only a short time ago. The only boy in the school likely to know anything of your son is that young sneak who stands yonder, avoided by every one. For further information I refer you to Doctor Whackley.'

Baynes, Senior, raised his cane, but Frank Egerton looked so dangerous that he thought better of it, and walked away towards the house.

What took place in the house was never known, except that very angry voices were heard in the study by the servants.

Later in the day, however, the doctor informed Frank and two or three others that young Baynes had not been home to his father's house, and there was reason to believe that the youth was still in Ballsbury.

"Indeed!" exclaimed Frank, "then I can understand now why——"

He paused, and slightly changed colour.

"Why, what?" demanded Doctor Whackley.

"Why that ruffianly captain so persistently waylaid and illtreated our boys. He was a great friend of Baynes, who owed him, I believe, a great deal of money, lost at billiards."

"Then the unhappy boy became a thief to cover his losses as a gambler. Oh, let this be a warning to you all."

"We have established a custom, sir, in the upper forms never to play for money. Baynes seldom played with us, but I believe it was he persuaded this Robinson to pitch into our fellows because he was afraid to do so himself."

"Of course, you have no proofs of that?"

"No, sir."

"You must be very cautious, for, though that man Robinson is not likely to be at large for a long time to come, Baynes has a very revengeful disposition, and might find other agents to work you harm."

"I don't think he will risk a personal encounter with me, sir, and I'd like to catch him hurting a little chap."

Doctor Whackley smiled.

"Well, be careful, for he is a thoroughly bad and revengeful boy."

"Very good, sir. You may depend on our avoiding him as much as possible."

* * * * * *

That same evening, Frank went to see his darling Kate Conway.

Now some of you may think, perhaps, that Frank was acting in an underhand way to thus keep up an acquaintance which his mother had once so strongly condemned.

But it was not so.

Frank, of course, had heard from Kate's own lips the story of her meeting with Mrs. Egerton, who, it must be remembered, had said nothing to her son on the subject.

The King of the School was too high-minded to take advantage of that.

He wrote home to his mother, telling her that he loved Kate Conway more than his life, and that——Well, it would be useless to repeat all the young fellow said about the girl he was so fond of. However, he wound up by saying that until he had explicit commands to the contrary, he should continue to look upon the milliner as his betrothed.

That was the only letter of Frank's that Mrs. Egerton ever neglected to answer, and our readers may well guess that the hero of this little story was not greatly displeased at the very unusual silence.

And so it came to pass that he boldly visited the object of his affections whenever he had a chance, and generally found that she was quite as rejoiced to see him as he was to have an opportunity of seeing her.

On this present occasion Kate was alone, and in tears.

Frank at once asked the cause of her distress, and with many sobs she told him that she had only just returned from the house of a lady who lived about a mile out of town, having been there on business.

While returning by a rather lonely pathway across the fields, she was overtaken by a well-dressed young ruffian, who had followed her for some distance, and caused her great annoyance.

"Tell me what he was like?" asked, Frank, and Kate immediately gave a full description of her persecutor.

"It must be Baynes, the villain!" our hero immediately exclaimed. "The coward? I'll horsewhip him."

"Don't quarrel with him, Frank, darling," said Kate, putting one arm round his neck, and resting her face on his shoulder.

"But I must, my love; when I see him, or you will be subjected to some other outrage."

"No, dear; my father has gone to tell the police."

"And I'll tell them what I know about him, the scoundrel!"

A few minutes afterwards Lizzie Conway came in, accompanied by the Earl of Pembridge.

Lascelles also came, in the hopes of meeting the young lady who had so fascinated him at the pic-nic; but was disappointed.

As happy an evening as mortals could wish to spend was passed by these young people.

But at length the time came when it was necessary to part.

Kate and Lizzie would accompany the youths a short distance, trusting to each other's protection on the return journey.

The Earl of Pembridge and Lizzie walked some distance in front of Frank and his sweetheart.

Lascelles had gone on a-head to be out of the way.

Presently Frank saw Lizzie tripping back in the uncertain light, she having undergone the terrible trial of parting from her lover.

"He's waiting for you," she said, "Come, Kate, let us get home."

"Good bye, darling," whispered Frank, putting one arm round the waist of the fair girl, and kissing her.

"CATCHING HOLD OF THE WHEEL, HE WAS LIFTED OUT OF THE WATER."

No. 8.

Then he started off to overtake his companion.

He was very near the cathedral precincts, and hoped to overtake Pembridge before he entered the playfield.

Suddenly the sharp report of a pistol rang through the clear night air.

Frank turned suddenly as the bullet hissed past his ear, but could see no one.

" Hollo ! what's the matter ?" shouted the earl, who had loitered for his companion, and consequently was not many yards a-head.

" I have been shot at !"

In a few seconds more the earl was by the side of his companion.

Together they searched the dense shrubbery by which the cathedral was bordered on one side. But no sight could they obtain of the intended assassin.

" It must have been Baynes. Who else would have thought of such a thing ?" said the earl.

" I shall go and report the circumstance to the police."

" Right. I am with you."

The two boys then walked direct to the constabulary office, and informed the sergeant on duty of what had taken place.

In reply to the question of that official—" Did they suspect any one ?"

—Frank boldly replied that he did, mentioning the name of Baynes.

"Very good, young gentleman. I'll do all I can to find out whether you have guessed right. Good-night. Shall I send a man with you up to the college ?"

" No, thank you," replied both.

In getting from the police-station to Lexicon College, the two boys had to pass by the end of the street in which the riot took place.

Of course they could not help slackening their pace a little, and, glancing down towards the scene of their late encounter, were not a little surprised to see two persons standing a short distance down the road.

These two persons were Baynes, senior, the father of our black sheep who bolted from the fold, and Crawley.

" It is as I thought," whispered Frank, " that fellow knows all about Bully Baynes."

" It seems so. I wonder what sort of a plot they are concocting."

" I can't guess; but I feel pretty certain that Crawley will *not* get the best of the bargain whatever it may be."

" Here comes the little sneak; let us get away before him."

They walked on and soon were inside the school.

CHAPTER XXIX.

BLACK VILLANY.

Two days elapsed and no tidings of the assassin who had so nearly taken Frank's life.

Doctor Whackley had received a letter from Mr. Baynes, which he eventually laughed at, though the first perusal made him seriously angry.

It ran something like this—

" SIR,—I have found my boy whom you left to starve. He had not a penny in his pocket when you expelled him from your school. I shall not fail to let the world know how you have behaved in the matter.

" H. BAYNES."

Yet, strange to say, the following

day, Baynes, Junior, was seen in the town, walking about as carelessly as though nothing had happened. He even spoke to some of the smaller boys, and told them that he was now a gentleman, his father supplied him with plenty of money, and he intended to remain for some time in the town.

This state of affairs caused Doctor Whackley and his senior scholars some uneasiness.

Having made some enquiries, the police had come to the conclusion that Baynes was not the person who fired the pistol-shot, but the doctor was not so well satisfied on that point.

The boys, on the other hand, though they had no fear as to what would be the result of a personal encounter, did not like the idea of the younger boys meeting him, arguing that as he was bad he might corrupt others.

Next day—that is the morning after Baynes was seen in the town—old Mr. Conway called upon Frank at a very early hour in the morning.

The old gentleman appeared very much excited.

"Have you seen my daughter?" he asked, grasping Frank's collar.

"Not since the day before yesterday. Why do you ask, Mr. Conway?"

"Are you telling me the truth?"

"Yes; but what is the matter?"

"I believe you are honest," continued the old gentleman; then, after a pause, he said, in lower and hoarser tones—

"She's gone."

"Gone! Where? With whom?"

"Would to Heaven I knew."

Frank dropped the old man's hand, and stood staring at him.

The world seemed turned completely upside down, now that the load-stone of his life was snatched so suddenly away from him.

Suddenly, however, he roused himself.

"She must be sought and found. Have you been to the police? Have you any clue?"

"This letter was thrust under the door; but it is not her writing, I am certain."

The letter referred to stated that the writer had grown tired of living at home, and had gone to London with some friends. Her father might, perhaps, hear of her in a year or two.

"Kate could not write such a letter," said Frank, indignantly.

He then hurried away to Doctor Whackley's study, and, on the plea of important business, obtained permission to be absent from school that day.

"Come along with me to the police-office," said Frank, when he had gained his liberty.

The sergeant he had seen before was there, and, of course, thought Frank had come to speak about the shooting affair.

"A very serious matter, indeed," said he, when he had been undeceived, and the real state of affairs had been related to him. "And you suspect the same fellow—Baynes?"

"I do."

"I'll put my men on the business at once. In the meantime you must get some bills printed and posted over the town, and should also send advertisements to some of the London papers."

"Thanks. That is Mr. Conway's address."

So saying, Frank led the old gentleman away towards his cottage, and when they arrived there made him detail once more all the circumstances of the loss so far as he knew.

It appeared that about twilight the the previous evening, Kate had put on her hat and mantle to go out and procure sundry little trifles upon which she had set her heart, the shop being about a quarter of a mile from home.

She was gone some time, but at first Mr. Conway felt no alarm, for some of her young friends lived near, and he thought that perhaps she might have met with some of them.

But at eleven o'clock, finding that she did not return, he went out to seek her, not thinking it right that she should be out alone at so late an hour

On reaching the friend's house, he heard, to his utter astonishment, that his daughter had not been there. He then tried the shop, knowing well that the proprietor's wife had taken a great fancy to Kate, but was informed that Miss Conway had not been seen there that evening.

More astonished than ever, he returned home, only to find, not his daughter, but the letter, we have before spoken of.

And that was all that he knew, except that his darling Kate couldn't be wicked and cruel enough to write such a letter, or to go away from her poor old father.

Frank at once saw that the plot was concocted by some most unscrupulous person. There was nothing to be done, however, but wait the course of events.

On their way home they had called at a jobbing printers, and ordered some hand-bills to be printed and distributed, and were waiting to see a first impression.

Before that arrived the police-sergeant made his appearance.

"Any tidings?" asked both.

The man shook his head.

"Have you made any inquiries?"

"Yes. I have been to the railway station, and ascertained that no such person as your daughter was a passenger by any train last night."

"Then she must be in the town."

"So I thought at first."

"She could not walk to London."

"Whoever took her away might have money enough to hire a vehicle and drive to Winton, or some other station on the line. I have sent a man round to all the hotels and stables to know what vehicles were hired out yesterday; the man will come here to make his report to me."

Soon afterwards, the man who had been detailed to perform this special duty, made his appearance.

"Well?" asked the sergeant.

"I have been to every place in the town, and find that no licensed vehicle was out after six yesterday evening."

"Then she must have been taken away in some private trap. Back to the station, and send Ralph here as soon as he comes in."

With a clumsy bow the constable departed.

During the time that elapsed between his exit and the arrival of the man called Ralph, many schemes were anxiously discussed by Frank and Mr. Conway, all having for their object the recovery of the fair girl who had been stolen away.

The police-sergeant listened, and when they had finished, politely informed them that before any of their plans could be carried out, it would be necessary to discover in which direction the fugitives had gone.

Old Conway gave a deep groan.

"Don't despair, sir," said the official. "We shall find her. Here comes Ralph."

A loud knock was instantly heard at the door, and the individual so named entered.

"Any news, Ralph?"

The man shook his head.

"Did you find out where that Robinson lived before we provided him with lodgings under the town-hall?"

"Yes; at the 'Spotted Dog.' And that young chap you told me about, he's there."

"Was he there last night?"

"So they say. At all events, I saw him there this morning myself."

"How about the pike-keepers?"

"None of them had noticed anybody like you described going out of the town. I have been round to all the main roads leading out of Ballsbury."

"Then she must be in the town now," exclaimed the sergeant. "The villain has hidden her away in some snug corner."

"She *may* be in town," observed Frank.

"She must be!"

"Why must?"

"Because she has not left it by rail, nor by any hired vehicle, and, as she can't fly, it stands to reason she must be somewhere in the neighbourhood.

Frank and Ralph, the constable, shook their heads.

"What do you mean?" asked the sergeant.

"There is another method of getting away."

"What's that?"

"By water."

"But she can't swim, can she?" asked the sergeant, opening his eyes with astonishment.

"No; but there are plenty of boats about Ballsbury, some of them owned by people of not the best character.

"By jingo! yes, and about seven miles down stream is Winton, with a railway station. The night mail stops there about ten. Go, Ralph, telegraph over —you know what to say."

"But if she was taken to London at ten, how does it happen that this letter was not put under my door till after eleven?" asked old Mr. Conway.

"That is a puzzler, certainly. I should have thought that after saying she had gone to London, the letter would have been posted there. He ain't such a clever fellow after all, and we shall nail him."

All the forenoon, and two or three hours after mid-day, these three people sat and consulted and made inquiries, but all with the same result.

About three o'clock in the afternoon, Frank, whose heart seemed ready to burst with the accumulated load of anxiety, took up his hat and walked out.

He felt that he would burst into tears if he sat there much longer watching the haggard woe-begone features of old Mr. Conway; and although there would have been nothing very disgraceful in his weeping, he was too proud to do so in public.

So he walked away with rapid steps and had soon got clear of the town.

People who saw him striding along fancied that there was another such a fight as they had witnessed a few days before. This fiery young champion was going to the rescue of his comrades.

No such thing, however.

When he had got quite a mile beyond the town, it suddenly occurred to Frank that he was walking more like a lunatic than a rational being.

He slackened his pace, then halted and turned.

"What an idiot I am to walk out here!" he exclaimed to himself. "What a waste of time, too! Why, I might have been watching for Baynes all this time."

Less than twenty minutes afterwards Frank enter a little street running parallel to that in which the "Spotted Dog" was situated.

He paused before the back entrance of a public-house, which had another frontage exactly facing the low hostelry in which young Baynes had taken up his abode.

There was great rivalry between the two houses, and when Frank explained that he wished to watch the "Spotted Dog," the landlord of the "Brindled Cat," whose only and daily prayer was that the opposition establishment might loose its license, at once showed him into a private parlour from the window of which he had a good view.

"That's a great willin, sir, as keeps the 'Dawg,'" observed the man. "He and his pot-boy was amongst the crowd as you fought the t'other night.

"Was he?"

"Yes: and their pot-boy, which is a duffer, told my lad as how they were all set on to it by a young gent as runn'd away from your school."

"I thought so; and I want to see that young gent, as you call him."

"I seed him there not a hour ago. and I don't think he have been out since."

"Thank you for that piece of information."

"Welcome, sir. Take anything, sir?"

"Yes. You may bring me a bottle of stout and a biscuit."

"Got the best of both in the house, sir," was mine host's exclamation, as he rolled out of the room

The refreshment was brought, but Frank felt too excited to feel able to eat or drink much.

Being so near Baynes, the villain he suspected of having spirited away the beautiful, bewitching Kate Conway, kept his nerves in a constant tremour.

"Is it possible she can be *there?*" thought he. "Has he taken her to that low place?"

More than once he felt very much inclined to rush across the road, and insist upon thoroughly searching the house.

But then he knew pretty well what would be the result.

At length, after watching for some time, Frank's patience was rewarded by his catching a sight of Baynes's face at one of the windows on the ground floor.

Our hero at once concealed himself behind the curtain, and Baynes at the same moment withdrew.

The King of the School fancied that perhaps his adversary had seen him. He continued to watch, however, and in a short time the young villain again appeared, this time wearing his hat.

"Going out, are you? Then I'll see where you go," Frank thought.

And then he rang the bell.

The landlord appeared.

"How big is your pot-boy?"

"About your size," replied the man, rather astonished at this strange question.

"Then lend me a rough-looking old coat of his. Here is a half-a-sovereign as security that I bring it back."

The landlord looked puzzled.

However, he went away, and soon afterwards returned with the shaggy garment of ancient fashion and appearance.

When our hero had put it on no one could have identified him at a few yards' distance.

He then hastily walked out into the street and followed Baynes, who was some yards a-head.

One thing rather puzzled Frank. The youth he was following carried a leather bag by his side slung by a strap across his shoulder.

What he could want with such a piece of luggage, Egerton could not imagine, unless Baynes was going out of town.

But that could not be, for he was walking in the wrong direction; going towards the waterside instead of to the railway station.

The best way to find out what he was up to would be to follow him.

Baynes very soon reached the river, which was not very far from the public-house at which it seemed he was staying.

He jumped into a boat, unmoored it, and began to row slowly *up* the stream.

"What shall I do?" thought Frank. "If I follow him on the water, perhaps he will recognise me, for I could not row in this great thing of a coat."

After a few minutes' consideration, he came to the conclusion that he would walk; there was a road running almost parallel with the river—about a hundred yards from it—and as Baynes, being compelled to work against stream, was not going very fast, he would have no great difficulty in keeping up.

He did so, keeping his enemy in sight for more than three miles.

Presently Baynes pulled across to the opposite side of the stream, and, tying his boat to the root of a willow tree, landed.

"Oh, what a fool I was! I shall lose him now!" exclaimed our hero.

Baynes, however, instead of making off across country kept by the river bank.

He carried his bag with him, and walked on for at least a mile before Frank could form any idea as to his destination.

"The old ruined mill! She is there!" at last burst from Egerton's lips as he saw in the distance an ancient building, which did not bear the best reputation, being looked upon by the rustics of the neighbourhood as the abode of ghosts, goblins, and evil spirits.

CHAPTER XXX.

THE ABDUCTION.

BEFORE we follow Frank Egerton any further in his adventures, it will be necessary to carry our readers back to the previous evening.

We must see what had become of Kate Conway, whose sudden disappearance from her home and friends had caused so much consternation and grief.

The girl had gone out, as she said, to purchase a few little ornaments wherewith to render herself more charming, if possible, in the eyes of her young lover.

She had completed her purchases, and was about to return home, when a sudden fancy possessed her to stroll along by the banks of the river, and look at the spot where she first met Frank, on that eventful afternoon when he saved her life and her father's.

The sun had hardly gone down, and the moon would soon rise, and give almost as much light as the greater luminary; so there would be no danger in taking a little walk alone, especially as Ballsbury was now considered free from the few bad characters who had for some time past made it their head-quarters.

At least, so argued the girl.

The night was still; hardly a breath of wind stirred the sere and yellow leaves of the great elm trees that stood on either side of the road.

Kate's footsteps, light and tripping though they were, sounded very distinctly on the hard sandy road.

Suddenly she fancied she heard another and a louder tread behind her.

She turned sharply.

The shrubs and trees threw strange, weird shadows upon the roadway, but no human being was visible.

"It was but fancy," she thought, and, summoning up all the courage her little heart possessed, climbed over a stile, and took the foot-path across a meadow towards the water-side.

All her fears vanished as soon as she found herself in the fair open moonlight which now illumined the face of nature.

On she tripped like some fairy vision, till at length the river-side was reached.

Yes, that was the spot!

It was just where that big eddy was circling round and round that the boat was overturned, and there, beneath that drooping willow, Frank brought her to land. It was there she first felt his arm encircling her waist, and heard his much-loved voice.

Bright and happy thoughts sprang up in her mind—soon to be rudely dispelled.

While in the midst of her meditations, a rude hand was placed upon her shoulder.

Giving a half-smothered shriek, she sprang round to find herself face to face with Baynes, and a low-looking ruffian who inspired infinitely more terror in her mind than his companion.

"Silence!" exclaimed the first-named individual, harshly. "If you utter another sound I swear I will kill you."

The command was unnecessary, for the poor girl was so terrified as to be utterly unable to speak.

"Come this way," continued Baynes, then seeing that there was great danger of her fainting, he said to his companion—

"Hold her up on the other side, Bob, and bring her along as quickly as possible. There may be some one about, and it would never do to be seen."

"Right you are, young guvnor. I ain't nowise in any partickler hurry to wisit the beak again. We'd get seven year a-piece, make no bloomin' horror!"

"Hold your tongue, and come along," replied Baynes, who shuddered when his companion mentioned the punishment that would be meted out to them.

Between them they hurried the poor, helpless girl along, till they reached a point about a quarter of a mile up the river.

A boat was there, moored to a bush upon the bank.

"In with you."

This rough command was addressed by Baynes to poor Kate, who was too far overcome by fear to be able either to comprehend or obey.

"Bob,"

"That's me, young guvnor."

"Come here and lend us a hand."

Bob had taken his seat in the boat, but immediately stepped out, and helped his ruffianly young employer to place his prey in the stern sheets of the craft.

"Now pull as hard as you can."

Bob did so, and the boat silently shot up stream.

"Did you get those padlocks and keys?" asked Baynes, when they had journeyed about two miles in silence.

"Yes, guvnor."

"Because it will be necessary to keep this young lady quiet for a time, till she has got over her excitement."

"Axing yer parding, young guvnor, but where are you going to take her?"

"Up to the old ruined mill."

Poor Kate, though a good, and generally speaking a very sensible girl, was not altogether free from superstition.

She had often heard the character borne by the place to which her captor was taking her.

No!

Rather than be imprisoned in that weird, spectral building, the outlines of which were now becoming dimly visible in the moonlight, she would end all her troubles in the glistening water.

She jumped up from her seat suddenly, and would certainly have carried out her rash resolution had not Bob, the boatman, dropped his oars and seized her.

"You must take better care on her, young guvnor," observed the man. I vos honly hingaged for abduction, and don't know nothink about suicide or murder."

"Hold your tongue, you fool," growled Baynes, and passing his arm round the girl's waist, he held her close to him by main force.

Then, for the first time, Kate spoke.

"You will repent this vile outrage when Frank comes," said she.

"Frank will never know what has become of you, unless——"

"Unless what?"

"I will tell you presently; but don't think Egerton will ever find your hiding-place. Water doesn't leave any track, you know, and that is why I brought you by boat."

"Let me go. I will promise to tell no one."

"Perhaps I'll let you go, presently, if you are good."

"Help! help! help! Frank!" she screamed.

"Silence!" said Baynes.

And to enforce his command he thrust a thick handkerchief into her mouth, thus effectually gagging the poor girl.

The boatman pulled away stolidly, and in a short space of time landed his living cargo at a spot about fifty yards below the old mill.

This structure was situated on a little island in the midst of the stream.

There was just room enough for the mill itself and a little plot of garden, now, however, overgrown with weeds and sedges.

A rude bridge, composed of two

planks, supported on piles, connected the building with the main land.

As before said, the mill had for a long time been deserted.

A dreadful tragedy had taken place there some years before; the miller, his wife and servant, had been found brutally murdered, and the place plundered.

Who did the deed was never known, but a few days afterwards dense clouds of smoke proclaimed that the place was on fire.

It seemed as though incendiarism had tried to obliterate the track of murder.

The fire, however, only partly destroyed the interior of the building, and ruined the machinery.

The outer walls were almost as good as ever.

Some few months after the fire just mentioned, a good gossip from Ballsbury was returning home one night from the neighbouring town of Haftsbury, and, having partaken plenteously of strong ale by the road, managed to take a wrong turning.

That, however, was an affair of little consequence, as he knew the bearings of the country; but to get home from the place where he first discovered his blunder, the poor fellow had to pass by the ruined mill.

As he neared the building, strange sounds of unhallowed merriment were heard, lights flitted to and fro, and dusky figures were seen inside the building.

The man told his tale, and was laughed at for his pains.

Sceptics said that the light was Will-o'-the-Wisp, and the laughter only the harsh cry of some waterfowl.

And yet from that time the old mill bore the reputation of being haunted.

*   *   *   *   *

Baynes, still keeping his arm fast round Kate Conway's waist, hurried her along till they came to the bridge of planks before mentioned.

Then he halted.

"Lift her up, Bob, and carry her over," he then said.

Bob caught up the girl in his arms,—Baynes feeling not quite up to the task,—and trotted with her across the frail bridge.

Kate made one struggle to throw herself from his arms into the stream, but the boatman was too strong for her.

The door of the old mill opened to Baynes's touch, and Kate found herself in the interior of the building.

A most desolate place it was, though some slight attempt had been made to render it habitable.

Doors and windows had been constructed, and a few rude articles of furniture were there, but the beams and rafters, blackened by the action of the fire, looked terribly grim.

Round the walls were nets and rods, betokening that the old mill was sometimes the resort of salmon-poachers.

Bob the boatman placed his burden upon a chair, and then stood waiting the further commands of his employer.

"Leave the place," said Baynes.

"All right, guvnor, shall I wait at the boat?"

"No, go home. I shall walk back."

The man gave a rude bow and withdrew.

As soon as he had gone, Baynes turned to his captive with a smile, and, coming close to her, said—

"Do you know why I have brought you here, Kate?"

"I do not; but unless you let me go you will be punished for this outrage."

"I brought you here because I love you, Kate."

"You have chosen a very strange method of showing your love, Mr. Baynes; but as I cannot possibly care anything about you, pray be kind enough to allow me to depart."

"No. You cannot go till you promise to become my wife."

"A boy like you to talk of marrying! The idea is absurd."

Kate spoke with a sneer, which cut Baynes to the heart.

However, swallowing his rage, he replied—

"Has Frank Egerton never said anything of marriage ?"

At this insolent query Kate Conway's temper was fairly aroused.

She clenched her little fist, and struck at Baynes with all her strength.

Disregarding her impotent rage, the young ruffian continued—

"I know he has promised to marry you in a few years' time, but he shall not do so. *I* will marry you when I am of age, and in proof that I am in earnest, I swear by all the powers that be, you shall not leave this place till you have signed this letter, promising to become my wife !"

Baynes's recent reverses of fortune, together with the quantity of bad brandy he had swallowed during the past day or two, had rather muddled his head, and made him speak like a melodramatic madman.

But Kate thought him the most cool and determined ruffian imaginable.

"I will never sign any such letter !" she boldly replied.

"We will see. Twenty-four hours in this dreary old den may induce you to alter your decision."

He then went out, leaving the hateful letter he wished her to sign upon the table, with a pen and pocket ink-bottle.

Kate heard sounds like the fastening of chains and locks, as Mr. Baynes departed.

She was a prisoner then.

As soon as his footsteps had died away, she began to examine her prison, a feat rendered possible by the bright harvest moon.

The room she was in was some distance above the water, and had apparently once been a kind of storeloft.

The door was fastened securely, and, there was no way of escape but by the window.

Kate looked out.

Immediately beneath her was the huge water-wheel, which had escaped the ravages of the fire, and since then had hung and turned at the will of the waters, with a restless, never-ceasing rumble and splash.

It was evident she could not escape that way.

She returned to the table in the centre of the room, and catching sight of the hateful letter Baynes had left for her signature, tore it into fifty pieces and threw it out into the stream.

Then to secure herself from intrusion, she piled all the furniture she could move against the door, and tried to rest.

But the mournful creaking of the water-wheel, in its never-ceasing revolutions, and the strange noises caused by the wind as it whistled through and around the ruined old building, together with the many strange thoughts that kept rushing through her brain, effectually prevented Kate from sleeping.

Not till the sun had fairly risen did she close her eyes.

CHAPTER XXXI.

FRANK TO THE RESCUE.

OF course you have guessed by this time that Frank Egerton was quite right in his supposition that Baynes was going to the ruined mill.

The promising young scoundrel who had planned and executed the abduction of Kate Conway, suddenly chanced to remember the following afternoon that his fair prisoner had neither food nor drink.

Not that the recollection troubled him much.

"Starvation will do her good," thought he; "will bring her to her senses, and show her how completely she is in my power. Then, perhaps, she will consent; not that I care much about her, but it would be a blow at Egerton's heart."

He leisurely collected some food, which he placed in the leather bag before-mentioned, and started.

Frank, as we know, followed.

Baynes, after landing, walked up to the mill, and had just set his foot on the bridge of planks, which communicated only with his side of the shore, when he caught sight of Frank.

There was no possibility of reaching the mill from Egerton's side of the stream, except by boat, or by swimming.

"Stop, villain!" shouted Egerton.

Baynes made no reply, but with a threatening shake of the fist, darted across the bridge and entered the mill.

"How can I reach the scoundrel?" exclaimed Frank.

A moment's hesitation, then he plunged into the water and began to swim across.

Baynes saw his object, and, rushing out from the mill, broke down the bridge.

"You shall never see her again, Egerton! Rather than surrender her

to you, I will plunge her into the stream!" he shouted.

Frank made no reply, but changed his course.

Instead of swimming towards the bank, he made direct for the mill itself, which, as before said, stood in the centre of the stream.

A piercing shriek caused him to lift up his eyes as he bravely struggled against the flood.

Baynes had thrown open the wooden folding windows of Kate's prison-chamber, and there he stood angrily clutching her by the arm.

"Tell him to keep away," he said.

"Frank, Frank! help me!" cried Kate.

"By Heaven! if he approaches nearer, I will shoot him! Keep back, Egerton, if you value your life!"

As he spoke, the young ruffian drew a small pistol, and took aim at Frank's head, which was the only portion of his body visible.

Frank heard the threat, and saw the levelled weapon, but he did not heed either.

"Bang!" went the weapon, as a puff of white smoke polluted the air, and the bullet splashed up the water close by Egerton's ear.

"Perdition seize him!" muttered Baynes, as he hurled the empty and now useless weapon at his foe, with no better aim.

"Frank, are you hurt, darling?" exclaimed Kate. "Quick, dear, and save me. He is hurting me."

"Patience a moment, love," replied Frank.

Making a desperate struggle against the swift waters, he swam right up to the wheel, which still continued its revolutions, and, catching hold of it, was thereby lifted bodily up out of the river to nearly a level with the floor on which stood Baynes, still holding Kate Conway by the arm, and apparently endeavouring to throw her over into the water.

Making a desperate spring, Frank leaped off the wheel, caught the side of the open window, and scrambled in.

"Now, villain, it is my turn!"

"Ha, ha, ha! follow me if you dare!" laughed the unhappy youth, as, finding his plans foiled, he leaped out of the opening by which Frank had entered.

Egerton saw the foaming tide close over his rival's body, then he turned his attention to Kate, who had swooned from the excitement to which she had been subjected.

He knelt down by her side, kissed her lips and cheek, calling her by every endearing name he could remember, and soon had the pleasure of seeing the flush of consciousness returning to her brow.

In a few minutes more she was able to sit up, and then to stand erect.

They then began to look round to find some method of escaping from the mill, and also to see what had become of Baynes.

That young gentleman, however, was nowhere to be seen.

"How are we to get away from this horrid place, dear?" asked Kate, who clung close to her lover, although his clothes were dripping with water.

"I can't think for a moment. But what has become of Baynes, I wonder?"

"Drowned, I expect. I saw his head strike against the wheel as he jumped out."

"I am afraid he has not met with any such good luck. You know darling, there is an old proverb to the effect that those born to be hanged can't be drowned."

Kate laughed slightly.

All her courage had returned now that Frank was with her.

After the King of the School had looked round for a few minutes, he said—

"I fancy those planks will reach the shore. If they won't I must swim out and put up the bridge again."

A short spell of work convinced him that he was right in his estimate.

The planks he had alluded to formed a first rate bridge over which they had both passed, and in a very short space of time the young folks were on their way back to Ballsbury, Kate telling Frank as they went along all that had happened.

CHAPTER XXXII.

LEGAL ADVICE.

FRANK did not remember anything about Baynes's boat till he reached Ballsbury, and began to tell his tale to the sergeant of police.

A constable was at once despatched to secure the craft, and find out its owner, who, no doubt, was implicated in the plot.

When the man reached the place no such boat was to be found.

Strict search was made for the body of young Baynes; but although the drags were used unceasingly, it could not be brought to light.

No one doubted that the young ruffian had met his death in the stream that had witnessed so many of his villanies.

A man, supposed to be the boatman who had aided him in carrying Kate away, was soon afterwards apprehended and brought before the magistrates.

When told the charge against him, he simply smiled and requested to be allowed to communicate with Mr. Bateman, an attorney very much sought after by the criminal classes.

Mr. Bateman, for the defence, called upon Kate Conway to swear that the accused was the man who had been employed by Baynes.

This, the girl declined to do, though she felt convinced, in her own mind, that he was the guilty party.

Still, remembering that it was night time, and that she was dreadfully alarmed, she declined to run the risk of accidentally perjuring herself.

"To the best of your belief was it this man?" asked the lawyer.

"Yes."

"Now don't you think it might have been *this* individual, or *this?*"

As he spoke, Mr. Bateman waved his hand, and two men came forward from the body of the hall.

Both, strange to say, strongly resembled the prisoner in dress, figure, and countenance.

Kate was perfectly confounded, and the more she looked in the three grimy, cruel, but stolid faces before her, the more was she puzzled to know which of them had been her companion on that memorable moonlight evening.

"You cannot say which is the man?" suggested Bateman.

"I cannot."

"Then, of course, the prosecution cannot be sustained, and your worship will discharge the prisoner?"

"I suppose I must do so," replied the magistrate. "The prisoner may leave the dock."

The man did so, but, as soon as he had reached the body of the hall, the police-sergeant stepped forward.

"I am determined to have the man who committed the outrage, so to make sure, I arrest all three of you."

"Not so fast, my good friend," said Mr. Bateman. "You have no power to do anything of the kind."

To tell a policeman that he has not the power to do certain things, is, of course, to put him in a violent passion. Our friend, the sergeant, was no further removed above earthly passions than the rest of his profession, and therefore, he grew very red in the face with anger.

"What do you mean by interfering with me? Constable Jones, step this way."

The urbane lawyer, however, only smiled the more.

"You are doing an illegal action, my friend of the police," said he, holding up a warning finger.

"How illegal?" demanded the sergeant, while the poor constable who had been called started back as though the three prisoners had suddenly been transformed into as many vipers.

"You have heard this young lady's evidence?"

"I think she swore that there was only *one* man in the boat besides Baynes."

"Certainly she did."

"Then you must not arrest these persons at the same time for an offence committed by one. These three men could not have been rolled into one for the occasion.

The sergeant was puzzled, and scratched his head in hopes of extracting an idea.

"What am I to do?" he at last asked.

"As soon as you have paid my usual fee—you know the amount—I shall be most happy to advise you," replied Mr. Bateman. "I don't do business on credit."

A roar of laughter, in which even the magistrate joined, made the policeman more furious than ever.

Frank Egerton at that moment fortunately came to the rescue of the unhappy official.

THE KING OF THE SCHOOL; OR, WHO WILL WIN?

"Here is your money," said he. "Now be kind enough to give the sergeant the advice you promised."

"Certainly," said Mr. Bateman, testing the coin between his teeth. "The officer can take either of the men into custody, separately, but he cannot apprehend them all at once. And if he fails to establish the charge, he is liable to be cast for damages."

The worthy sergeant, after consideration, wisely declined to have anything to do with the three individuals who so much resembled each other, and so the case came to an end.

Frank escorted Kate home, and, after a tender adieu, returned to Lexicon College.

A surprise was in store for him.

A letter was lying upon his desk, the address written in a hand he well knew.

Several of the boys had gathered round to look at it, for they, too, recognised the florid penmanship.

To keep the reader no longer in suspense, the letter was from Baynes.

Feeling no small amount of curiosity to know what he could have to write about, as well as to know how he managed to escape the watery grave every one thought had received him, Frank opened the billet.

As he read it, his brow grew stern.

The tone of the letter was threatening, and Frank was not accustomed to receive threats calmly.

It ran something in the following style:—

MR. EGERTON.—No doubt you fancied me dead, but you will find that I yet live to be your evil genius. You have baulked me this once, but next time I shall triumph. Kate Conway shall never be your wife.

"H. BAYNES."

Frank then looked at the envelope again, and, to his great surprise, found that it bore the Ballsbury post-mark.

First of all he consulted with the doctor; but that worthy gentleman could not understand it at all.

Only one thing appeared at all clear to his mind: that was that Baynes had by some very marvellous mischance escaped the death he so richly deserved.

Frank then proceeded to the residence of his friend—the sergeant of police.

That worthy looked at matters in a more worldly way.

"Did you watch to see what became of the young ruffian after he leaped out of the mill window?" he asked.

"No," replied Frank.

"Then it is very clear to my comprehension. While you were attending to Miss Conway he must have risen to the surface, and got to the bank. It would then be very easy to reach the boat, in which, with a swift current in his favour, he could soon reach town."

"But do you suppose he is hiding about here now?"

"I should hardly think so; but I will have a good search made."

The search was made and maintained, but nothing was seen or heard of Baynes, and every one began to fancy that he must have enclosed the letter to some confederate, who posted it in Ballsbury.

Nevertheless, about a week after this event, as Frank was returning from Mr. Conway's house one evening, he was again fired at, a circumstance which convinced him that his foe was still in the neighbourhood.

CHAPTER XXXIII.

A LOT OF MAGIC.

FOR some time everything went on very quietly at Ballsbury, both as regarded the town itself and Lexicon College.

Baynes kept out of sight, and his threats came to nothing; though Kate Conway still had a suspicion that the villain was lurking about the neighbourhood to pounce out and carry her off at the first opportunity.

To guard against any such nefarious designs, she never went out for a walk beyond the town alone at any time, nor would she even trust herself in the streets of Ballsbury after sunset without a companion on whom she could rely.

We need hardly say that Frank Egerton was the escort she most preferred.

The time drew on towards the holidays.

Anxious youngsters consulted almanacs, and immense calculations were made as to the exact number of weeks, days, hours, minutes, and seconds that had to pass away ere the happy time would arrive.

Freddy Webber especially performed prodigious feats of arithmetic.

According to his computation, 2,678,400 seconds were wanting to bring them to "Cock-hat Sunday," from which day to that on which they were actually to depart for home, 432,000 seconds more must be counted.

Cock-hat Sunday was that immediately preceding the holidays, on which day the pupils were accustomed to wear their hats in a very jaunty style.

There had, in days past, been a still more offensive custom, but Frank, on hearing of it, had determined that it should not be continued.

As the holidays drew nigh, the discipline became more lax.

Professor Moeritz, who in his manners was as much a boy as any of them, encouraged all sorts of extraordinary sports and pastimes.

One evening he gave a grand exhibition of magic.

After the usual sleight of hand performances, passing coins, burning pocket-handkerchiefs, &c., he announced that he would transform himself into a giant of monstrous stature.

"Please don't eat us!" groaned Freddy Webber, pretending to be horribly frightened.

"Dat Ich shall nichts!" rejoined the professor. "Zo do not be afraid."

Freddy promised not to tremble very much, and the professor then commenced his preparations for the crowning feat of the evening.

He procured first of all a thin, transparent sheet.

"Oh! it's only a magic lantern dodge," observed Lascelles.

"Dere is no magic in dis lantern," replied the professor, exhibiting a common policeman's bull's-eye, which certainly was all the light he proposed to take behind the scenes with him.

Freddy, being very sceptical, went and had a thorough search amongst the professor's paraphernalia, but could discover nothing more than the lantern before-mentioned.

Having hung his sheet across the room, Herr Moeritz went behind it.

Suddenly a strong ray of light announced to the boys, who remained in front, that the lantern was at work.

Then the shadow of the professor was seen upon the screen.

At first it was about life-size, but gradually it grew larger and larger, till the worthy German, if his shadow might be believed, was fully ten feet high,

"'OH, MY HAT!' SHOUTED THE PROFESSOR. DANCING ROUND"

PRICE ONE HALFPENNY.

[Published Every Monday.]

and proportionately bulky in circumference.

Then it gradually reduced to a more natural size, suddenly became greatly elongated, and as suddenly diminished.

Having continued the performance for some minutes, the professor re-appeared before the curtain, looking rather red in the face.

" He can't make himself big *this side*," grumbled one or two of the very junior members of the fraternity.

" No," replied the professor. " It is all von optical delusion. I gets behind ze curtain, shtands between it unt ze lantern ; den if I comes near ze curtain I grows little, and if I steps back to ze lantern I gets big. Ven I shoomps up I am big and little both."

" That is not a very clever trick, sir," observed Freddy Webber, with a grave face.

" Can you play tricks ?"

" Yes. Much better than that."

" Petter as dat. Let us see, let us se."

" Excuse me this evening, sir. I will perform *my* trick in the light of day, without the aid of any curtain, lantern, or other means of deception."

" You are a clever boy."

The boys looked out bright and early in the morning ; for though Freddy had not told any one his plans, they all guessed that Professor Moeritz was to be made the victim of some practical joke.

" Your game must be a gentle one, Freddy," observed the King of the School. " I don't like any sprees that result in personal injury."

" I would not injure him for worlds," replied Webber; " but *I'll have his hat !"**

A few minutes afterwards the breakfast bell rang, and the merry, hungry boys trooped into the dining-hall.

One of the number remained behind, however.

That one as you may guess, was Webber.

* This is the real, authentic origin of the slang phrase now so popular.

But what was Freddy doing? you may naturally ask. He had taken two or three of the brass rings from his fishing-rod, and was busily engaged in screwing them into the ceiling of the room.

What was his object in so doing we shall see.

Having arranged the rings to his satisfaction in a row from the centre of the room to near the door, Freddy passed a long piece of thread through them, and secured both ends to the roller of a map that hung upon the wall.

A final look round to see that all was right, and then our young friend marched into the dining-hall, and made as vigorous an attack upon the bread and butter and weak tea as though he had spent the morning in the performance of a variety of virtuous actions.

Professor Moeritz seemed to have some vague idea that he was to be victimised.

When the morning meal was over, and the boys had returned—some to the play-fields, some to the school-room —he kept very carefully in the centre of the apartment devoted to learning, not daring even to sit down, lest pins should have been stuck in his chair, or some other joke played.

" Just what I want," muttered Freddy, as he prepared for his magic.

" Tell me ; I'll lend you a helping hand if possible," said Fitzgerald, who loved a joke dearly.

" You won't blab ?"

" No—on my honour."

" Then stick this fish-hook into the crown of old Germany's hat."

" Give it here. Why, you have some cotton on the end of it."

" Of course. A hook is no use without a line."

Fitzgerald, under pretext of asking some question, went up to the professor, and, when his back was for a moment turned, inserted the fish-hook in the little ventilator in the crown of the professor's hat, accomplishing his work without exciting the slightest suspicion.

A few minutes afterwards, while the

professor was explaining to a few of the boys the principles of the *handeludes seitwort transitivum* (active and transitive verb), his hat suddenly flew from his head.

" *Wer hat mein hut?*" (Who has my hat ?) he inquired, looking round the room without being able to see the article he required.

" I really don't know, sir," replied Egerton, who had not been enlightened as to the joke.

" Here it is," said Fitzgerald, restoring it to the professor's head.

Moeritz continued his lecture, but in a few seconds the hat again flew away.

" Der teufel !" he roared. " Dis hat has bezauberung !" (the hat has enchantment).

Strange to say, it was brought back to him, this time from the opposite side of the school.

Our young friend, Fitzgerald, for the second time placed it on the head of the professor, who in rather angry tones exclaimed—

" Now you all shall leave me. I vill not have one near so as to touch me."

In obedience to this order, they all stood some distance from him.

" Now, Master Webber," continued the German with a chuckle, " you shall pe at ze bottom of all this, but——"

" But it seems you can't keep your hat. Is not mine a better trick than yours ?"

" Yes, yes," said Moeritz, as he stared round and at last caught sight of his chapeau, which seemed to adhere to the ceiling. " How have you done it ?"

" That is my business, sir ; but am I not a clever magician ?"

" Very."

Freddy would not explain the secret, and for a long time the professor was in ignorance of the means by which the trick was played. The joke being at an end, however, more serious business occupied the attention of our young friends.

They had to prepare for the half-yearly examination, which always occupied the week immediately preceding the holidays.

CHAPTER XXXIV.

A DAY'S SPORT.

ONE of the most popular games at Lexicon College was hare-and-hounds, the hare being one of the boys considered a good runner, and the hounds all the others who thought fit to follow.

I suppose you all know how the sport is managed ; but in case this should fall into the hands of any young ignoramus who has never participated in the pastime, I will just state that the scent by which the hounds follow is composed of small shreds of paper ; the hare takes a large bag of this, and scatters it as he runs, being allowed (generally) ten minutes' start of the hounds.

The hare gives an indication of the course he intends to take, and where he intends to stop if he is not run down.

On a fine Wednesday morning Frank Egerton announced that there would be hare-and-hounds at Hatfield chalk-pits at four o'clock in the afternoon.

Every spare moment the small boys had was occupied in tearing up old newspapers, exercises, and other old papers into "scent" for the hare, on this occasion personated by our friend Lascelles, who was a splendid runner, keeping his wind any number of miles.

It would be a "twister," as Marsham expressed himself, especially as the hare had decided to take the race-course, and then get down into the village of Stratford, where there would be plenty of work for them after their three mile chase over the downs, in the shape of meadows, plentifully crossed by wide dykes and artificial water-courses.

Four o'clock came, and the chalk-pits were thronged with boys.

Professor Moeritz, who saw the con-course from the garden of the college, imagined that another fight was about to take place, and started with the laudable intention of putting a stop to it.

After toiling up a steep road for a mile or more, the worthy German came upon the group just in time to see the hare buckle a bag of the paper scraps over his shoulder, and start at a long, slinging trot across a stubble field, towards the high, furze-covered downs we have before spoken of, while Frank Egerton and the Earl of Pembridge consulted their watches, and restrained some of the younger hounds, who wished to be off at once.

"You'll have quite enough running before you get back," said the King of the School.

"Bah!" exclaimed Webber, "It is nothing."

"You won't be in at the finish of the run, Freddy."

"Won't I! Just you wait and see."

"Wat is dis?" inquired Professor Moeritz, coming up at the moment. "You are not at ze box."

"No, hare-and-hounds. Won't you join the pack?"

"Who is hare?"

"Lascelles."

"Then I will. He can run nicht mooch good."

Egerton and one or two others laughed rather at this.

They knew what sort of a runner Lascelles was, much better than Professor Moeritz did.

However, after some other chat, Frank announced that time was up, and the whole party started across the field.

Some of the younger ones darted ahead at once and outstripped the more experienced runners, who knew that the pace had to be maintained for some miles.

A heavy breathing told Frank that the German professor was keeping close to his heels.

At the spot where Lascelles had vanished from their sight they found the scent thinly scattered upon the ground, and followed it right up the side of the steep hill till they we fairly among the furze bushes, and the keen pure air of the hills whist shrilly about their ears.

Suddenly, Freddy Webber, who managed to keep up very well, consi ing that his legs were shorter and body fatter than any of the others, up a shout of triumph.

His keen eyes had discerned the figure of the flying hare, about a mile-and-a-half a-head, pegging along at quite as good a pace as when he started.

"Forward! forward!" shouted Egerton, and the whole pack quickened pace as they dashed along the old Roman road, which ran in a straight line for miles.

The hare heard the cry, and turning aside, leaped over a wattle fence with a ditch on either side.

Some of the youths attempted to cut him off by taking a diagonal course, but they made a great mistake in their calculations, and were seen no more during the chase.

The fact is, the hare, after crossing a turnip-field on his right, doubled back, crossed the Roman road again and made off across the fallows for Stratford, which village he reached about the same time that the cunning ones found themselves at Queenhampton, a place about four miles in the opposite direction.

Continuing his rapid career, Lascelles led the way across a huge pasture, in which a few stunted old elms were scattered about, and, having dashed through the hedge at its further extremity, was lost to view.

The few harmless cows grazing in this pasture threw up their tails, lowered their heads, and galloped about in a sad state of mind, as the thirty or forty yelling boys, who still followed, charged across the field; but in a few minutes the pack swept out of sight, and followed the scent which led them towards the Stratford water-meadows.

Freddy Webber and Professor Moeritz had managed to keep pretty well up, and when they crossed the road that separated the uplands from the valley, overtook some of the leading hounds, who, in their impetuosity, had overrun the scent, and were "trying back."

Scarcely thirty out of the sixty original starters were to be seen, the others having giving up the chase long since.

Frank, after a hurried look at his watch, announced that they had done something like four miles in less than forty minutes; not a bad pace, considering that our young friends are not professional pedestrians, and that most of them had been hard at work "Gradus grinding" for the examination, and are consequently slightly out of training and scant of breath.

Having well quartered the meadow in which the scent was lost, the cry of "*Forward!*" is again heard on the extreme right, Fitzgerald being the lucky hound to hit the trail.

Forward they all went, Professor Moeritz much regretting that he had allowed himself to be persuaded to take part in such a wild-goose chase.

There is good reason to suppose that hereabouts the hare found his stock of paper getting short. At all events, the scents did not seem so thick.

That was a matter of small consequence to the experienced hounds, who could guess pretty well which way the course would be—straight through the water-meadows for two miles, and then up a hill; but which side of the hill would it be? If the hare was very cunning, he might baffle the hounds very considerably.

It was thoroughly understood that the run was to end at one of two public-houses—the "Fox and Goose," or the "Black Bull."

These houses stood in different roads, which ran in almost parallel lines towards Ballsbury, some half-mile or more of stiff clay, deeply ploughed, separating them.

Egerton kept on running well in front of the pack, leaping the water-courses with ease, and firing every one with emulation; but all were not so lucky, and several falls took place, of which we shall have occasion to speak presently.

At length the hare was viewed again going right up the side of Alderburn Hill.

Cunning hare! Would he bear off to the right, and end the run at the "Black Bull," or would he keep to the left and patronize the "Fox and Goose."

That was a question could only be decided by following the scent.

At the moment that Lascelles disappeared over the crest of the hill it struck Egerton that in a few minutes time it would be dark. He shouted to the Earl of Pembridge, who was not far behind, to apprise him of this fact.

"I know it," was the response.

"Shall we put the steam on?" asked Egerton.

"Yes; let me come up to you, then drive a-head."

Frank slackened his pace for a few seconds till the young earl once more was by his side.

Each then drew a long breath, braced up his belt, and rattled up the side of the hill.

"There he goes!" shouted Frank, and, as they were descending on the other side, they taxed their legs and lungs to the utmost.

It seemed almost certain that the "Black Bull" would be the finish of the run, and Marsham, who, with Fitzgerald, kept close behind our two young friends above-mentioned, dropped off to make the nearest possible cut to the haven of rest.

Frank scorned all such devices, and pertinaciously stuck to the scent, knowing that if he could only hold on for ten minutes more he would run down the hare, and thus bring the chase to a close.

He was fast gaining on Lascelles, who, though he had led the hounds a good chase of seven or eight miles, seemed almost exhausted.

Suddenly, however, he changed his direction, turned back, and made for the "Fox and Goose."

Thinking that, in the fast gathering gloom, he had deceived the hounds, he slackened his pace, a fault which was at once taken advantage of by Frank and the earl.

The "Fox and Goose" was only about a hundred yards distant; could he reach it before either of the hounds?

He would make a trial at all events; so he "put on the steam," as Frank called it, and started as though he had only just started from Lexicon College.

Unfortunately for the success of his gallant attempt, his foes (for the occasion) were just as sound of wind and limb as himself, and they, too, increased the speed.

Twenty yards to the house, but Egerton is not six feet behind him. Ten yards more! Frank is already extending his arm—two yards only from the doorstep—ah! a hand upon his shoulder!

Caught!

Lascelles gives up at once, staggers up against the doorstep, and as soon as he can, says—

"Well, you have had a good run for it, at all events.

"The best of the season!" gasps Frank, wiping the perspiration from his brow.

Then, without any more ado, the three boys walked into the parlour of the little inn, and ordered some mulled ale.

The Earl of Pembridge feebly hints at a good draught of porter, but Egerton reminds him that cold drink, in their perspiring state, would be very dangerous.

After an interval of something like twenty minutes, Marsham and Fitzgerald appeared, having walked over from the "Black Bull;" all five then sat till it wanted but half-an-hour of the hour when they must be in school, wondering what had become of all their companions, and especially of Freddy Webber and Professor Moeritz.

While they are wondering, let us retrace our steps and see, if we can, what has become of our fat young friend and the German tutor.

Both of them found that the water meadows before-mentioned formed the stiffest portion of the course.

The water-drains and dykes were many of them half-full of water, and a short jump or a false step would certainly subject the unfortunate hound to a very severe ducking.

The professor was the first to come to grief.

He had made a leap, and a good one, but, unfortunately, as he was in the act of alighting on the opposite side of the open drain, his heels slipped up, and Herr Moeritz went souse backwards into the water, which fortunately was not deep enough to drown him.

Freddy endeavoured to pull him up but was unfortunate enough to slip forward, and went sprawling on top of the professor. There they lay, sprawling in the mud, weeds, and water, like a couple of amphibious beings rather than Christian gentlemen.

"Ach! Mein Gott!" ejaculated Moeritz, as at last he rose like an ancient river-god, with a crown of reeds and water-cresses on his head. "Webber, where are you?"

"Here!—Oh! Jupiter, what a sight! I beg your pardon, I meant Neptune, for I am sure you only want your trident to look the character exactly. Hi! Chawbacon, bring that pitchfork this way!"

The rustic thus addressed did not condescend to reply, and having freed themselves from some of the filth that had encumbered them, Freddy suggested that, as they were both drenched to the skin, it would be advisable to quit the chase and make for Lexicon College by the nearest route, in order that they might change their clothes, and so avoid all chance of rheumatism, and other kindred ailments.

"Good advice, Freddy, but why not ask Chawbacon to direct you, for you have never been this way before, and may take a wrong turning?"

Freddy, however, was confident that he knew the way, so off they started.

Both our travellers, who saw that night was quickly coming on, were aware that a hill had to be climbed before they could get to Ballsbury, consequently, when Freddy led the way up a steep miry lane the professor followed with implicit confidence.

However, after a mile or two of stiff walking, they found themselves on the downs before alluded to, but at what part of them was rather more than Master Webber could tell.

"Dere is ein haus?" suddenly exclaimed Professor Moeritz.

"A house! where, sir?" asked Freddy.

"See, see!"

And the professor pointed towards a spark of flame at some distance.

"Let us go there," said he, "unt see if dey can direct us."

Freddy assented, and on they walked till it became evident that the light did not proceed from any house, but from the camp of some gipsies, who very frequently pitched their tents on the wild heath.

Now Webber, though brave enough in general, had a few cowardly points in his character; for instance, he was desperately afraid of frogs and toads, and, moreover, believed that gipsies travelled the country for the whole and sole purpose of stealing the eldest sons of rich gentlemen.

The author, having met a good many of the wandering tribes in the south of England, is able to state that they do nothing of the kind; they may be poachers, but not kidnappers.

Freddy halted as soon as he had a good view of the camp.

"Why, they are gipsies!" he said.

"Ja! Bohemisch peoples. But dey knows dere way about, as your friend Marsham shall say. Let us go unt ask dem."

Freddy felt just as if he had been walking into a lion's den; but he did not care to confess his cowardice, so he walked forward, keeping just a pace behind the professor, however.

Professor Moeritz, probably only knew fear as a lexicographical definition, and could give no description of it from personal knowledge; he cared as little for gipsies as he did for unruly schoolboys, and probably if the chief of the gang had offended him, would have commanded him to learn one of the odes of Horace by heart.

As it proved, however, the children of Ishmael were extremely civil (not so their dogs, which had to be severely beaten ere they would hush their noisy barkings), and, when the professor inquired the way, directed him.

A lucky chance it was, too, for our friends, for they had been walking the wrong way ever since they had been on the downs.

The gipsies, however, pointed out the constellation of Ursa Major; by keeping just a little to the right of that, the benighted ones would be able to strike the Queenhampto

Road, and get into Ballsbury by that way.

So they lumbered along painfully across the furze-covered plain, then through a turnip field. As they emerged from it into another miry lane, they heard a faint "halloo!" some distance from them.

Freddy answered the cry.

A few minutes afterwards Crawley emerged into the road and limped up to them.

The youth was in a terrible pickle.

In forcing his way through some of the quickset hedges, with which the face of nature was in that region adorned, he had torn his trousers and jacket in a most dreadful manner. Moreover, in crossing some stiff clay land he had lost a shoe (serve him right, the young fop, for not wearing thick boots like the others), and, having suffered two or three tumbles, was plentifully plastered with Mother Earth from head to foot.

All this he explained as Webber and the professor came up, and I am in duty bound to say that the sight of his forlorn schoolfellow cheered Freddy in no small degree.

It was a treat to see some one several degrees more wretched than himself.

Crawley also cheered up; being no longer alone in those huge, gloomy fields his spirit rose, and, as Freddy seemed to have forgotten their late disagreements, they walked along as jauntily as the state of the road and their wearied limbs would permit.

So they trudged along till at last they came into the turnpike road.

Then they paused, quite bewildered, for they had lost sight of Ursa Major, and did not exactly know in what part of the heavens to find him.

Consequently, having missed their bearings as well as their great bear, they stood bewildered on the edge of the turnpike road, not knowing whether they ought to turn to the right hand or to the left.

Their indecision was soon at an end, however.

A rattle of wheels and horses' hoofs was heard, then a light was seen.

"The 'wheelbarrow,' by Jove!" exclaimed Freddy.

The "wheelbarrow," was the epithet contemptuously applied to a lumbering old two-horse coach that ran every day between Ballsbury and a town some fifteen miles distant.

As it strolled along the two boys screwed themselves, and made a run to catch hold of it behind.

Freddy succeeded in so doing; but Crawley being less fortunate, had another tumble.

Half-an-hour later Webber reached Lexicon College just five minutes before the gates were closed.

Crawley was, at that moment, fully a mile away.

The gallant hare and the other hounds had been home some time, and, stiff and tired with their day's run, were sitting round the tables discussing the various incidents of the chase.

"Ah, here comes Freddy; now we're all in," exclaimed the Earl of Pembridge, as the young joker entered the hall.

"It looks as though he had been too tired to walk, and had *rolled* home," observed Egerton.

"A nice *crusty* roll he is too. Won't even speak to us."

"Where is your human kindness?" groaned Freddy. A poor fellow comes in half-dead, and instead of sympathising with him you only perpetrate puns of the vilest description. However, if I am in a pickle, Crawley is in a worse."

"Crawley!" exclaimed half-a-dozen of the boys.

"Yes. I left him limping along with only one shoe."

Freddy then ascended to his bedroom, changed his clothes, and got down again just as the supper-bell rang.

At that meal the head of each form

had to present a list of any who happened to be absent.

The doctor scowled as he saw Crawley's name; but at that moment the door-bell rang, and the servant who answered it, returning, announced "Master Crawley."

"Bring him in," said Dr. Whackley; and in another minute the hapless urchin stood before all the school.

CHAPTER XXXV.

HOME FOR THE HOLIDAYS.

THE appearance Crawley presented when brought before the assembled masters and scholars of Lexicon College, was certainly not a very pleasing one.

As before stated, the youth had "come to grief" in various ways. His clothes were torn and soiled, and his face had on it a look betokening that he apprehended serious consequences.

What excuse should he make? was the question that puzzled his mind.

"You are late, Crawley," observed Doctor Whackley, after severely looking at the youth for a few seconds.

"But I could not help it, please, sir."

"How is that?"

"I joined the hare-and-hounds chase this afternoon, sir."

"That is no excuse. Several boys younger than you were out, but managed to get back in proper time. You know the rules."

"Yes, sir : but please I could'nt——"

"Silence ! unless you can make some better excuse."

After a minute's pause, as it seemed that Crawley could offer no better explanation, the doctor continued—

"You will remain in the school-room after all the others have gone to bed. I shall flog you for being out of school after the appointed hours."

"Please, sir——"

"Once more I say silence!" exclaimed the doctor, who was evidently very angry, and then strode out of the room.

"He's gone to tell Thomas to prepare a bran new bundle of twigs," said Freddy, in a low voice, but quite loud enough to be overheard by the unfortunate culprit, who stood trembling in the middle of the room till Professor Moeritz told him to sit down.

The King of the School, Lascelles, and one or two others, though they joined in the laugh caused by Webber's comforting remark, inwardly resolved to make an effort to obtain a remission or mitigation of the sentence Doctor Whackley had pronounced.

Crawley was not liked by them, but then his offence was simply the result of a mischance that might have befallen any of them.

So, after a little consultation, Frank and Lascelles proceeded to the doctor's study.

"Well, my boys, what is it you want?" he asked, kindly, as they entered, looking up from the book he was reading.

"We want to speak to you about Crawley," replied Frank, plunging boldly into the business on hand; and explaining the circumstances under which they supposed the unhappy youth had lost his way.

"It appears to me that he did not play the game fairly," observed the doctor, when Egerton had finished. "It seems that he did not follow the chase in a legitimate manner, but wandered off towards a point where he supposed it would end, and was mistaken in his calculations. Well, I will not flog him; ring the bell."

A few minutes afterwards Thomas, the footman, entered.

"Tell Crawley to come here," commanded the doctor, and a few minutes afterwards Thomas proclaimed before all the school—

"Master Crawley, you are wanted in Doctor Whackley's study."

The wretched boy followed the footman, not before Freddy Webber had quietly observed that the head of the college always flogged harder in his own private room than in the public school-room.

On arriving in the awful presence, however, his fears were slightly relieved when he saw that the frown had partly vanished from the doctor's face.

"I have—through the intercession of these young gentlemen—resolved not to flog you; but, to mark my sense of your conduct, I shall insist upon your writing two hundred lines. Now go, and never let such a thing occur again."

The doctor waved his hand, and Crawley departed, glad that he had escaped the threatened flogging, but angry that he owed his escape to Frank Egerton.

* * * * * *

Time marched on at his accustomed pace, but to many of the boys he appeared to be dragging slowly.

Two young ladies in Ballsbury complained, on the other hand, that he was much too fast; and, of course, the reader at once guesses that I allude to Kate and Lizzie Conway.

Holidays to them meant separation for a period from those youths whose constant society now seemed so necessary to their happiness, that Kate and her sister used sometimes to wonder how they managed to exist before Frank Egerton and the Earl of Pembridge became known to them.

A promise of constant correspondence was, of course, given on both sides, which partly reconciled the girls to their hard fate.

The examinations took place the week immediately preceding the holidays, and resulted in Frank Egerton being proclaimed premier scholar in classics, mathematics, and modern languages: Fitzgerald coming next in the first-named studies, Lascelles and the earl winning the other second honours. Freddy Webber received honourable mention, so did Marsham, to his great astonishment.

A grand supper was always given to the boys the night before they left school—all the luxuries of the season and plenty of wine.

Doctor Whackley always headed the table, with the boy who had won most prizes on his right hand.

On this occasion, of course, Frank Egerton, the King of the School, was that honoured individual.

The cloth being removed, the healths of the Queen, Royal Family, army, navy, and church, were drank in one bumper, and then came the toast of the evening—Frank Egerton, the King of the School.

"He has proved a wise and a strong king," observed the doctor; "wise in encouraging those younger than himself to act in a honest, brave, and manly manner—strong to protect them from bullies and evil associates. His influence and example have done wonders in improving the general tone of the school." (Loud cheers and musical honours.)

Frank replied—

Well, we can't afford much space for reporting speeches, but not to give a few extracts would be unfair.

"The doctor has rather over-estimated my influence and exertions, I fancy," said he; "though I certainly have tried to do as much good, and give as little trouble as possible. When I came here the school was divided into three or four cliques or factions, and the consequence was that we were afraid to play a game with that wretched academy for young gentlemen up town, or even with our own 'nightingales.' I am happy to find all that is changed; we are a united band now, and either in school-room or play-field a match for any educational establishment of the same size in England." (Cheers, prolonged and uproarious.)

Frank then proposed the health of Dr. Whackley; and, after that, the health of Professor Moeritz, of whom he spoke so flatteringly that the bashful German could only reply—

"*Sie machen mir da ein kompliment worauf ich nichts zu antworten weis.*" (You make me a compliment to which I know not what to reply.)

Freddy Webber then sang a comic song, so did some one else, and—well, after a great deal of merriment, they went to bed.

Frank Egerton and his immediate friends had a long discussion in their bedroom as to the different ways of getting home.

The direct line to London ran one train to London at a very early hour, then no more till past midday — an arrangement which did not suit our friends.

"I tell you what it is, boys," suddenly said the earl; "I thought of all this yesterday, and made an arrangement which I fancy you will approve of."

"What is that?"

"I have engaged the old Bath coach, which you know has not been running for some months: the springs and wheels have been thoroughly looked to, and a relay of horses sent on to the half-way house. It will be here at eight in the morning, and take us over to Hendover, only sixteen miles, in time for the ten o'clock South Midland train."

"Hurrah! But you can't take all the school," said Freddy.

"Of course I mean our own form. We shall be in London before this lazy West Midland train has fairly started."

So they all agreed to patronise the coach, and then retired to rest; but very few of them slept much that night.

The great day at last dawned, fine and clear, with the least suspicion of frost in the atmosphere.

Every boy was out of bed as soon as it was light, and more than one fierce bolstering encounter took place.

After breakfast, which was not partaken of with usual appetites, the rattle of wheels announced that the coach had arrived.

A very dashing turn-out had been made of the old Bath Express. Four very decent horses had been harnessed to it, and the former driver, now keeper of a small beerhouse, sat on the box, arrayed in all his ancient glory.

Up clambered the boys, many of them being armed with pea-shooters, with which they fired a succession of volleys at poor Thomas, the footman, who was busy with the luggage.

"Now, gentlemen, don't if you please!" the poor fellow exclaimed, as the missiles stung his face and hands.

"Hold hard a minute, boys," said Frank. "We must give Thomas something better than peas as a parting present. Shell out you fellows."

Throwing half-a-crown into his hat by way of example, the King of the School made a collection for the serving-man amounting to about thirty shilling.

"Half-a-sov. for Tiddy (the boot-cleaner)," our hero remarked, as he handed him the money, which was received with profuse thanks.

"And mind you don't spend it all in beer," said Freddy, with his mouth full of peas.

"Right, sir,—all right, coachee!" The driver motioned to the man who stood at the horses' heads, gave the leaders a flick with the whipcord, and away they went.

People in the market-place cheered as the vehicle dashed along, but the peas soon sent them into their shops again.

Close by the turnpike gate they met a party of the choristers, who returned their fire with pebbles, one of which gave Freddy Webber a black eye.

But they were soon out of range, and out of the town also, though that was not the only adventure they were destined to meet on the road.

For some time they spun along all jolly.

The coachman was as pleased as Punch to be at his old trade again, and even the horses seemed to partake of his enjoyment.

At last they came in sight of the tumble-down hostelry, deserted since coaching times by all save a few grooms from some neighbouring racing-stables, and touts who strove by fair or foul means to give some information regarding the horses.

The "Druid's Head" was, however, on the present occasion in a state of excitement. The coach was to stop ten minutes, and the host, knowing that our young friends of Lexicon College were generally pretty free with their money, calculated upon doing a good trade during that short period.

As they neared the house a respectably dressed youth was seen to emerge from it, and take the road towards Hendover.

"That looks like Baynes!" exclaimed Egerton.

"It does—but it can't be the young ruffian," replied Lascelles.

Frank was of a different opinion, however.

"We shall soon overtake him when we have changed horses," said he, "then, our doubts will be decided. But I really think it is Baynes."

The discussion ceased as the coach pulled up at the "Druid's Head."

Frank Egerton took an opportunity of asking the landlord if he knew anything of the youth who had just left, and received a surly "no" for answer.

After a brief interval devoted to the demolition of biscuits, cheese, and ale,

the coachman announced that time was up, and our friends once more clambered to the box.

The Earl of Pembridge, who had heard the foregoing discussion, without taking part in it, was of the same opinion as Frank. He thought it just possible that Baynes might be in a very desperate state of mind, and thinking of making another attack on Egerton.

So to guard against mischief as much as possible, he changed seats with Frank, by which piece of strategy the King of the School was placed between two other boys, against whom Baynes could have no particular enmity.

Then off they started again.

After proceeding about a mile, they again caught sight of the doubtful person in front of them.

At the same time Freddy called attention to a gentleman shooting in the fields on the right hand side of the road.

The youth in front of them climbed up on the bank to look at the sportsman, and seemed not to hear the wheels of the coach.

Presently the gentleman's dog came to a dead point, and the next moment a partridge rose, flying not many feet above the ground, almost directly in a line for the youth on the bank.

Baynes—for he it was as they could all see—jumped back into the road to avoid the shots from the sportsman's gun.

"Hi! Out of the way!" shouted the coachman, pulling hard at his horses.

Too late!

The near leader knocked him down, and, before the coach could be stopped, the wheel had passed over his right thigh and shoulder.

All the fun of the day was spoiled at once.

The boys jumped down, and clustered round their late schoolfellow, who lay insensible on the hard road.

Only a slight movement of lips told them that Baynes still lived

"We can't leave him here," said Frank Egerton; he must be taken back to the "Druid's Head."

"But how?" asked Freddy.

"You had better let him remain a few minutes," said the gentleman, whose gun had, to a certain extent, been the cause of the mischief. "I will send some of my labourers from the next field with a hurdle on which he may be carried back to the inn."

He was as good as his word, and in a few minutes the bad boy of my tale was being borne along on a rude couch formed of great coats and wrappers spread on the hurdle.

Frank Egerton returned with him to the "Druid's Head." The others went on their way.

Two hours afterwards, the doctor, who had been called from Ballsbury, sent down word that Mr. Egerton was wanted in the sick-room, a summons which he readily obeyed.

Consciousness had returned to the poor, crushed form.

The surgeon had seen that the sufferer's hours were numbered, and had told him so.

The terrible fear of death had at first convulsed him with horror, but after a few kind, Christian words from the doctor, Baynes evinced a desire to make restitution as far as possible.

As soon as Frank was in the room, his former schoolfellow commenced a confession, in which he recapitulated the many dastardly and dishonest acts he had been guilty of.

"But the worst remains to be told," he gasped, sitting up feebly. "Your inheritance was wrested from you by fraud, Egerton; those mortgage deeds were forged! That's why your lawyer never heard of them till your father's death."

"Forged! Great Heavens! By whom?"

"May the powers above forgive him. My father, instigated by me, in revenge for the well-deserved thrashing you gave me. A man named Compton, living in Drury Lane, helped to do it.

You must catch him and extort—a confession. But, as I have told you this, be merciful—to my father. Forgive me. It was a race for superiority—you won—because—you were —brave and honest."

"I forgive you, as I hope to be forgiven!" exclaimed Frank fervently.

"He has not heard you; he is dead!" observed the doctor.

*　*　*　*　*

A day afterwards Frank with Mr. Throckmorton, the family solicitor, and a couple of shrewed detectives, encountered Compton in the neighbourhood of Drury Lane.

Hearing that his little game was up, the man volunteered every information he could give, and produced some documents which left no doubt of the elder Baynes's guilt.

The next thing was to seek that gentleman, who was found at the "Druid's Head" superintending his son's funeral.

The police did not interfere till that was over, when they informed Mr. Baynes the object of their visit.

At first he bullied and swore, but soon found that would not do; the evidence against him was too strong.

Then he was taken into a private room with Mr. Throckmorton and Frank Egerton.

"Well," said he, "what do you mean to do? Prosecute or make an arrangement?"

"I hardly think we should be justified in coming to any arrangement with such a scoundrel," replied Throckmorton.

However, after some consultation, it was arranged that, on consideration of his giving up the whole of the Egerton property, and paying down the sum of a thousand pounds, he should be allowed to go, giving his word to leave England at once.

Mr. Thockmorton was prepared with all the necessary documents, and the two constables were called in to witness the signatures.

Mr. Baynes was then allowed to

depart, and we believe he left the country. At all events he was no more heard of.

Frank then went home to see his darling mother, for so busy had he been that he had not been able to call upon her. She forgave him when she heard how he had employed his time, and that he had regained all his father's estates.

She clasped him in her arms, and kissed her own dear boy over and over again.

* * * * * *

It is now necessary to skip over a space of time.

Frank went back to Lexicon College for another half-year; but no one dared dispute his position as King of the School.

Then he graduated at Oxford, along with his friends the earl of Pembridge and Fitzgerald, the latter youth being deeply in love with Lady Florence Walworth, the young peer's sister.

All three left the university in triumph, with the proud privilege of writing B.A. after their names; and then——

Frank began seriously to think of marrying, while the Earl of Pembridge was all impatience to lead Lizzie Conway to the altar.

The two girls, it should be understood, had paid more than one visit to Mrs. Egerton, and that lady had quite overcome her prejudices against the milliner.

Amongst those invited was professor Moeritz, who one day was observed to be very intently studying a scrap of paper.

Suddenly a hand was passed over his shoulder, and it was snatched from him—by Mr. Conway!

"That writing!" said he. "Say, Herr Professor, where did you get it?"

"On the Konigsthul by Heidelsberg. I *know* it was written by Laura Wertheim, and was, I believe, given by her to an Englishman named Fairfax Egerton. I loved Laura."

"So did I; and she afterwards became my wife. For *I* am Fairfax Egerton, uncle to this gallant young man who is about to wed my daughter."

"You are not the Englishman with whom I fought!"

"Am I not? see."

Mr. Conway, alias Egerton, tore off a huge false beard and whiskers, displaying features very like those of our hero, who immediately asked—

"But why have you so long concealed yourself from us, dear uncle?"

"Because I dreaded lest my pure-hearted children should hear of the vices and follies I was guilty of in my youth, and despise me. But it matters not now; you will love Kate none the less for finding that she is your cousin. No, rather the more."

Three days afterwards three weddings took place; Kate Conway became Mrs. Frank Egerton, Lizzie found herself Countess of Pembridge, while Lady Florence Walworth disgusted several titled old tabbies by wedding Fitzgerald, a mere commoner.

Happiness was the lot of each, and happiness surely they deserved, none more so than THE KING OF THE SCHOOL.

Next week we shall have a New Story to introduce to you, entitled,

"UNLUCKY BOB; OR, OUR BOYS AT SCHOOL."

No. 2 we shall give away with No. 1, and the price will be the usual modest ½d. per week.

If you have enjoyed "The King of the School," follow on every Monday with its successor, "UNLUCKY BOB."

UNLUCKY BOB;

OR, OUR BOYS AT SCHOOL.

CHAPTER I.

A MYSTERY OF LIFE.

WILDGORSE HEATH, with its thick, stunted patches of heath, and the long range of hills behind it, was bathed in a flood of golden light from the slowly sinking sun, that had all day long been burning with an intense fierceness, threatening almost to fire the parched-up herbage.

The heath itself was of great extent, and ended at one part at an old-fashioned building known as Wildgorse Hall. The hall was very rarely visited by its owner, Philip Aubrey, who, with his wife, from some inexplicable cause, resided principally on the continent.

The lands formerly belonging to the Hall had gradually been sold by its successive inhabitants, so that very little income was derived from the estate.

Afar off, on the summit of a lofty hill overlooking it, stood the palatial mansion belonging to the Wilder family, who were, by distant ties of consanguinity, related to the Aubreys.

But it had never been known that the stern, dark, morose man who now stood at the head of the Wilder house had ever claimed any acquaintance with Philip Aubrey at the Hall.

Only an old man, who had once been steward, resided at Wildgorse Hall, and he on market days drove over to the town in an old chaise drawn by a pony almost as aged as himself.

The old man never entered into conversation with anyone in the town, but having purchased the articles he required, left as silent as he came.

Upon the day that we speak of, as the sun began to decline, upon a slight knoll of grass, screened by a thick gorse bush, a man sat looking, with a smile of derision upon his face, at the old Hall.

He was alone upon that wild heath, for the labourers had long since wended their way to their humble dwellings.

It was a singular picture to see that man seated there with the darkness gathering around him.

He was tolerably well dressed—the slouched hat looked as though it had seen roughish weather, and so did the face beneath it ; but the velveteen coat, the leggings, and everything else showed that the man had not poverty to contend against.

He cast his eye searchingly round the horizon.

"The sun won't be long afore it has done its day's work, and then I guess mine must begin. You've had a long time, Jem Greenwood, to beat about, and yet you're sound in wind and limb, although there's one part about you that has been aching and panting and struggling."

Here his head sank deeper into his hands, as he muttered—

For continuation see next week's number